I0719328

Sparks

by

Maren

Anderson

Published in the United States by
Not a Pipe Publishing, Independence, Oregon.
www.NotAPipePublishing.com

Paperback Edition

ISBN-13: 978-1-948120-30-2

Dedication

To the ranch women
who can toss 100 lbs. bales over a fence
and fix their own damn tractors.

Y'all rock.

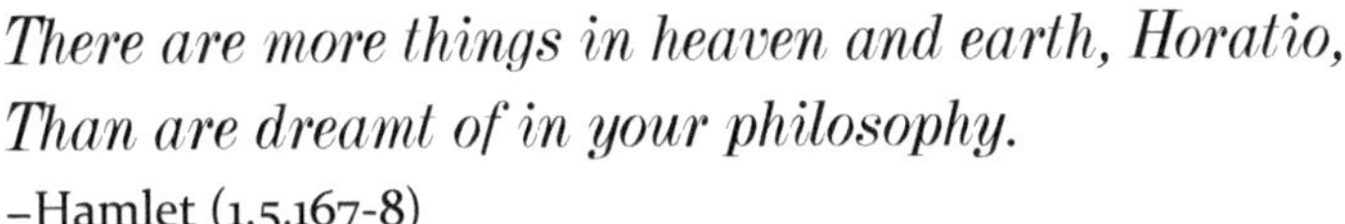

There are more things in heaven and earth, Horatio,
Than are dreamt of in your philosophy.
–Hamlet (1.5.167-8)

CHAPTER ONE

Problem Children

The ancient cowshed tumbled down so slowly only an immortal could see it collapsing. Rosie was not immortal, so she merely noted every month or so that the roof had sunk lower or another board had twisted loose. Blackberry vines thrust between the slats like tentacles, so the shed had spidery legs at twilight. Even with prickly appendages, the structure leaned heavily against a more ancient oak tree as if it were tired from collapsing and needed a rest.

Rosie stood in front of the old building. It was low and long, designed for milking ten cows at a time as they munched hay or grain in the troughs. She suspected the cowshed was actually the oldest building on her property. The original farmhouse might have been older, but Rosie had no way of knowing. It had burned down eight years ago.

Ed stood next to her, eyeing her crowbar. "I sure wish you'd think about this," he said. He pushed back his tattered ball cap and rubbed his eyes again. "It's bad luck to tear down a barn."

Rosie tried not to grin. She knew Ed believed this superstition and took it seriously. He lived next door and had adopted Rosie as family after Ben had died, even though her own father only lived ten minutes away. She accepted Ed's friendship and his help, but not always his advice. For instance, Ed had tried to give her a rabbit's foot like the one he had in his pocket to try to protect his calves from the cougar that had been prowling the hills that winter. She didn't think a rabbit's foot had been so lucky for the rabbit.

"Ed," she said. "It is not bad luck to tear down a barn." Still, she took one more opportunity to knock the dirt off of her boots with the curve of the crowbar.

Ed pulled his cap back over his white hair. His eyes wouldn't stay still.

"This is the best place to build the round pen," Rosie explained again. She swept her arm to show her horse ranch and boarding facility, the place she'd been developing for years on her own. "There is no place else."

"I know," he said. He shuffled his feet and then turned. "It's getting late."

Rosie shoved her cold hands into her pockets as she watched him go. Ed readily shoveled manure and fixed frozen pipes for her, but today — indeed, every time she'd tried to remove the shed — he excused himself at the last minute and went home with hunched shoulders, kicking rocks. She sighed and let herself believe the early spring afternoon was growing dimmer. She leaned the crowbar onto the side of the shed and stood a moment in the doorway.

It was dark in the shed, made gloomier still because the weak spring twilight merely glowed between the warped slats. Today, there were no bright shafts of light slashing through the dark making the dust motes dance like pixies. Her biggest hay barn had light like that sometimes, but the cowshed never did. It always seemed dark, especially in the back near the floor. The blackness and the cold draft that breathed out of the doors made the building Rosie's least favorite, and she had never used it for anything but storing broken machinery.

She cleared out the old tractor and broken long-handled tools last winter when she couldn't go out on the trails with her horses and the lessons had dwindled. Rosie busied herself those cold months planning the new round pen where she would train mustangs. She had always wanted to try her hand at taming a wild creature but had never had the correct facilities to do it properly.

Of course, the money she could make selling beautiful, well-trained horses would help a lot toward paying off the bills accrued from her father's heart attack last year. His meager health insurance had been affordable because of its outrageously high deductible. Rosie had taken out a HELOC on her ranch, but the added payments had stretched her finances very thin, indeed. She needed more income from more boarders and lessons, and the mustangs represented another badly needed source of revenue.

A round pen was one crucial step in that plan. At fifty feet across, it wouldn't be too big, but finding a place for it on her hilly property was nearly impossible unless she knocked down the cowshed. Even though she liked the romance of having a 150-year-old building on her property, she wasn't going to allow nostalgia to stop her from moving forward.

That back corner was very black this evening and looked even more ominous than usual because it was empty. Cold air wrapped around her ankles, and she shivered. She wondered again if the perpetual cold was from a hidden well or spring at the back of the shed and if that would mess up the ground of the round pen. She shook her head and leaned against the doorframe. An endlessly muddy pen would annoy her.

"You certainly are a thorn in my side," Rosie said to the building. She ran her hand over her head and drew her long ponytail across her shoulder so it draped down her front. "It would be so much more convenient if you would just fall down on your own."

A puff of cold air on her calves seemed to acknowledge her departure as she turned, but Rosie had long ago discounted any thought of anthropomorphizing the creaky buildings on her property. If she had spent the last fifteen years guessing what each creak and groan, what each dropped nail or swinging door had meant, she'd be in the loony bin by now.

Still, she said, "Goodnight, Cowshed. I guess I'll tear you down tomorrow," as she turned to go inside.

Bobby, her cattle dog, waited for her on the steps of the triple-wide modular home that she and Ben had chosen to replace the burned-down farmhouse. They had only lived in it a few months before Ben was killed. Still, Rosie thought of the house as "theirs." Bobby was only five years old, so he was "her" dog. Ben would have liked him, though.

She patted his head. "You chicken shit," she said smiling. Bobby refused to go anywhere near the cowshed. He had never liked it. Rosie assumed that a board had fallen on him or something when she wasn't around, but she was only guessing. Whenever Rosie went to the shed, Bobby waited for her on the porch, sometimes whimpering, never venturing closer than the bottom step. She shoved her cold fingers into his fur to warm them for a moment before she stood up and opened the door.

They went inside the house, and Bobby bounced and laughed with his dog mouth and dog tongue until Rosie put his food down on the floor. Then she contemplated her own supper by opening the freezer and regarding the stack of TV dinner boxes. She only cooked when she had company, and she had not had company in a long time. She chose her favorite — Chicken Parmesan — and popped it into the microwave. She rubbed her hands together and then sorted the mail as she waited for the ding. Bills, bills, bills. She wished that she just once she'd get something other than a bill in the mail.

Across the room, her cellphone rang. "Damn," she said as she looked around for it. It rang again from somewhere near the door. Rosie stepped around Bobby as she navigated around the dining room table to the coat tree. She fumbled through the pockets with fingers that all felt like they were thumbs as the phone shrilled again. Finally, she found it in the breast pocket, and even though the call was from an unknown number, she answered it.

"Hello, this is Rosie."

"Oh! Hello. This is Patrick."

"Hi, Patrick," she said. "How can I help you?"

"Let's see. This is Equestrian Heights, the horse training and boarding facility on Highway 223, right?" He sounded like he was reading from one of her cards.

The microwave pinged. Rosie decided the food needed to sit for a while, anyway.

"That's me," she said. After a moment she repeated, "How can I help you, Patrick?"

"Oh, yes!" Patrick said. "I just bought a horse, and I need someplace to put her. I found your card at the feed store, and thought I'd give you call."

Warning flags leaped up in Rosie's head. "You bought a horse before you knew where you'd keep her?"

"Well, yes. It was a little spur-of-the-moment," the caller Patrick admitted. "She's at my aunt's place until I can find a stable."

"I see. So, you will require boarding. Do you think you'll need training for her or perhaps lessons for yourself?"

"Well, yes. I was thinking of both of those things," he said.

Don't do it, a little voice whispered to her. Don't take on another novice who bought too much horse. He'll just blame you when it doesn't work. Just like all the others.

Rosie shook her head, but her eyes fell on the pile of bills she'd been sorting through. It had been a lean winter. "Can you come visit tomorrow?" she asked.

"I'll be there with bells on," Patrick said.

Rosie hung up and sighed. Another problem child to take care of. She patted her cowardly dog and took her pre-packaged dinner out of the microwave. Problem children seemed to be her specialty.

The sprite watched the woman who loved the horses lean the metal bar on his shed and walk to her house where the canine waited for her. The sprite didn't mind the canine, but when it had been puppy the sprite had needed to frighten it once.

If he could have sighed, he would have, but he was not a creature that needed to breathe. Instead, he pulled back into the quiet darkness of the corner of the cowshed nearest the biggest root of the oak tree where the tree spirit faintly pulsed. Turning the woman away from the shed was tiring, but necessary.

He continued his vigil, checking the animals within its territory. This included the horses in the barn and also the beef cattle in the field next door which belonged to the cattle-loving human named "Ed." These animals were not dairy cows, the sprite's favorite, but since there were no milk cows, he watched the other domestic livestock.

The sprite could tell that the neighborhood cougar was miles away, but the cat was hungry and possibly injured after a long winter. The cat knew better than to bother the animals near the sprite, though.

All was quiet, so he sank deeper into the damp and waited.

Patrick was due "first thing in the morning," in his words. When he pulled up in a white pickup, Rosie — already done with morning chores — was sitting on her porch with Bobby, her hands wrapped around a mug of coffee, enjoying the warm steam as much as the hot drink. He hopped out, smiling, and strode over to her, hand extended. "Hiya! I'm Patrick!"

Rosie stood and shook his hand. "Hi, yourself," she said. Then she handed him the other mug of coffee steaming beside her and sat down again.

He stood a moment with the mug and then sat one step below her. He rubbed Bobby, and the dog nearly died in ecstasy. Patrick took a sip. "Nice place you've got here."

Rosie smiled into her drink. "Thanks."

Patrick didn't seem to know what to do next, so he fondled her dog. "What's your name, buddy?"

"That's Bobby," Rosie said.

"Bobby's a handsome boy." Patrick smiled at Bobby and scrubbed him at the base of his tail.

Bobby groaned, and his tongue lolled out and hung to his knees.

"You found his favorite spot," Rosie said. "It looks like you've got the magic touch."

"Maybe I do," he said. "I like animals."

She stood and stretched a little. "I assume you want a tour?"

"Okay. Yes."

Rosie strode off the porch toward the horse barn, mug in hand. Patrick, Bobby close at his heels, followed, but when they passed the falling-down shed, he stopped and blinked.

"You don't keep animals in there, do you?" he asked.

"Not on your life," Rosie said. She stood next to him as they regarded the shed together. She noticed that they were nearly the same height, she five four, he maybe five six. His haircut made her suspicious of a military background, but it wasn't so short that she couldn't see that he had been blond as a child. She decided there was something both old and decidedly young about him.

He looked at her, and his gray eyes smiled. "What kind of ghosties live in there?" he asked.

Rosie smiled back. "I don't know. I've been trying to bring myself to tear it down for a while. I need the space for a round pen. Something always comes up, though." She let her gaze return to the shed. Today it looked as though it were trying to push the oak tree out of its way. She shrugged and turned.

Patrick, with Bobby trotting at his heels, followed her to the twenty-stall barn slash indoor arena that had been Rosie and Ben's pride and joy. It had taken them years to scrape enough together to buy the materials for the barn, and then it had taken months and every favor from every friend they ever had to put it up. The ordeal never seemed like work, though, Rosie told herself.

Patrick was impressed. "This is way nicer than where Sunny is boarded now," he said. "My aunt has her behind her house, but there's no shelter except a tree. It's really muddy, too."

"Just a tree?" Rosie clenched her teeth and let out a slow breath. "I do my best to take care of my boarders like they were my own." Her face brightened. "Speaking of my own..."

A huge horse head swung over the stall nearest the tack room. The pert ears swiveled, and a hearty whinny shook the glass in the skylight.

"Hi, Caesar," Rosie said. She stepped up to the stall and rubbed her friend's head between his ears; they drooped, and his eyelids slid down.

"Wow, that's a huge horse," Patrick said.

"Caesar? He's chunky now, but you should have seen him when we were competing." She slipped the horse a sugar cube from her pocket.

"What did you compete in?"

"Oh, three-day eventing mostly. Some Dressage," Rosie said as if she were describing a car wash and not a grueling test of horse and rider.

Patrick was oblivious, as Rosie thought he might be. "Maybe you'll show me pictures someday."

Rosie smiled and gave Caesar a last rub. "C'mon. I'll show you the available stall."

She led him to the end of the row where a stall door stood open. The rubber matting was clean and dry. The last border, Ellen, had been forced to sell her gelding months ago because she had injured her back. The new owner had taken the horse to her own farm in October. The box had been empty since then.

Before Patrick had arrived, Rosie had pulled out the random broken tack and cracked buckets she had stored there and then swept out the stray bedding. As he looked around pretending to know what he saw, Rosie idly pushed on the automatic waterer to make sure the pipe hadn't frozen over the winter. Water filled the muzzle-sized pan.

"So, um, there'd be straw or something on the ground?"

"I use fir shavings from the mill usually, unless there's a reason to use straw."

Patrick nodded as if this satisfied him. Then he looked concerned, and Rosie knew a novice question was on his lips.

"Um, do the horses get exercise, or are they just locked up all day?"

"They spend most of their time in the winter in the stalls," she said. "In a couple weeks, when the pastures dry out, we turn them out. In the summer, they like to sleep outside. We can exercise your horse if you like, but that'll be extra. There are different levels of boarding: the most basic is just room and board and stall cleaning. Those owners come in every day to exercise and ride."

"I'll be in every day." Patrick smiled at her like he thought this information would please her. "I love Sunny."

"Right." Rosie stepped out of the stall to hide her face. He didn't know it, but he was lucky he'd worn a knit cap and not a cheesy new cowboy hat or else her head would have exploded with contempt.

Patrick followed her into the arena where a woman was lunging a ropey gelding in a seemingly lazy circle.

"The indoor arena is open all year, but most people only use it in the winter or when it is super-hot."

"Hi!" called Patrick. "What's your horsey's name?"

The woman looked up and smiled a tolerant smile. "This is Talent. Don't come much closer. He's a bit testy today."

"Come into my office," Rosie said. He followed her into the tack room. On the back wall, nearly hidden among a wall of English and Western saddles, Rosie pushed open a door and went into her office. It was a weird setup, but she kind of liked the hidden nature of the room. It felt like a little safe, hidey-hole.

She had turned on the electric space heater before she had started chores, so it was toasty warm inside. She re-filled her mug of coffee from the coffee maker and topped off Patrick's, too. Patrick sat in the chair in front of her desk, and Rosie noticed that Bobby ignored both the ratty sofa and his soft dog bed in front of the heater, instead flopping at Patrick's feet. Patrick smiled and rubbed the dog's back with his toe.

Rosie sat behind her desk and forced herself to smile warmly at the handsome novice on the other side of her desk.

"Now, what exactly do you think I can do for you?"

"Well, I bought this horse," he began.

"Yes, tell me about that."

Patrick shifted a little in his seat. "I was thinking about buying a horse for a while, you know, since I've been back, in fact, so I went to an auction."

Rosie cursed in her head. An auction horse? "And?"

"And there was this guy in the parking lot."

"Oh." Rosie set her mug down.

"I know I shouldn't have bought her on the spot, but she is so beautiful, and we have a real connection."

"Did you at least ride her first?" Rosie asked, fingers crossed.

"No. I'm too new. I wouldn't know from straight up. But I watched him ride her. She seemed sound."

"And where is she now?"

"My Aunt Nan lives outside of town on an acre."

"And the only shelter is a tree?"

"Yeah. It's been kind of cold this week, too."

Rosie picked up her long braid and began plaiting the loose hairs on the other side of the rubber band. Finally, she sighed. "Okay. You have a horse. Now what can I do for you?"

"I like your place," Patrick said. "I like how clean it is. I like how you treat your horse. I'd like to bring Sunny here."

"And?"

"And I'd like full board, lessons for me, and training for her."

Rosie chewed on her lip.

"What's the problem?" Patrick said. The brightness was gone. "I can pay you for your services."

"That's not it," Rosie said. "I am happy to take your money. I am happy to give you lessons and train your horse, but I need one condition from you."

"Yes?"

"You have to promise me that you'll sell the horse if I tell you that she's going to kill you."

"I'm sorry, what?"

"The only way that I'll take you on is if you will trust me enough to sell the horse if I tell you that she's too wild and is going to kill you. If you don't promise, or don't sell the horse, I'll evict the both of you."

They regarded each other a moment before Patrick nodded and said, "Yes, Ma'am," without a hint of sarcasm.

That was the first time Rosie thought that they might be able to work together.

Bobby interrupted the moment by thrusting his head under Patrick's hand. He laughed and rubbed the happy dog's ears. Rosie sat back with her mug and smiled.

"You're one of the chosen," she said. "Bobby is wary of new people."

"Oh, I have a way with animals," Patrick said. "Always have."

Rosie watched him rub Bobby into a drooling coma, and she didn't doubt it. It reminded her of other men and different dogs. She swallowed the lump in her throat and said the first thing that flew into her head.

"Where did you come back from?"

"Huh? Oh, Iraq. The first one and the second." He was scratching Bobby's chest and the dog was orgasmic, but Patrick was perceptively more tense. "Retired Army. As a civilian I'm working as an analyst at HP in Corvallis." He sighed, then half-smiled which made his eyes crinkle. "I'm looking to forget the Middle East, you know?"

As Patrick signed the boarding agreement, Rosie wondered where the idiot who had bought a horse in a parking lot had gone. Who was this man? Patrick was suddenly interesting.

CHAPTER TWO

Liar's Club

Patrick was due at 9 a.m. sharp, and Rosie didn't doubt that he'd be on time. Something about the way he called her "Ma'am" whenever she told him to do something made her confident he'd always try to be on time. It also made her smile. She felt a little silly when he called her "Ma'am," but she also kind of liked the term of respect. A woman in the livestock business had to work twice as hard to get any respect, so it was nice to have it handed over so readily.

She had been readying the stall for Patrick's horse, and had realized that the water pan had a leak. After she fixed that with some epoxy, she began spreading fresh sawdust in the stall. She stood up and stretched her back after the first wheelbarrow load was spread.

"This is going to take forever," she said to Talent, who was watching her from across the hall. "I think I'll use the tractor instead." The horse shook his head. "What could go wrong?" she said. She rubbed his forelock.

She walked outside to the tractor, an old red thing that was last washed when Ben was alive to care how it looked. She started it and drove it a little too fast over to the huge pile of shavings in its little shed. She scooped up a bucketful and drove much more slowly back inside the barn. The aisle way was technically big enough for her compact tractor to get through, but it was always a tight squeeze, especially if there were any saddle blocks down or random buckets in the aisle.

She stopped the tractor by the stall door and looked at Talent. "That's saved me three trips." He nodded, so she began to shovel the shavings from the bucket.

She had just begun to get a rhythm going when her cell phone rang.

"Gah."

Answering the phone involved leaning the shovel against the tractor, shedding her gloves, and fishing the phone out of a deep inside pocket. She didn't bother looking at the caller id.

"Yes?"

"Hey sweetie. It's Dad."

"Oh, hi." Her dad, Lew, was quasi-retired but still helped out around the alpaca farm he lived on.

"You sound busy."

"No more than usual," she said. "What's up?"

"Well, I'm over here talking to the guys."

"Wasting time at the coffee shop with the Liar's Club, you mean," she said.

"Hi, Rosie!" called the old men. She could imagine them sitting around a big table in the cafe. They were usually there after morning chores, trying to out-bullshit each other and share the old tools they discovered in their workshops.

"Anyway, Ed was telling them about your milking shed. How you can't bring yourself to tear it down."

"That makes me sound sentimental," she said. "I'm not. I just ... something always gets in the way."

"I know. You're the least sentimental woman I know." She could hear the teasing note in his voice, not that that note ever completely left. "Anyway, the general consensus is that you can't knock it down. It's bad luck. You might anger a sprite under your barn."

"Anger a what?"

"Alix says you might have a sprite, a — what was it, Alix? — A cow sprite under your barn."

"I think I can handle a sprite," Rosie said with a smirk. "What are they, like made of vapors? I'll be fine. Can I go now?"

"No, no, no!" She could hear Alix protesting in the background. The rest of his tirade was in his native language — he was from some part of Eastern Europe, though no one was sure exactly which part — but she did catch the word "Revenge" near the end.

"Can you tell Alix that I'm not changing my mind, no matter what foreign words he flings at me?" she said gently to her father.

There was some muttering. Rosie leaned against the doorjamb and rubbed her tired neck. There was sawdust in her hair, and she wondered if there would be time to shower before Patrick arrived.

"Dad, I've got to go."

"Wait, Rosie. We're coming out to your place."

"Who's 'we'?"

"The Liar's Club."

"What? All of you? Why?"

"Alix wants to hex your cowshed."

"And we want to watch!" came a chorus of old man voices.

"What?"

"I'll hex it for you, Rosie!" Alix called, still a distance from the phone. "I'll hex it good!"

"Fine," Rosie said. "That's fine if I can just get off the phone with you now."

"Okay. See you in a bit!" said her father cheerily as he hung up.

For a moment she stared at the load of sawdust still in the tractor bucket and felt suddenly weary.

"So much for my shower," she said to Talent.

Then she realized that the old men would probably arrive while Patrick was still there.

"Shit," she said to herself.

Patrick arrived on time in the same white pickup but towing a beat-up trailer, which looked like it had been used as a chicken coop for part of its life. He sprang from the cab in the same giddy-teen-girl manner as before. Bobby beat Rosie to his truck and nearly tackled Patrick as his enthusiastic tail wagged. Fortunately, Patrick returned the dog's enthusiasm.

Rosie never took that shower, but she had spent five minutes brushing sawdust out of her bangs. She'd re-done her braid, too. She didn't know why; she just felt like doing it. If she couldn't shower, she wanted to at least look presentable. But she was still grumpy about her dad's friends coming over uninvited.

Finally, Patrick stood up and smiled at Rosie. "And hello to you, too!"

"Hello," she said. "I'm sorry I didn't have time to shower after chores."

"I didn't notice," Patrick said. "Do you smell bad after chores?"

She almost laughed. "No, I was just covered in sawdust. Why did I just say that to you?"

He shrugged. "I don't know why you do anything yet."

"Okay. Well, just so you know, a caravan of crazy old men is on the way here to exorcise my barn, so we should..."

"Wait, what?"

Rosie shook her head. "It's my dad and his loopy friends. They think that there is a ... oh, it doesn't matter. They're just coming over, so we should get your horse set up quickly."

Patrick was looking at her queerly.

"What?" she said. "Don't you have crazy relatives?"

"Did you say 'ex-_or_-cise'? Not 'exercise' like running around?"

"Yeah. Nutty, huh? I've found that just letting them do their thing is easier than trying to keep them out."

"Well, this should be fun," he said. She couldn't interpret the look on his face.

"I'd used the word 'annoying,' but that's family for you," Rosie said. "Now, let's see this horse of yours."

Patrick brightened. "I can't wait for you to meet her!" he cried. He flung open the rusted trailer doors, and Rosie peered inside. "This is Sunny."

"My Lord," Rosie breathed. Inside was the most beautiful horse she had ever seen. Sunny turned her elegant head towards Rosie, and her copper hide glinted. Her mane was golden, and she had a soft, kind eye.

Rosie looked over at Patrick who was watching her. "Could you unload her?"

Patrick smiled and stepped into the trailer. He backed Sunny out and walked her a moment before stopping her in profile in front of Rosie. At last, she let out an impressed whistle.

"I have to admit, Patrick," she said. "I might have bought this horse in a parking lot."

"I know, right?" Patrick gazed lovingly up at his horse. Sunny stood very erect, ears on alert, taking in her surroundings. Rosie noted how tense the horse was.

"Mind if I feel her?" Without waiting for an answer, Rosie stepped up and said "Hello," by offering the mare her palm to sniff. Then she ran her hands over every inch of the horse, feeling the mare's joints, picking up her feet, rubbing her ears, covering her eyes, putting her ear to the horse's ribs. Finally, she stood up and leaned against Sunny's flank.

"How is she, doc?" Patrick asked.

Rosie smiled. "I think you got lucky and bought a relatively sound horse in a parking lot." She wagged her finger at him. "Don't ever do that again."

"Stop encouraging me," Patrick said and winked at her.

"I will never encourage you. Welcome to the family." Rosie thrust out her hand.

He held the lead rope in one hand and reached to shake her hand with the other. When Patrick took it, she felt a shock, but instead of leaping back, it made her grip Patrick's hand tighter. Her eyes grew wide, and she stared at him. He seemed surprised, too.

"What?" she managed to say.

Bobby barked. The sound made her jump, and she let go of Patrick's hand. Bobby wagged his tail and gazed adoringly first at her, then at Patrick.

"Did I shock you?" Patrick said. "That happens with certain people sometimes. Sorry."

Rosie stood blinking a moment. She'd had static electric shocks before, but this, this was more like a "zing!" that flooded her from fingertips to her hair follicles. "That, that happens to you ... frequently?" she managed to say finally.

"Oh, not frequently," Patrick said, slipping his hands into his pockets. "There's only maybe ten people I've met that get shock as big as you just did."

"Lucky me," Rosie said. She was warmer than before she touched Patrick, and she still felt a buzz. She forced a smile, but leaned against the trailer, away from him. "Um, let's not do that again for a while, okay?"

"Sure," Patrick said. He smiled and stepped out of her way. "After you."

Rosie was still buzzing when she heard a car crunching down the driveway. When it stopped in front of her house, the doors opened, and a surprising number of old men clambered out. Had they been wearing funny pants and big shoes instead of bib overalls and work boots, she'd have believed the circus was in town. Her father stepped out of one of the pickups that followed them.

Sunny did not like the spectacle and threw her head up and shook her halter. She pinned her ears back.

"Watch her," Rosie said, stepping forward in case the mare bolted. But Patrick put a hand on the mare's shoulder, and she instantly softened. Rosie's jaw dropped. "How did you...?"

But Patrick smiled at his horse, unaware that he had surprised Rosie — again.

"Is that the exorcism committee?" Patrick asked. He waved to the old men. "Looks like a good show."

"Uh, yeah," Rosie said, still blinking. "That's my dad and his silly friends."

"Whoa! I don't know if I'm ready to meet your parents. We just met."

Rosie rolled her eyes to cover her surprise. She wondered if that zapping thing had an intoxicating effect. She shook her head and walked over to her dad. Lew was white-haired, tall and thin, with a permanent teasing grin on his face. When he saw Rosie with Patrick and his horse following her, he said the one thing she hoped he wouldn't.

"Say, Rosie. Who's your new boyfriend?"

"Dad, this is Patrick Ecklund. He's just brought me a new horse to board."

"Hey, Patrick!" Lew shook Patrick's hand, and Rosie noticed he didn't wince even a little. "Nice looking horse you have there. What do you think of our little Rosie ... quite a looker, isn't she?"

Rosie sighed deeply. "Patrick, you have parents, right?"

"Just the two."

"Then you understand."

"Absolutely. Nice to meet you, sir. I assure you that my intentions toward your daughter are completely reprehensible, and I wouldn't have you even guess what I've been thinking of doing to her when you're not looking."

Rosie's jaw dropped as Lew bristled, but the other little old men laughed heartily, their voices echoing around her little bowl valley. Soon enough, Lew was laughing, too.

Ed swung a meaty arm around Rosie's shoulders. "That one's a keeper," he chortled as he steered her to the cowshed.

"Shush, Ed. I met him, like, two days ago." She tried to shrug his arm off her shoulders, but he didn't budge.

"Aw, let the old men have some fun, Piglet," he said, using Rosie's childhood nickname. "You know we all love you."

"I know," she said. She watched the crowd of old guys bonding with the new guy as they made their way to the shed. Military branches and ranks were being discussed, and Rosie overheard that Patrick had made Captain before he was discharged because of shrapnel in his leg. He caught her watching and smiled. Rosie was aghast when she realized she was blushing.

How dare Patrick say such a ... a crass thing? How dare he embarrass her ... in front of ... *with* her dad? How could she ever have thought him attractive? She decided she was relieved she'd seen his true colors before she'd actually begun liking him or something.

"Alix?" she snapped, jerking herself from Ed's grasp. "What exactly are you going to do here?"

"Me? Oh. I'm hexing shed." He looked at her riding arena. "That is one huge shed."

"The shed is over there." She pointed behind her house at the ancient leaning collection of boards. "Can we get this over with?"

"Oh. Okie. Let's take a looky at the place." Alix limped to it like it was calling to him.

Alix walked with a limp because of some war injury, although, like his origin story, the war story got stranger and more exciting each time he told it. The old men parted in front of him as he jerked his way over to the door of the shed where he set down the worn doctor's bag he held in his hand.

The rest of them circled around Alix, and as one, the group peered into the long, straight building. The morning sun slanted in from the left, but as Rosie had noticed before, there were no dust motes to illuminate the beams, so the light just striped the floor where it fell. In the back, where they wall slats fit better, it was very, very dark.

"Huh," Alix finally said. "Too dark back there."

"Yeah," Rosie said. "Even when I had stuff in here, that corner never..." She was going to say "felt right," but that would only encourage this silliness. Instead she said, "It's really damp back there, too ... because of the spring."

"Huh." Alix tapped his bag with his toe without looking down at it. "How old ist barn?"

"Don't know. I think it's probably the oldest building on the ranch since the house burned down."

"Huh." Alix hadn't taken his eyes off the dark spot in the back corner, and his face hadn't changed, but Rosie notice with alarm that beads of perspiration had sprung to the back of his neck.

"Alix?"

The old man wiped his neck with the cuff of his shirt. Then he looked up at her. "When were animals last in here? Slept in here?"

"I don't know, but I've never kept animals in here. It was falling down and too damp when we moved in."

"How long ago?"

"Fifteen years, at least."

"Huh."

Rosie wished he'd stop saying that.

"Do you have cow?"

"Me? No."

"Goat?"

"No."

"Huh."

"I have a dog, a few barn cats and horses."

"You got a little girl horse?" Alix asked.

"Um." Rosie turned to look at Patrick who stood holding Sunny's lead rope behind the group of old men.

"Wait, what's going on?" Patrick said.

"Oh, yes. Bring pretty horsey. She is perfect."

"What do you want to do?" Patrick's grip on the halter tightened.

"Lead her inside."

"I don't think..."

Alix looked Patrick in the eye. "Horsey will be fine. Put her inside."

Rosie sighed. "Let's just put your horse in there, Patrick. The sooner this nonsense is over, the sooner we can put her in her stall." She gently took the lead from him. "I wouldn't hurt your horse. You know that, right?"

Patrick's face was stony, but he let go of the rope. Rosie led Sunny around Alix and into the shed.

"Take off halter and come back here."

"O-kay." Rosie unbuckled the halter and gave Sunny a pat. Then she ducked out of the shed and stood next to a very tense Patrick.

"I need a program," he said to her. "Who's the Eastern-European shaman?"

"Alix," she whispered. She'd never heard Alix called a "shaman" before, but she supposed the title fit. She bent her head to peer inside the door.

Sunny stood in the shed watching the humans watch her. She stood, but her skin twitched, her ears rotated. She pawed the ground with one hoof.

That was the point when Patrick brushed Rosie's shoulder and zinged her again. Rosie gave a tiny yelp the same instant he whispered, "Sorry! There was sawdust on your jacket."

Sunny pricked her ears and looked at the pair, but a moment later, the blackness behind her became blacker. She swung around to face it and planted her feet. The humans felt a chilly draft wafting from the shed door. They all shivered.

Sunny spun and bolted out the door, scattering the old men like so many bowling pins, and took off running toward the pasture, mane and tail trailing like banners.

"Sunny!" Patrick yelled, his eyes wide. "Sunny! Come back!" The horse slowed to a lope at the sound of his voice but kept moving away.

"It's okay, Patrick," Rosie said, almost laying a hand on his arm before she remembered what touching him was like. "That pasture is fenced. We'll let her run and go catch her in a minute."

"Damn!" Alix had stood up and brushed dirt off of his overalls. "I was hoping a little girl horsey would be enough."

"Enough for what?" Rosie and Patrick were watching Sunny slow to a canter and then stop to graze spring's first green shoots in the muddy pasture.

"Enough for to calm the sprite." Alix peered inside the shed again. "Sprites protect the animal. This one in a cowshed probably protects cows, female cows."

"So, it's lonely? For a cow?" Rosie said.

"Get a cow. We'll see."

"I don't want a cow."

"You're sure she's okay?" Patrick said. "What if she's hurt?"

"She is not hurt. Sprite would not hurt horse or cow or animal that lives here. It might hurt a person who hurt an animal." Alix rubbed his bald head and then tugged his mustache. "You sure you don't want a cow?"

"I need the opposite of that. I want to knock this building down so I can put a round pen here. I have a truckload of mustangs arriving that need training."

"No, no. Don't. Leave building up. Please, Piglet. Feel the cold? That's not a good sign."

"It's always cold in there!"

"Right!"

"Maybe I could go get Sunny now."

Rosie whirled on him. "Patrick, will you hush! Your horse is fine. We will get her in a minute."

His look got suddenly steely. After a beat, he said, "Yes, Ma'am."

Then she turned to Alix. "I'm not getting a cow. Can you get rid of the sprite?"

Alix looked at the shed again. "Fifty years? Yes. Hundred years? Maybe. Hundred fifty? I don't think so."

"Okay, Alix," she said. "Let's say that I went ahead and tore down the barn. What would this hundred-fifty-year-old sprite do?"

"Bad luck," he said.

"Like, animals get sick kind of bad luck?"

"No, no. Sprites love animals and like people who take care of them."

"So, it shouldn't be a problem, then."

"Ach! Lew! Make your girl understand! Please!"

"Yes, Dad. Explain this to me."

Lew had his empty pipe clamped in his teeth, and he was staring into the dark shed. He turned to Rosie and said, "This is all hogwash, Piglet, but you should do what Alix says."

Rosie squeezed her temples with her fingertips and shut her eyes. "Thanks for your help, Dad."

Lew shrugged. "What can I say? It's creepy in there. Your dog and that mare don't want to be in there. Hell, I don't want to be in there. 'There are stranger things in heaven and earth than are dreamt of in your philosophy.'" Lew liked to quote Shakespeare; in mixed company he quoted the dirty parts.

"Why don't one of you carve that into a sign and I'll hang it over the door?" Rosie said. "If we're done here, I have coffee and donuts in the house. Dad, can you set them up? We have to round up Sunny, or she'll founder on the new grass."

She strode to the far pasture where she could just see the mare. Patrick followed a pace behind her. She thought maybe he was angry at her for not getting Sunny sooner, but she was still fuming at Alix's foolishness and her Dad not contradicting him. A sprite? She would have used a stronger word than "Hogwash."

"So, that *was* quite a show," Patrick said. "I don't get why Sunny had to be a part of it."

Rosie stopped and faced him. "I am sorry I involved your horse. I was one-hundred percent sure that Alix was full of hooey, so I didn't expect her to get frightened. I would never have put her in any danger. Still. You were reluctant, and I should have respected that."

"Jesus, you're good at apologizing," Patrick said.

Rosie shrugged. "Lots of practice, but I only apologize when I mess up. I also expect apologies."

"Yes, Ma'am," he said.

"That should annoy me, but it doesn't," she said. "Let's get Sunny."

After a couple steps, Patrick said, "So, you don't believe that there is a sprite under your shed?"

Rosie waved a dismissive hand. "Like Dad said: Hogwash."

"Really? I mean, here we are chasing Sunny who charged out of that shed like a bat out of hell. And didn't your dad say that Bobby won't go in there, either?"

"Bobby's a coward. Aren't you?" she asked the dog as he appeared at their heels now that the excitement was over.

"Oh, I don't think he's a coward. He seems pretty bright to me." Patrick gave Bobby's ears a quick rub and then jogged to catch up with Rosie's big stride.

Sunny ran up to Patrick after a couple more bites of grass, and he slipped the halter back over her head. They walked back toward the barn, but Sunny started dancing on her toes as they got closer to the shed.

"Easy, Sunny," Patrick said.

Rosie watched the mare. The second time Sunny laid her ears back, Rosie said, "Come on. Let's go in the back way." She led them around the barn to the back door.

Every horse in the barn swung its heavy head over its stall door when Sunny walked into the room, not because she was a supermodel, but because they were curious about everything that happened in the barn, and a new horse was the most exciting thing that had happened in months. Caesar was especially taken with Sunny and pranced in his stall as she passed. Rosie smiled because Caesar had been a gelding longer than most of the other horses in the barn had been alive, but he seemed to forget that on a regular basis.

Rosie had put a thick layer of shavings on the floor of the stall and once they took off her halter, Sunny threw herself onto the floor and had a good roll, kicking her feet into the air and scraping a giant horse-angel onto the floor. Rosie and Patrick laughed.

"She likes it here," Patrick said.

"I'm glad she's relaxing now. I was afraid it would take a while for her to settle down," Rosie said.

After they had filled Sunny's hay bin, Patrick turned to Rosie.

"One thing I don't understand is why you had the old guys come over today if you don't believe them."

"Oh, Ed won't help me take the shed down because he believes it's bad luck," Rosie said. "These guys are like family. I guess I hoped Alix's 'ritual' would calm them down so I could get on with tearing it down in peace."

"Really?"

Rosie slammed the stall door's bolt closed. She wasn't sure why she felt so defensive. "If you have something to say, then say it," Rosie snapped.

"Sorry, Ma'am," Patrick said, but he didn't back down. "That just doesn't seem like the whole truth."

"You really want an answer?"

"Yes."

"Fine. I can't knock it down by myself."

"Why not? You run this whole place by yourself."

"Something stops me every time I try to wreck it." She leaned against the stall and ticked off on her fingers: "My phone rings, the sun sets, Bobby hurts his paw, or, I just decide to put it off until tomorrow. Only, the next day, I can't do it for some other reason." She shrugged. "Taking care of this shed has been on my to-do list for months, but it's like the universe is conspiring against me."

"Do you think it is?" Patrick's face had a strange brightness to it.

"No, that's silly," Rosie said. "I just don't like the cold air, and I tend to procrastinate on things I don't like."

"That doesn't sound like you," he said. "You seem remarkably direct. I like that."

Rosie's breath caught a little, and she couldn't help smiling for an instant.

"Well, I've made a point to face things. Instinctively, I want to avoid things like cold, creepy barns that don't want to be torn down."

"What did you say?"

"About avoidance?"

"No, about the barn not wanting to be torn down." Patrick leaned closer. "How do you know?"

Rosie could sense more than feel Patrick's warmth. "I don't know. It's always been there, and it seems like it wants to stay. It's not like it whispers to me or anything."

She didn't understand why a flash of disappointment crossed his face. She wanted the other look to come back.

"Plus, the last time we tried to knock it down, Ben died."

"Ben?"

"My husband."

"Oh, I'm sorry."

Rosie tried to shake off his sympathy and told her well-rehearsed version of the story. "We'd torn a plank or two off of the shed to see what it would take to tear it down. Later that week, Ben was ... breaking ... a stallion and took him out on the trail too green. The thing spooked and threw him in the ditch. I'm sure it was just a coincidence."

"I'm sure you're right." Patrick didn't look sure at all, but Rosie let him reassure her, anyway.

"Listen, I need to go back in to my house before the Liar's Club eats me out of house and home."

Patrick smiled. "Okay. But I'm not leaving without a donut and a peek inside your house."

Rosie shook her head. "You can come in only if you ignore everything the Liar's Club says."

"Oh yes, Ma'am."

The old men fell silent when Rosie and Patrick stepped inside the house. Rosie had the distinct feeling that she had been the topic of discussion, and she could tell by their serious faces they had not been speculating about what she and Patrick had been up to in the barn. She almost wished they had been. She knew how to handle dirty old men. She didn't know what to do with deadly serious old men.

Her dad walked up to her. "Rosie," he said. "The fellas here are really against you tearing down that building."

Rosie didn't even say anything before her dad raised an arresting hand. "Now, I see that stubborn crease in your forehead. Just listen to them for a minute before you dig your heels in."

"Dad, I don't need to listen to this. I let the guys come over to look at the barn because, well, mostly because I was railroaded, and partly because it sounded fun. But I'm not going to change my plans because there's a cold draft coming from a damp building."

She saw that someone had put her coffee pot on her mail pile, and now there were coffee rings on her bills. "I need that round pen to train the mustangs because I need the money to pay for..." Rosie trailed off and looked at her toes. She saw her dad's feet shuffle a little, too.

"I know, Piglet. Just listen to Alix, please?"

Too ashamed to say anything else, Rosie said, "All right."

Alix stood before her and opened his black bag. From it, he pulled a worn leather-bound book and a strand of coarse, braided, and knotted hair. Then Alix began singing or chanting in his native language. Rosie wondered again which language it was.

Alix's voice rose and fell with the almost monotone melody, and he swayed slightly, hands palm up, arms bent at his side the braid in one hand, the book in the other.

Then, there was a flash of light. The braid of cow hair had changed color from black to blond. She looked at Lew who looked as astonished as she felt.

"That's some cow hair. From the tail," Alix said as he handed it to her. "Please hang that in the dark corner.

"And this is my Book of Lucks. Maybe it will help you." Alix gave Rosie the book, which she immediately realized was in some Coptic script.

"Alix? What happened?" she asked.

Alix closed his black bag and set it on the floor. He picked up another donut and said, "What? You wanted a hex. There's your hex." He waved the donut at the cow braid and then took a bite, powdering his mustache with sugar.

"This is a hex?" She pinched the hair and held it high. "I guess if I'm worried about a little sprite, a little hair can't hurt."

"Alix, that charm will make the sprite leave?" Lew asked.

"Maybe, yes. Just hang in corner. Then wait. Sprite will think cows are gone and will leave."

"Okay. So, how long? A couple days? A week?" Rosie asked.

"No, no. Not that strong. Year, maybe."

"A year?" Rosie flicked the charm onto the dining table in front of her and sank onto a chair. "Right. A year. I have five mustangs arriving in the middle of next month, and I have to wait a year before I can put up a round pen to train them in." She laughed a little. "I don't think that's going to work."

"Rosie," Alix said, wiping his mustache. "Please. I know what I say. This sprite is bad luck. He's, uh, mean. I'm surprised he hasn't caused trouble before."

Rosie stiffened and glanced at her father.

"Wait, her house burned down, remember?" Ed said. "You guys didn't do anything to the shed before that happened, did you?"

"I don't know," Rosie said. She picked up the end of her braid and fiddled with the curl of her hair. "It was full of rusty stuff by then. We pretty much ignored it except to stuff more crap into it."

"Were any animal sick on farm?" Alix asked.

Rosie looked at her feet as she thought. "That might have been the year Charger broke his leg in a gopher hole. He had to be put down."

"Near the shed?"

"Yeah."

"Anything else?"

Rosie couldn't look at her dad again, even though he stood quietly just to her left. She couldn't look at him because he remembered that year as well as she did, and even if she hadn't told him every detail, he knew enough to leap to the same conclusion she had.

Ben had been neither kind to animals, nor kind to her. The year the house burned had been the worst.

She reacted to her shame with her usual anger.

"This is bullshit." Rosie stood. "I love all of you guys, but you need to leave and take your special kind of crazy with you."

As one, the pack of old men recoiled from the angry woman, stood, and shuffled out of the door. Alix turned on the porch and said, "I know what I say, Rosie! Put charm in barn for year!"

"I heard you!" Rosie called back.

When she closed the door behind them, she turned to find Patrick still in the living room, feeding bites of a bear claw to Bobby.

"Ahem!"

"Oh, sorry," he said, standing. He brushed his hands off on his jeans and hurried to stand beside her at the door.

"Hey, I have a question for you before I go," he said.

Rosie found herself glaring at him, so she took a deep breath and forced a smile. None of this was his fault, she reminded herself. "Sure." She smiled. "What is it?"

"Will you have dinner with me Friday?"

The smile dropped into a surprised "O."

"Excuse me?"

"You know, on a date?"

Rosie squinted at Patrick as if that would make his words make more sense.

"A date? Really?"

"Sure. Why not? I'd really like to get to know you better."

"Even after this morning?"

"Especially after this morning," he said.

"Aren't you mad about Sunny?"

"How could I be after that stellar apology?"

Rosie almost laughed, but then her eyes drifted off into the middle distance.

"What is it? You look sad."

"Hm?" Rosie looked at Patrick like she'd forgotten he was there. "Oh, nothing. Thank you, but I can't."

Patrick's smile changed to a mask that didn't manage to hide his disappointment.

"Well, another time, perhaps." He stepped close and kissed her forehead so it tingled. "Think of that the next time I ask you out," he whispered, and then he left.

She heard the door click as he closed it, and she stood for a moment as the buzz from his kiss warmed her face and neck and then her arms and legs. She swallowed once or twice and blinked. "Wow," she said.

She walked to the living room and flopped on the couch. Bobby insinuated himself into her lap, so she patted him for a while as the morning sank in. Soon he was asleep. She envied him.

She tried stretching to reach the TV remote, but she couldn't reach it without waking the dog. Instead, her hand fell on the Book of Lucks, so she opened it, resting the spine on Bobby's sleeping back.

As she expected, she couldn't read the book. The letters and words swam in front of her, foreign, or perhaps even alien. She shook her head, not really frustrated because she didn't expect to understand anything in it. Still, she flipped through the pages, looking at the woodcut pictures.

One picture stopped her. It was old and crude, but unmistakable. There was a barn. There was a man whipping a cow. There was a monster crawling out from under the barn, claws extended, heading for the man from behind.

A shiver danced down Rosie's back.

The caption beneath the picture stopped swimming and resolved itself into a word she recognized.

"Sprite."

The sprite hadn't meant to frighten the mare, but the new man surprised him into his solid form. The man had so much power that it leapt through the woman who loved horses and buzzed in the air around the sprite.

It made him uneasy, so he'd shifted, just a little. The horses on the ranch knew he was in the shed, but few had ever seen him, not since the violent man had died. The new mare hadn't known the sprite existed.

When darkness fell, after all the old men left and the woman was asleep, the sprite lifted himself from the corner and slid into the night for patrol. The carnivores in the area knew the sprite's territory and usually made a wide circle around the ranch. There was a young cougar in the neighborhood that he was watching carefully, but the coyotes were no longer a problem. The sprite tolerated the barn cats, and they tolerated him because each knew the necessity of the other for the protection of the farm.

Usually, the steel barn was closed up, but tonight, the sliding barn door was open an inch. Perhaps the woman had been distracted by the troubling new man. Whatever the reason, the Sprite let himself in to visit the horses and say hello to the new mare.

The sprite checked on each horse for the pleasure of its company. The new mare at the end of the aisle was nervous and banged her hoof against the stall. He went to her and mooed, and she put her head over the stall door. She relaxed when she saw him.

Welcome, little one.

Thank you.

I am sorry for frightening you this morning. The new man surprised me.

You are not the same as the last guardian I knew.

I am for milk cows. But I am here for you.

Sunny nodded, shook herself, and sighed. *Then this is a good place.*

It is.

The mare said, *You do not like my friend.*

The sprite considered a moment. *He has much magic and anger. He makes me nervous.*

He loves me, she said.

Then he must be good. Good evening, little one.

Good evening.

All was well, so the sprite went back to the shed and sank into his cool spot again. To wait.

Rosie was laughing. She sat across from her friend Meg in the same coffee shop her dad and his friends occupied earlier. It was the only coffee shop in town, but at two in the afternoon, it was pretty empty. Only the waitress and the owner's posters of *Casablanca* saw her trying to make light of the morning's events.

"Can you imagine people believing this shit?" she said, watching her friend. She'd told Meg about the hexing, but she left out the part about the Book of Lucks changing to English. She was still trying to convince herself that hadn't happened.

Meg smiled. "I thought horse people were a pretty suspicious bunch," she said. "I mean, even you have a horseshoe hanging over your door, right?"

Rosie's face fell, and she looked over Meg's shoulder. "That was Ben's doing. He was the superstitious one. He even made sure to hang it pointing up...so the luck wouldn't run out."

"Oh, right. Sorry."

Rosie smiled. "Oh, I don't mind. You never met Ben, and it has been eight years. I should get over myself and not freak out every time he's mentioned."

Meg shook her head. "Don't be so hard on yourself."

"Oh, I'm not, really," Rosie said. "It still catches me by surprise, sometimes."

"Yeah." Meg stirred her mug of tea. "Every now and then, I think I hear Martin's voice at the back of the house. He's never even been here. If I hadn't caught him with the housekeeper, I'd never have left him, and I'd never have come here, either. It's triple-weird that he still occupies that part of my brain sometimes." She smiled at Rosie. "Martin's still alive, though. I can't imagine..."

Rosie stopped her with a raised hand. "Let's not compare former husbands," she said. "Cody more than makes up for the bastard in your past."

Meg laughed. "He does." Cody was the local veterinarian. When Meg first moved to town, Rosie had helped her understand Cody's shy ways because long ago, she and Cody were briefly together.

"I'm glad you set us up," Meg said. Then she leaned forward. "I wish you would let me fix you up."

Rosie tried to avoid the question by looking around the coffee shop. She pretended to see a movie poster that was new to her.

"Rosie? Why won't you let me arrange a date for you?" Meg said again.

"Who would you set me up with? I've lived here my entire life. I've met or dated every man in fifty miles." Rosie shook her head. "I'm pretty happy with my life. I'm content."

Rosie caught the twinkle in Meg's eye.

"Lew says that you've got a new boarder with a pretty handsome owner," Meg said.

"My father is not a fair judge of man-flesh."

"But I am," Meg said. "He was the one you were giving the tour to while I was longeing Talent, isn't he? That man was very cute."

Rosie sighed her defeat. "Okay. He's cute."

"What was his name? Patrick?"

"Yeah."

"You're being kind of cagey about him," Meg leaned farther across the table. "Did he ask you out or something?"

Meg saw the look on Rosie's face and laughed. "I knew it!"

"How did you know?"

"Oh, years of hanging out in bars watching men, hoping they'd look at me the way Patrick was looking at you."

"How was he looking at me?"

Meg cocked her head to one side. "I keep forgetting that are out of practice."

"I didn't spend my youth hanging out in bars, if that's what you mean."

Meg laughed. "Touche. But you did go to school in psychology. Didn't they teach you anything about body language?"

"Apparently nothing useful." Rosie gave in and scootched her chair closer to Meg's. "Okay, spill. How was Patrick looking at me?"

Meg grinned. "He was watching your every move. Whenever you'd look away from him, he'd be checking out your hair or your ass, which looks spectacular by the way," Meg added.

Rosie felt herself blush, thinking about Patrick's eyes raking over her body. Then she thought about his hands raking over her body.

"So, when are you going out?" Meg asked.

"Huh? Oh, I don't know that we are," Rosie said. She began tearing up her napkin.

"I thought he asked you out."

"He did. I said no."

Meg sat back, wide-eyed. "Why'd you do that?"

Rosie twisted long strips of napkin into snakes. "I don't know. It was just after the whole hex thing, and I was kind of annoyed with the old men, and he asked, and looked at me, and..."

"And?"

She glanced at her friend. "And it felt good. Good like when Ben looked at me, and I was sad. So, I said no."

Meg chewed on her lip. Rosie knew by now that that meant that Meg was trying very hard not to say what she was thinking and thinking very hard about what to say.

"Let me have it," Rosie said.

"When was the last time anyone made you feel as good as Ben did?"

"Eight years."

"Eight years is a long time, Rosie," Meg said. "If there's a spark, why not follow it and see where it goes?"

"Funny you should say that," Rosie said.

"What?"

"Sparks. Not the sort you're talking about."

"What kind of spark, then?"

"The zapping kind."

"Really?"

Rosie tried to explain how it felt when Patrick touched her, how shaking his hand made her hold tighter, how brushing her shoulder had made her yelp, how his simple kiss on her forehead tingled for hours.

"Whoa," Meg said. "I've heard of chemistry, but this takes the cake."

"I know. He says that there are about ten people he's met that he zaps."

"Makes me think of auras and energy fields and stuff."

"Oh, that's all a bunch of hogwash."

"You just got done telling me about it," Meg pointed out.

"I know." Rosie's forehead warmed where Patrick had kissed her. "It's just, I don't know. My life has been so normal, and now I have a haunted barn and there's this guy who zings me. Where did normal go?"

Meg shrugged. "First define 'normal' for me." She smiled. "So, what are you going to do?"

"About the barn or Patrick?"

"Either. Both."

"The barn needs to go. I need that round pen for the mustangs."

"And Patrick?"

Rosie shrugged, but smiled. "I guess we'll see. He said to think about it until he asked again."

"When do you see him next?"

"He has a lesson tomorrow."

"I have a good feeling about this," Meg said. She nodded her head and her short dark curls bobbed. "I can feel the dry spell about to end!"

Rosie let herself laugh with Meg.

"Here's to tomorrow!" she said.

They tapped their paper cups together.

Rosie had always had a thing for mustangs. Maybe it began the first time she saw a documentary about Wild Horse Annie and her fight to save them. Maybe it began with *My Friend Flicka*. As long as Rosie had loved horses, she had loved mustangs. She had done all she could over the years to donate to wild horse causes and had taken on one or two at a time as training projects for charity, but she'd never owned a mustang.

Over the winter, she'd had the opportunity to "adopt" five mustangs that needed a home and training. She'd leaped at the chance, but she really needed a round pen to get them started right.

Rosie had a corral behind the barn, but it was made of fence panels, so the horses could see everything on the outside. She'd trained horses there, but it was a real pain and took twice as long because the horses wouldn't pay attention.

Some of the wilder ones thought that they could escape by jumping over or through the fencing. Unfortunately, that corral was built over the septic tank. Rosie couldn't sink posts down into the earth for the round pen without landing in a certain creek without a paddle.

Since Rosie had nearly twenty acres, no one could be blamed thinking that there was another spot she could put a round pen. Logistically, however, the paddock where the mustangs would live had to be close to the round pen because none of the creatures was halter broke.

There was one spot for the round pen, and that was right where the cowshed was leaning against the oak tree.

Rosie was all set, too. A stack of new lumber sat beside the tree. She planned to use good boards from the cowshed as uprights. All she needed to get started digging post holes was a bare stretch of ground.

She thought about the horses as she stood, again, in front of the cowshed that evening, beer in hand. The herd included a stallion (which she might geld), three mares, and a yearling colt. All of them were beautiful dun Kiger mustangs. The stallion, colt and one of the dams had the distinctive zebra-striped legs, even.

Rosie fingered the crowbar in her left hand and took a swig of beer. Then she peered at the darkening sky.

"You win for another night, Sprite," she said and tossed the bar in the dirt at the entrance. She drank the rest of her beer and walked back to her porch where Bobby was waiting, ecstatic at her return.

"Yeah, I escaped the sprite's evil clutches again, no thanks to you," she said as she rubbed his ears. "Come on."

A shower was in order. Ranchers need two showers a day: a shower after morning chores and a shower after evening chores. She had to hurry a little since she was due at her dad's for dinner in an hour. She turned on the water and shed her clothes. She loosed her braid and let her hair hang down to her waist.

Before she stepped into the hot water, she caught a glimpse of herself in the door mirror, which hadn't steamed up completely yet. She almost never looked at herself in the mirror anymore; a woman who works with her hands and shovels shit every day doesn't usually worry about what she looks like to other people.

Today was different, though. Today was different because the man she would see tomorrow had asked her out on a date.

She decided that she was much like the young woman in love who'd married fifteen years ago, and perhaps prettier than the sad widow of eight years ago because her heart was lighter.

She closed the toilet lid and sat on it, chin in hand. Her hair fell along side of her like a screen so she could only see her toes and the worn bath mat. How old was she? She'd been a thirty-year-old widow, much to her surprise. She supposed that meant that she was now a thirty-eight-year-old widow. That didn't seem right, but she counted on her fingers and toes, and that's what it came out to. Thirty-eight.

That was an ugly number. Unwieldy. Weighty. Two years from forty, for heaven's sake.

Rosie heard the door creak open and then felt a wetness against her bare skin. Bobby shoved his nose under her hand. He panted dog breath next to her face, so she patted him, stood up, wound her hair up into a bun to keep it dry, and stepped into the shower.

The hot water rinsed away the day's layer of dust and mud and unmentionables. Rosie watched the dirty water go down the drain and thought about the next day. Patrick, assuming he was actually an eligible bachelor and not a married cad, had expressed an interest in her thirty-eight-year-old husk of a self. He'd wanted to buy her dinner. There were reports of him checking out her ass. This made Rosie smile.

Then she felt ashamed, like she was fantasizing about someone other than her husband. Her dead husband.

"You are still dead, right, Ben?" she asked.

Not hearing an answer, Rosie wondered if she should put on eyeliner in the morning, or if that would be trying too hard.

Molly was an excellent cook. Rosie grinned like a grade-schooler when she opened the door to her dad's trailer and the scent of dinner enveloped her.

"Oh, my God. What are you cooking?"

Molly grinned back. "I thought I'd try some ostrich curry tonight," she said.

"You should have seen her trying to pluck that bird," Lew said from his overstuffed chair. "Those things can kick!"

Rosie looked at Molly who said, "If you believe him, I'll lose all respect for you."

Rose took her place beside Molly in the kitchen. "Oh, I know better. Where'd you get the big bird?"

"The bird farm on Highway 99 butchered their market chicks a week ago. I have another ten pounds in the big freezer. Want some?"

"Maybe. We'll see how this tastes."

Rosie wasn't surprised that the ostrich curry was excellent. Molly could take the rankest game and make something sublime out of it. She'd spent her youth cooking the boars and bears and pigeons her father and brother brought home from hunting trips. Ostrich was so bland to Molly's palate that she put it in a spicy curry.

"Pretty good, Molly," Lew said. "I can't taste the feathers or eyeballs at all."

Molly and Rosie both rolled their eyes. They shared Lew's sense of humor, but they also knew that eye-rolling was often the response he was hoping for.

"What do you think, Rosie? Should I take it to the pot-luck on Sunday?"

Rosie swallowed her mouthful. "Absolutely. But I'd probably just label it 'chicken curry,' or something."

"Don't label it at all, and make it extra spicy," Lew said.

"These are our friends," Molly reminded him. "We don't need to torture them."

"My friendship is torture enough." Lew's eyes twinkled as they always did when he was provoking her.

"I'll help clear the table," Rosie said, mostly to avoid being hit with a napkin in the cross-fire.

Molly picked up a couple plates and with a parting wink to Lew, followed Rosie into the kitchen.

"So, what will you bring to the pot-luck?" she asked.

"Molly," Lew called from the table. "Don't start on her again."

"Lew, I'm just worried about her is all," Molly said.

"I'm fine, Molly. Really," Rosie said. "I don't need to go to the potluck."

"There are some really fine men, single men, there."

Rosie tried to laugh. "You know, for someone who isn't actually my mother, you fill that void pretty well."

Molly shrugged and scraped rice into the compost bin. "I just worry about, you know, your happiness."

Rosie hugged her. "You don't need to worry. I'm happy. I'm happier now than I was when I did go to church."

"I don't think you understand what you're missing. It's different now."

"Perhaps," Rosie said. "But I've spent years in and out of congregations. So far, I'm happiest not going to church."

"But maybe you could get over Ben if…"

"Molly," Lew was standing at the entrance of the kitchen. "We've talked about this, honey. 'What wound did ever heal but by degrees?'"

"I wish he quoted scripture like he quotes Shakespeare," Molly said.

"Shakespeare is scripture," Lew said, serious as a dramaturgist.

"It's just that every time I see that new pastor…"

"Not interested. Not my type," Rosie said.

"And you can't make a silk purse out of a sow's ear," Lew said.

"Oh, so now I'm a pig's ear?" Rosie laughed.

"Your words, not mine." Lew's eyes smiled as he gathered her up into his arms and squeezed. "And I'll love you even if you start sacrificing calves to the earth-goddess."

"You don't have to worry about that," Rosie said from her dad's comfortable embrace. "I'm a long way from any of that craziness."

CHAPTER THREE

Sunny

Patrick was more of a rank amateur than Rosie had guessed. He arrived early for his lesson so he could pet Sunny. He wore jeans and what looked like out-of-the-box new black cowboy boots. At least he continued to wear a knit cap and not a Stetson. Still, the fact that his eyes lit up around Sunny like a nine-year-old girl's was both charming and annoying.

"So, do you ride English or Western?" she asked from the tack room door.

He frowned and said, "Which is the one with the handle?"

"A saddle horn?"

"Yeah, whichever one that is."

"Right." Rosie shook her head and pulled down a saddle from the wall that seemed about the right size for both horse and rider. She found a bridle with a nice gentle snaffle bit and walked to Sunny's stall.

"Let's put her in the cross ties," she said.

"The what?" Patrick poked his head out of the stall and then said, "Oh! That looks heavy. Let me help."

Before she could protest, Patrick was at her side, hefting the saddle and trying to take the bridle from her other hand.

"Patrick!" she said. "What do you think I do for a living? When I can't carry tack for a horse, I'm going to retire. Give me that and bring your horse over here."

"Oh. Sure thing, Ma'am." Far from being chagrined, Patrick handed her back the saddle and winked. "Anything you say."

Rosie watched him walk back to Sunny's stall — which he had left open — and found herself admiring the way the new boots made his ass flex. She shook her head, but smiled. What was he doing to her?

He led Sunny to where Rosie waited. She put the saddle and bridle onto racks and then clipped the horse into the two short ropes in the middle of the aisle. She pointed to them. "Cross-ties," she said.

"Cross-ties, Ma'am."

"Brushes." She held up a curry comb and finishing brush, one in each hand. She wasn't going to fuss with the technical names yet. She moved the curry comb in circles against the nap of the horse's hide and then followed with long, sweeping strokes of the finishing brush. Then she handed them to Patrick.

"Ma'am!" He grinned like he had just opened the best Christmas present ever, he went to work on Sunny's coat.

When he was finished brushing both sides, Rosie handed him a towel. "Shine her up."

"Yes, Ma'am!" He simonized the horse like she was a '57 Chevy destined for a show, and she glowed when he stepped back.

"That'll do," Rosie said. She then threw on the horse's borrowed blanket and saddle and slipped on the bridle.

"Let's go."

"Do I get to ride her now?"

"No. We need to longe her first."

She let them into the arena and clipped a longe line onto Sunny's halter. Rosie held a long whip in her hand. She walked to the center of the ring, but Patrick stayed on the wall.

"You coming?" Rosie called.

"Ma'am!"

She had to smile as he trotted out to where she stood. It didn't even annoy her when he "Ma'amed" her.

"We're going to turn in a little circle while she runs in a big circle, so keep your feet moving, or else she'll tie us together. Okay?"

"Yes."

"Ok. Let's see what we have here."

Rosie clicked and flicked the longe line.

It took a little work, but eventually the coppery mare was walking, trotting, and generally showing off at the end of the longe line. Rosie wasn't about to say it out loud for fear of jinxing it, but she thought Patrick had been lucky. Sunny had good ground manners.

When the horse's head dropped and Rosie saw her brain go into working mode, she said, "That's enough. Let's see what she does with a person in the saddle."

"Where do I get on?"

"You don't," Rosie said. "I'm not having you break your neck before I see what kind of animal we have here."

Rosie coiled up the longe line and hung it from a hook. Then she sat Patrick down in a folding chair on the perimeter and led Sunny to the center of the ring.

She stood at Sunny's head and looked her in the eye. "Hello, sweetness. How's Sunny? How's the baby?" The horse looked back at her and Rosie relaxed a little. There was no suspicion or fear in her eyes, which was a good sign. Too often, Rosie had seen horses' distrust before she was even near them, but sometimes the horse hid his intentions until he could do damage. Sunny seemed curious.

Still, Rosie was careful when she put her foot in the stirrup. Sunny skittered a little as she swung up into the saddle, and danced on her toes, but that was mostly pent-up energy and not animosity as far as Rosie could tell.

However, whatever manners Sunny had on the longe line evaporated when Rosie asked her to move forward. Rosie squeezed her legs, and Sunny laid her ears back and took one step forward. Another squeeze, another step. Another squeeze, and Sunny started walking, but not before rudely flipping her tail.

After two slow circuits around the arena, Rosie asked Sunny to turn and go the other way. Sunny pinned her ears again, and Rosie asked again. Sunny turned and flipped her tail. Rosie asked the mare to trot, and Sunny flipped her tail and chomped on the bit. The fighting was exhausting. Rosie never worked so hard to get a horse to canter slowly around the arena. Sunny defied her every move. Rosie could feel Sunny tire, but the fire never left the horse.

Sunny fought Rosie's every direction.Rosie found herself becoming angry at Sunny, and this made her angry at herself. Anger did not train animals, love did, but each time Sunny rejected her direction, Rosie found herself a step closer to telling Patrick that he couldn't keep her. Rosie found the idea of disappointing him too much to take. She blamed the horse.

Finally, Rosie leapt off. Sunny stood lathered. There was a new, flinty look in Sunny's eye as she regarded Rosie. Rosie gave the horse a steely stare, but then her eye fell on Patrick who was standing, concerned, at arena's edge. Rosie choked up.

By the time she had wiped her eyes and discovered that eyeliner smeared when wet, Patrick was at her side, gently taking the reins from her. Their hands brushed, a tiny "zing" chased through Rosie's hand, and she had to wipe her eyes again.

"How did it go?" Patrick asked.

Rosie managed a slow head shake. "She's too much horse for you," she said.

"What do you mean?" His voice clicked up a note.

"I doubt you'll ever be able to ride her, Patrick," she said. "This horse fought me every time I asked her to do something. She'll need an experienced rider who asks for all the right things at all the right times. Otherwise, she'll just take off with you wherever she wants to go."

"No, no that's not right," Patrick said. "This horse loves me. I love her."

Why was it so hard this time? Rosie had had to talk a number of stupid novices into selling their stupid impulse purchases because they'd bought a pretty, unrideable beast. Why was it so hard to tell Patrick this?

"It isn't true." Patrick's face creased with hard lines. "I'll show you."

Before she could stop him, Patrick swung up into the saddle and kicked Sunny in the ribs. "Patrick!" she called after him, arms outstretched as if she could catch him falling.

But Patrick wasn't falling. And Sunny wasn't running away with him. In fact, they were loping gently around the ring, each of them at ease and happy. Rosie turned in a little circle in the middle of the ring watching them. Every time they changed direction or gaits, Sunny would flick her ears at him, a horsey grin. Patrick bounced in the saddle like a sack of potatoes with no finesse at all, but otherwise, it was like he was an extension of the horse. By the time the two walked up to her in the middle of the ring, Rosie was convinced.

"What do you say, Ma'am?" Patrick asked, grinning and so happy it made Rosie's heart lighter.

"You were right," she said. "That horse was made for you. I can't believe it, but there it is."

Patrick kicked out of the stirrups and slid off.

"You have so much to learn that it isn't funny," Rosie said.

"I know you'll teach us everything in no time," he said, caressing Sunny's shoulder.

"It will take more than no time," Rosie said. "Connection or no, I don't trust Sunny yet. She has a long way to go, and you! Don't even get me started."

Patrick smiled and glanced at her sideways. "I know. I'm a mess."

Rosie laughed for no good reason. Relief maybe? "Come on. Let's rub her down and get her a snack."

"Yes, Ma'am." Patrick and horse followed her back to the cross ties.

Rosie showed him the steps in cooling down, rubbing down, and putting away a horse and then made him clean the tack before she let him out of the barn. He attacked each task with attention to detail and precision she wasn't used to but was grateful for. She'd had spent many a night re-cleaning tack that some teenager had half done in her hurry to leave the boring parts of horse ownership behind.

At the door of the barn, Patrick waited for her to exit first. Then they walked together to his truck. Patrick caught her eye as they approached the cowshed that seemed to sink lower into the ground as they got closer.

"I'm tempted to hold my breath when I pass that thing," he said.

Rosie smiled. "Well, you see where Bobby is." She pointed at the dog who had run a great arc around the shed and now sat on her porch.

"Seems like a good place to be."

Even though they laughed, they also gave the shed a wide berth. They were too far away to feel the cold air that always hung around the doorway, but something else made Rosie stop and stare a moment.

"What is it?" Patrick asked.

"Nothing," Rosie said. "I just thought I saw the shed move." She looked up at the oak tree. "It's not windy. My eyes must be playing tricks."

"Huh." Patrick looked at the shed, too, but didn't move any closer. "Haunted cow shed of Equestrian Heights!"

"Shut up." Rosie laughed, and they started walking again.

When they got to his truck, Bobby appeared at their heels.

"Bobby! I'll see you tomorrow, won't I?"

"Tomorrow? You want another lesson tomorrow?" Rosie frowned and ran her schedule through her head. "I might have time in the late afternoon, but I'll have to check."

Patrick smiled. "How about dinner?"

"I usually eat after chores ... seven or so. You want a lesson after dinner?" She frowned deeper. "It'll be pretty dark."

Patrick laughed. "No, I'm asking you to have dinner with me. Tomorrow night? After chores?"

"Oh." Rosie blinked and looked at Patrick. His head was still covered with his black knit cap, which made his laughing blue eyes stand out and twinkle impishly. "I..."

"I'm taking that as a yes." Patrick took her hands in his and her skin was alive with tingles. He leaned over and kissed her forehead. "Thanks for the lesson, Ma'am. See you tomorrow, Rosie."

She stood and watched his truck drive away, and then she sat on her porch steps petting Bobby until her skin stopped tingling. Every now and then her eyes would fall on the cowshed, which sat dark and probably not moving next to its tree. Then, she would look at the barn that held her horses and her boarder's horses. She smiled, thinking that Patrick riding Sunny may have been the most beautiful thing she'd ever seen.

It had been a long time since the sprite had felt power like that, and now it was on his ranch.

The shaman was not powerful; he was a human who knew something about magic. The charm he'd left was nothing more than ticklish, but this new man was different. He loved the mare, the sprite could feel that, but when the man stopped and looked at his house, the sprite could also feel the ground hum and the timbers around him itch with something like grief and hatred.

The surge of power he felt when the man touched the woman made the sprite shift again, just in case. The people didn't notice, and by the time the man drove away, the sprite was ephemeral again, resting on top of his house, watching the woman.

When the woman went inside, the unsettled sprite went to the barn, even though it was day, and through the open door. He went to Caesar who was glad to see him. The way the big horse chewed his hay calmed the sprite who thought of Brown Swiss milk cows and Guernseys with doe eyes and their methodical cud chewing. He missed methodical cud chewing.

When he felt better, the sprite swept the territory, even though it wasn't yet dark. He went back to his shed when he was satisfied that there was no danger lurking.

But he still felt the timbers of his shed itch.

The next day went slowly. Every time Rosie assigned herself a task which she thought would not only take forever, but would also distract her from counting the hours, it would take half as long as normal to do, and Rosie obsessed about the date the whole time. Bobby was at her heels, as always. It seemed to her that he had cued in on her anxiety and made sure to be at her side just in case she needed him.

She mucked out stalls, longed a few horses, gave a few lessons, ate lunch, gave a few more lessons, mucked some more stalls, repaired some tack. Except for the part where she checked the clock on the wall every ten minutes, the day would have been completely boring.

At last, the final stall was clean, the last hay bin filled, the last sugar cube lapped up by Caesar. Rosie turned off the lights and closed the barn door, Bobby winding around her ankles like a cat.

"What's up with you, silly?" she asked.

Bobby whined and leaned against her legs.

Rosie rubbed the dog behind his ears and started walking toward the house. She sniffed her fingers and wondered how long it would take to scrub the scent of saddle soap from underneath her nails.

She pondered this so fully that Bobby's single, sharp bark made her jump and squeak in surprise.

Bobby stood between her and the cowshed, his cattle dog intensity focused entirely on the black empty door three strides away.

He gave a low growl.

"Bobby?" She was confused. This was the dog who raced past the shed and waited for her on the porch, whining.

Rosie peered at the old building. It was blacker than it should have been that twilight, and another board had fallen.

"One less for me to pull down," she said to her dog, probably. Her voice caught as she tried to laugh.

Then one corner of the shed gently bowed and wobbled like she was looking at it from behind a wall of water or heat. Then it snapped back to attention. Cold licked her feet through her thick work boots.

"C'mon, Bobby," Rosie said, and they hurried to the porch. Bobby, for once, brought up the rear. He gave a last woof before he went inside with her. They didn't relax until the door clicked shut behind them.

"I need a vacation," she said to the dog. "That's the second time it looked like the shed was moving."

Bobby was still watching the door. He worked his jaw open and closed soundlessly—it was his tell that he was worried.

Rosie patted him again. "Thanks for having my back," she said.

Then her eyes fell on the clock. "Holy oats! I've got to get ready!"

Rosie hadn't fretted about what to wear in years. She had one or two dresses she used when she was required to be attired like a girl — horse association dinners and whatnot. The rest of her wardrobe consisted entirely of jeans and knit tops. Standing in her underwear in her room, she had the unfamiliar feeling that she had nothing to wear.

Patrick had been vague about his plans for the night other than "dinner," which in this one-horse town usually meant one of only a couple options: the casual dining place on main street that was filled with senior citizens and young families until eight o'clock, or the Mexican restaurant where you could order a margarita the size of your head.

Rosie decided that she'd be more embarrassed if she were overdressed, so she chose a long denim skirt and a white blouse she usually reserved for when she was judging horse shows. She pulled on a pair of tights and her calf-high English riding boots. She had polished them that afternoon as one of her distractions.

Rosie headed into the bathroom and pulled open the drawer of make-up. It creaked on its sliders, stuck from years of non-use.

"I should throw away half of this junk," Rosie said to Bobby who was curled up on the bathmat, watching her. "It's so old it smells like old lady." She held an offending rouge out to Bobby who tried to lick it.

She dropped the spoiled makeup into the trash. Rosie braided and wound her hair up in her favorite up-do. She pinned it in place and shook her head so a few tendrils floated down by her face. She decided a couple smudges of foundation to hide the circles under her eyes and some mascara would be enough.

"There, that's better," she said to Bobby, who wagged his tail every time someone looked his way.

Patrick had left a message on her machine saying he would pick her up at seven. At five to seven, Rosie stood in her living room, coat over her arm, purse in hand, wondering what to do with herself while she waited. Then she realized that her house was a mess. Truly, a disaster zone. She flung her purse and coat onto the couch and tried to clear a path within the eyeline of the door, ridding it of the barn coat, dog tracks, unopened mail and other clutter. She shoved books into shelves, stacked magazines on the coffee table, and flung the coats behind the door. She was contemplating the dirty dishes in the sink when Patrick knocked.

She answered it, panting a little.

Bobby shoved himself between them and tried to turn himself inside out when Patrick knelt down and let himself be licked. Rosie had to smile.

"Hello," he said when he finally stood. "What have you been up to?"

"What do you mean?"

Patrick smiled. "Well, I knocked three times before you answered the door, and your hair is a little..." He reached out and tucked an errant tendril behind her ear, which left a little thrill.

"Nothing," she said. "I was just waiting."

"Well, the wait is over," Patrick said. "You look wonderful. Shall we?"

"Okay." Rosie turned to get her coat and purse and succeeded in knocking down a pile of mail hidden on the seat of a dining chair.

"I'll get that," Patrick said, and was on his knees before Rosie could protest.

"I could have done that when I got home," Rosie said.

"But now you won't have to," he said. "Ready?"

She smiled and patted Bobby goodbye. So did Patrick.

Rosie could tell that Patrick had washed his truck. It gleamed white in the dusk. She glanced at the shed and realized that Patrick had parked as far from it as possible while still being in her driveway. Before she could comment on it, though, he trotted in front of her and opened her door.

"Thanks," she said, climbing in. "I though chivalry was dead."

"Nah," he said, as he slid behind the steering wheel. "Certainly not when you've been in the Army as long as I have." He started the engine and swung around the circular driveway.

"I thought maybe you were Army," Rosie said.

"Why's that?"

"Haircut. Plus, you said so."

"Oh, yeah," he said. He turned up the road, and then smiled at her. "I won't go into detail, though. It's not really first date material."

Rosie smiled. "You'll know more about that than me," she said. "I can count the number of first dates I've had on one hand."

"No kidding? I'm surprised. I figured you'd be beating them off with a stick."

"Aw, shucks," Rosie said.

"No, really," Patrick said. "I assumed the first time you turned me down was because you had a boyfriend already."

Rosie laughed. "A boyfriend? That's a good one."

"I'm not joking. Why wouldn't you have a boyfriend?"

"Well, for starters, I'm a widow. That usually puts people off."

He paused. "Not to be insensitive or anything, but wasn't that a long time ago?"

"Eight years." Rosie looked out the window as the darkening landscape swept by. "It doesn't seem like a long time, but I guess it is."

"Oh," Patrick said. "I see. People aren't put off by your widowhood. You are."

Rosie couldn't disagree. "Maybe I am," she said. She folded her hands in her lap and felt peculiar sitting in a strange man's car. *Poor widow me*, she thought. *Poor dead Ben.*

Patrick cleared his throat. "Well. The important thing is that you are here now. With me." And he reached into her lap and took her hand into his.

Rosie found it difficult to feel sorry for herself and think about Ben when her hand was vibrating from Patrick's touch. She smiled and looked at their entwined fingers.

"This might take some getting used to," she said.

"It's worth it. Honest." He winked at her. She nearly giggled.

When Patrick drove by both the Mexican restaurant and the old person mecca, Rosie turned to him and asked, "So, where are we going?"

He grinned. "You'll see."

"Am I dressed okay?"

He took his eyes off the road for a dangerously long time to examine her. Rosie felt her heart beat faster under his gaze.

"Patrick?"

He turned back to the road and said, "I think that will do."

"Don't do that," she said.

He just grinned at the dark road before them.

Patrick wore dark slacks and a button-down shirt with a pale check under a sport coat. He didn't have his knit cap on, so Rosie could see his closely cropped blond hair and a freckle behind his ear. She wondered if her lips would tingle if she kissed it. Then she blushed some more and was grateful for the gathering darkness.

They pulled into a parking lot in the middle of nowhere, the tires crunching the gravel.

"What is this place?"

"It's a winery," Patrick said. "I did a tasting here a while ago and found they have a restaurant tucked away back there."

The winery was a very plain, very large building. When they entered, Rosie discovered that there was only one floor with soaring ceilings. The high roof covered towering racks of wine casks, aging several vintages of pinot grape juice. "Holy mother of peanuts," Rosie breathed.

"I know, right?" Patrick stood looking up like he was admiring a gigantic tree.

He led her to the back of the huge room to a smaller addition with normal ceilings. This was carpeted, cozy and the large windows looked out over a nearly dark vineyard and city lights in the near distance.

"I didn't know this place was here," Rosie said.

Patrick beamed. "I hoped not. I mean, I wanted this to be a surprise. I really like it here."

They were seated at a window by a tall waiter. His shoes were muddy.

"That's the owner," Patrick whispered when they were alone.

"Why's he waiting tables?"

"I think he likes it."

Rosie ordered a duck and polenta dish.

"Can I have a rare steak?" Patrick asked. "And, will you just choose a wine for us?"

"Sure thing," the owner said. "You guys like a big wine or a fruity one?"

Patrick looked at Rosie who shrugged. "Surprise us."

"Gotcha!" The waiter practically skipped back to the kitchen.

"Okay, you've got a winner here," Rosie said. "As long as the food doesn't bite me back, this is my new favorite place."

"That's a relief," Patrick said. "You don't know how much I've been stressing about it."

"Really?"

"Oh, man," Patrick sighed. "I haven't been on a date since I moved here. Actually, for some time before that. I'm a wreck."

"I can beat that," Rosie said. Then she smiled. And he smiled back.

"Um, so, chit-chat. How long have you been here?" Rosie asked.

"Oh, six months maybe. I got a job running some computers over at HP. Before that I was in the Bay Area, hopping from one job to another. That was only a year or so. Before that I was in Iraq."

"I see." Rosie blushed because she didn't know what else to say.

"And you?"

"I've been here my whole life," she said. "I went away to school up in Portland, which is where I met my husband, Ben, but he was eager to move here. We worked a couple years to get a down payment, and then opened the ranch."

They stared at each other, aware that further questions would probe into the two topics that had already been declared off-limits: her husband's death and Patrick's service overseas. Rosie stopped watching her hands fiddle with her fork and looked out over the sparkly lights of the capital city in the near distance.

"It's pretty here," she said.

Patrick took her hand. She jumped a little and looked up to see him staring at her. "You're pretty here."

Rosie felt her fair cheeks flame red. She tried to pull her hand away, but he held her firmly.

"And I think it's charming that you are so ... blush so easily," he finished.

"It's embarrassing," she muttered. "I don't get flustered. I'm in control, always."

"Then it's all the more flattering that you are flustered." He smiled.

Rosie took a deep breath. She looked at their hands locked together and let the warmth of his fingers tingle up her arm. Then she smiled, too.

The waiter arrived with the wine, but Patrick didn't let go of her hand. The waiter/owner simply placed the glasses near their free hands as if this was nothing new to him. Maybe it wasn't. Or maybe he was just enjoying the show.

"Are we the only ones here?" Rosie asked.

"No, there's a couple over in the far corner by the windows. Behind you. I just tipped the owner $50 to pay special attention to us before we were seated."

Rosie grinned. "You did not."

"Did to. Want to ask him? Garçon!"

"No, no!" Rosie laughed.

Patrick waved the owner over. "Excuse me, sir, but did I not tip you a fifty when we came in? The lady here does not believe me!"

"Oh, he did." The owner pulled a bill from his pocket. "See?"

"Okay, okay! I believe you!"

"Make sure we get the most decadent dessert after dinner, too," Patrick said. "If you need to throw the soufflé in the oven, do it now."

"Oh, oui, monsieur!" The waiter was laughing now at his own terrible accent and left.

When Rosie could breathe again, Patrick started a story about a Chinese restaurant in Germany where he was once stationed where the waiters were more abusive the more authentic the food became. Rosie was laughing so hard when her duck arrived, she wondered if she would be able to eat it. She was.

The meat fell from the bone with a touch of her fork and melted on her tongue, gamy and good. Creamy polenta clung to the carrot spears and reminded her of the soul of the cornbread Molly made. She ate and drank, allowing herself the enjoyment of a meal that she didn't have to make or clean up after. As she pushed the last of the polenta around her duck bones, she thought of a question for Patrick.

"Why a horse, Patrick? Why now?"

Patrick's smile became softer and his eyes more distant. "That takes me back to Abarhim's horse farm in Iraq."

"Oh, I didn't mean to bring that up," Rosie said.

"No, this was a good part," he said. "When I would get some down time, I would just take drives around the countryside, the safer parts, anyway. I kept passing this one place that had these beautiful fat horses. Then, in the late winter, I drove by and the fat horses had foals. I didn't know from straight up, of course, but the fat horses were actually pregnant. Damn, the foals were cute, so I would park by the fence and just watch them bounce and play.

"Well, the third time I parked, out comes Abrahim from the house. You never know how an Iraqi feels about an American, and even though I was off-duty, it was safer for me to be in uniform off base, so I was conspicuous. I was nervous seeing this this huge guy come bustling out of his house, but I just stayed in the vehicle and waited for him.

"So, when he's close enough, he shouts 'Howdy!' at me." Patrick chuckled. "I have never been shot at by someone who shouted 'howdy!' first. Abrahim was the owner of the ranch, and apparently his horses were famous in the neighborhood."

"Were they Arabians?"

Patrick shook his head. "Hell, if I know. If you asked Abrahim one question, he'd launch into this lecture in Arabic and Pidgeon English that would last forever. I never caught more than a few words of any of it. He was so proud of his horses, though. He took me into see his favorite stallion. My God, that was a magnificent animal. All black with four white feet like he'd waded through paint. That horse ... he was the wisest creature I've known."

Rosie smiled. "I know that feeling. You've met Caesar."

Patrick gave her a queer look, then nodded. "Well, after that, whenever I got time off, I would go to Abrahim's to hang out with the horses. I would smuggle apples off the base and cut slices off for whoever came up to the fence. I was pretty popular."

"Did you ever ride them?"

"Oh, no," Patrick said. "I never asked, and it was never offered. Abrahim was proud of his horses, but he wasn't a fool. If something bad had happened while I was on one of his horses, there would have been hell to pay. Plus, we could barely talk. I was happy just making animal friends. They were a welcome distraction, and I wasn't going to jeopardize that."

"I see," Rosie said. "So, buying a horse wasn't a spur-of-the-moment thing, then?"

Patrick took her hand and squeezed it. "Not at all," he said. "I've been thinking about it for years."

"But why did you jump at the first horse you saw for sale?"

"Oh, I didn't." Patrick drew his thumb across the back of Rosie's hand, making her shiver a little. "I'd been to ten shows and auctions by then. She was the first horse who ... spoke ... to me the way that stallion did."

"That's why you bought her on the spot."

"Right. I don't care if I ever ride her out of doors. She speaks to me. I can't explain it."

"You don't have to," Rosie said, and squeezed his hand.

Dessert came and went, coffee came and went. Then it was late, and they were standing and shuffling on coats. As she walked beside him to his truck, Rosie tried not to feel anxious. She tried to enjoy the cool spring night and the rare treat of stars in the sky. She hadn't seen those for six months of cloudy Northwest winter. Still, her heart was fluttering as she climbed into the truck cab. Patrick started the ignition.

"So, uh, where to?" he asked, his voice catching.

Rosie knew what he meant. If he took her home, maybe the date was over. If he took her to his home, the date definitely wasn't over. If they went to a bar, they could talk more and drink more, but that was only delaying the choice.

Rosie wasn't in the mood for more talking.

"How old are you?" she asked.

"Me?" Rosie noticed he hesitated a moment. "Uh, thirty-six."

"I'm thirty-eight." Rosie paused. "I shouldn't be thinking about what my father might say at this moment, right?"

"No, not at all."

"Your place?"

"Done." Rosie laughed at the rooster-tail of gravel Patrick's tires left as he sped out of the parking lot.

Patrick's place was a duplex in Cynthian, a town near Rosie's ranch. It was completely nondescript. Gray paint, white trim, two story, garage. From the outside the place could have existed anywhere in North America. Not that Rosie was thinking about that. She was disappointed that she couldn't feel Patrick's zing through her coat as he took her elbow and led her up his walk.

However, before she slid her coat from her shoulders, she noticed a bookcase from Ikea full of horse bits.

"Are these what I think they are?" she asked. She strode to the case and stroked an ornate mouthpiece with one finger.

Patrick laughed and lifted one from the shelf. "Abrahim gave me this one because it was broken, and I thought it was cool. That sort of started me off." He handed her a standard snaffle bit, which was bent and weak at one end, but it had a certain grace to it.

"Nice," she said.

"Here, this one is interesting. Russian military from the 1800's I think." He handed her another, much more ornate bit with a lot of tooling on the side pieces. But, weirdly, it felt like a horse had just dropped it from its mouth.

"Wow, that's beautiful," she said. "What it is made of? It's warm in my hand."

"I don't know," Patrick said. Rosie realized that he was watching her carefully. "That one is a bit of mystery."

Rosie looked up and realized he'd made a joke. "Really? A pun?" She laughed.

Patrick grinned. "Sorry. Couldn't help myself. Look at this one."

"These are wonderful," Rosie said finally. She had held, caressed fifteen or twenty interesting or beautiful bits and listened to Patrick's impassioned retelling of how he acquired each one. Sometimes he knew the history of them, too. Three or four of them had been warm like he Russian bit. She'd never felt metal warm so quickly to the touch before.

"If I were a horse, I'd like a bit that warms up instantly," she said. "I wish we knew what they were made of."

Patrick shrugged. "I'm new at this," he said.

Rosie liked the sound of his voice. There was nothing remarkable about it — not a sexy baritone or radio-announcer grumble. It was just his voice, and he used it with great feeling and effect.

She also liked his hands, especially when they touched her, and little ripples of joy leapt up and down. She liked his eyes, gray now, blue outside, and looking at her.

"So, can I make you a drink?"

"Oh, absolutely."

Rosie followed him into the compact kitchen where he set up a couple glasses and began cutting up limes.

"What are you making?"

"Gin and Tonics. Wait, do you like gin?" His hands froze, knife in hand, hovering over the limes.

"Of course," Rosie said, though she couldn't remember the last time she'd had gin. "Mostly I drink bourbon, when I drink."

"I'm sorry, I don't have any of that," Patrick said. "Next time I will, promise."

"Next time?" Rosie smiled.

"Oops. Not supposed to make that assumption yet, am I?" Patrick laughed and handed her a drink. "Well, here's hoping," he said and raised his glass.

They clinked glasses and Rosie took a sip. "This is nice," she said.

"Thanks." Patrick took her hand and led her to sit on the leather couch.

"Look at you, all smooth." Rosie sipped her drink and hoped the ice cubes weren't clinking too loudly.

"Look at you, all nervous," he said. "See?" He held out his hand to show it shaking. "I'm a wreck. But, I'm brave in the face of danger."

He brushed a strand of hair and tucked it behind her ear.

"What's so dangerous about me?" Rosie asked.

"You might leave." Then he leaned in and kissed her.

Rosie had never felt anything like Patrick's kiss. The buzz of electricity, then the fire in her veins, and the urge to crush him to her all at once made her shake and splash some of her drink on her lap. She didn't react to the cold because she didn't care. She was floating, vibrating, losing herself, but gaining him.

Patrick put his hand on her cold, wet skirt and jumped back. "Oh, your drink!"

"It's okay," Rosie said. She leaned in again, but he was taking her glass and setting it on the table.

Then he looked at her carefully. "Are you going to leave now?" he asked.

She shook her head. "I have a question, though."

"Anything."

"Do you feel that?"

"The zing?"

Rosie nodded.

Patrick smiled and nodded. "I think it's different for me because I've lived with it so long. I feel it, though. It's like fire in my blood."

"I know how an electric fence feels," Rosie said.

Patrick laughed. "I haven't heard it put that way," he said. He cupped her face in his hand. "I'm glad you like it."

Rosie's cheeks burned and she felt ready to melt. She hadn't felt this good since...

"What's wrong?" Patrick was peering at her. "You're all stiff."

"I'm, uh, I..." Tears threatened. She pulled back and swiped furiously at her eyes.

"What? What did I do? Rosie, please!" Patrick grabbed her wrist.

Rosie could only stutter.

"Rosie, Rosie, look at me. Look at me." Patrick waited, repeating the phrase until she looked at him.

"You can go if you need to, but not until you tell me why."

She blinked at him. He gathered her into his arms, and she cuddled into his chest like a child.

"It's Ben, isn't it?" he asked finally.

"I don't know," she said. "It just suddenly felt like I was doing something wrong being here, with you..."

"Enjoying yourself?" he finished.

Rosie nodded. "It's silly."

"No, it's not." Patrick stroked her hair, making her scalp tingle. "I'm not a therapist, but I know that you deserve to feel good. I didn't know Ben, but if he loved you as much as you loved him, I know he'd want you to feel good, too. Am I right?"

Rosie nodded. This sounded like something from Grief 101. Even so, she wasn't 100% sure Ben would have wanted her to be happy this way. She decided that the topic of jealous dead husbands was not on the "first date" list, either.

"Do you feel better?" Patrick asked finally.

Rosie sat up and wiped her eyes. "Yes. Thank you."

"Good. Come on." He took her hand and they stood up.

"Where are we going?"

"I'm taking you home."

His words sucked the air out of the room. "Oh. I sort of killed the mood, huh?"

"No, that's not it. If you stayed now, I'd always wonder if I had taken advantage of you."

"I think I can make that decision myself." She lifted her chin an inch.

"You can make your half of that decision," Patrick said. "But I've made my half. I'm taking you home. But not before we schedule a second date."

Rosie smiled.

Rosie noticed the dark, unhappy building looking darker and unhappier than usual when Patrick walked her to her door. That was after a necking session in his truck as they sat in her driveway.

Patrick noticed it, too.

"The sprite is in a bad mood tonight," he observed.

She glanced at it and smiled back at him. "I'm so scared," she said, then giggled.

Rosie forgot about the cowshed entirely when Patrick kissed her goodnight on her doorstep. She was not even vaguely aware of the moths pinging again and again against her porch light and of the chilly air against the back of her neck because everything was zinging electricity in every part of her body as his lips touched hers.

"See you soon," he promised when he stepped off the porch.

Rosie closed her front door, and then watched Patrick walk to his truck out the window by the door, unwilling for the date to be actually over.

Then he drove away, and the shed deflated and leaned against the tree more heavily.

"It's the wine," Rosie said to herself. "Wine must make me hallucinate."

She poured herself a shot of whiskey and went to bed.

The very air told the sprite that the woman and the new man were returning. He could also tell that they had been in very close contact, and that was increasing the man's aura. It was the aura that made the sprite tingle and made his shed itch so.

It was the palpable animosity that worried the sprite the most. The new man had very positive magic, and while it seemed somewhat raw, it was the kind of power that the sprite normally found comforting, or at least benign. But it was not normally coupled with such hatred.

The sprite was not concerned — it was immortal and aware of the present only — but when the truck stopped outside the house and the people looked at the shed, the sprite watched them back. His feet touched the floor, and he felt his weight on the ground until the woman went inside and the new man drove away. Only then the sprite did let go of his solidness and went on patrol. He wished for the company of an animal, but the barn was locked, and the cattle next door had been moved to a pasture beyond his territory.

The sprite returned to the shed and murmured to the tree sprite, but the oak was not leafing yet, so that sprite was still asleep.

The cow sprite sank into his corner and recalled warm evenings when his cows had lowed to calves and a sweet girl with hay in her hair had milked each one twice a day.

A week later, Rosie was still reverberating from the aftereffects of the date. She smiled so much her face ached, but she didn't care.

The cowshed, however, looked the opposite of how Rosie felt: lopsided, worn out, grey. It also seemed grumpy, irritable. It was in a dark mood, indeed.

Ed wasn't going near it.

"You'll jinx us all, Rosie," he said. "Angus up the way lost three lambs to a cat last week."

"Now how does a cougar up at Angus's have anything to do with me?" Rosie asked. "And isn't the thing under the shed supposed to protect livestock?"

"I dunno. But you can't be too careful."

She smiled a truce at Ed. He had worked his whole life ranching and was barely getting by. She remembered her father's words about the comfort of something, even something not real, to blame for misfortunes.

"I know that's what you think," she said.

"You think we're all a bunch of stupid rednecks, don'tcha?"

"No, it's not that," she said. "I'm sure you all have good reasons to believe there's a pixie living under the shed…"

"A sprite," corrected Ed. "And if it's anything like the one Alix talks about, it's worth keeping happy."

"Right. A sprite. I need to keep the sprite happy." She sighed. She didn't even bother picking up the crowbar. She hadn't invited Ed over to contemplate the cowshed, anyway. She just wanted his help moving a manure pile. It was a job that was faster with two tractors.

She let her eyes sweep over the dilapidated building. She thought again how it seemed to be held together by sheer willpower.

"Wait, what's that?" She strode to he shed door and ran her hand along the jamb. She pulled out the cow braid. "How'd this get here?"

Ed shrugged. "Wasn't me. Last I saw that, you'd tossed it on the table."

"Huh." Rosie wondered who put the braid in the shed and why.

As she pulled the braid through her fingertips, she realized that the air in the doorway wasn't as cold as the day before. She put the braid back.

"As much fun as it is talking superstition with you, Ed, I need help with that mountain of shit behind the barn."

"Sure thing. Shit, I know." Ed grinned and Rosie got a glimpse of the little kid Ed once was. She thought for the millionth time that it would have been nice to know the Liar's Club members when they were still a bunch of young liars.

The two of them on their bucket loaders made short work of the manure pile, quickly dumping it into the spreader that Rosie would use later to fertilize the fields. Once the diesel engines popped and pinged to a halt, Rosie and Ed sat in the almost-warm spring sunshine and drank beer.

"So," Ed said after a prolonged sip. "Mabel and I saw you come home pretty late one night last week ... in someone else's truck."

Of course they had, Rosie thought. She reminded herself that she would have been much more embarrassed had they seen her come home before chores this morning.

"Did we wake you?" she asked, taking a swig of beer. "Sorry about that."

"Nah. We're old. We don't hardly sleep no more." He nudged her in the ribs with his elbow. "So? Was it this new boarder? Wassis name? Phil?"

"Patrick," Rosie said. "And, yes, it was him."

"Seems like a great guy," Ed said. "In the service."

Rosie had seen the tattoos that ran up and down Ed's arms and didn't want to imagine the ones on other parts of his body. Ed was in favor of people who were in the service.

"Army," Rosie said. "Served a couple tours in Iraq. I guess he saw some pretty rough stuff."

Ed nodded gravely. "Rough stuff happens," he said.

"Yeah. He won't talk about it. But he said that he fell in love with horses over there. They helped him deal with the stuff he was seeing. There was a friendly horse breeder in Iraq that let him hang around during his off times."

"I knew a guy in the South Pacific who found a kitten rooting around in the garbage and took it into the barracks. We all loved that cat, but it slept on his cot. It was a little piece of, I don't know, maybe home in a hell hole."

"What happened to the cat when you all left?"

"Dunno. I like to think that the guy hid it in his coat on the plane home. Most likely he gave it to one of the islanders to keep. Army's not going to pay to fly a cat home, no matter what the thing meant to a man."

"I suppose not."

"Good thing Patrick didn't want to bring a horse home with him!" Ed chuckled.

Something about that idea gave Rosie pause, but she pushed that out of her head. "Yeah, that's ridiculous," she said.

"So, did he kiss you?"

Rosie rolled her eyes. "Wouldn't you like to know?"

"I gotta know, Rosie. Mabel will have my hide if I walk in that door without some gossip!"

Rosie laughed. "I take it you haven't talked to my dad yet?"

"Had to miss Liar's Club this morning. So?"

"Yes. He kissed me."

"And?"

"And it was wonderful."

"Except?"

Rosie looked at Ed.

"What?" he said. "It's not called 'Liars' Club' for nothing. What happened?"

"I screwed it up. I thought about Ben."

Ed put his arm around Rosie's shoulder and gave her a squeeze. "I'm sorry, honey."

"We have another date, but..."

"It takes time," Ed said. "Grief never really goes away, you know. It just gets easier to deal with. It's not hard to deal with now, is it?"

"Not day-to-day anymore," she said. "Just when I'm in a room with a man I like."

"You'll get over it," Ed said. "You're ready. I can tell. You've been lonely."

"How could I be lonely with a pair of nosey neighbors, a gossip for a father, and Bob-o here?" She scratched her dog behind the ears and submitted to his zingless kisses.

"You deserve more than us lot. You deserve to be happy."
"Funny. That's what Patrick said last night, too."
"There you go," Ed said. "I knew I liked that kid."

CHAPTER FOUR

Whiskey

Ed left after his beer was gone, and Rosie watched his tractor putt-putt down her driveway and up the road. Slapping her knees, Rosie stood.

"Well, let's get this party started, Bobby."

Patrick and Rosie agreed to go out again after his lesson that day, which she scheduled for the last thing. Lessons and chores went more quickly than they had the last time she had been waiting for Patrick, but she still found herself watching the clock ticking slowly while a nine-year-old boy loped around the arena on Princess for his lesson.

Rosie's also mind turned in circles. Here was a man whose clothes she'd like to rip off, but as soon as she allowed herself to imagine him taking his shirt off, her stomach would knot.

She didn't believe in ghosts any more than she believed in sprites, but Ben was haunting her in a very personal way.

What had Patrick said?

"If Ben loved you the way you love him, he'd want you to be happy."

What a thing to say! Of course, Ben had loved her. He just loved her ... roughly, the way he had broken horses. Tough love, he'd called it.

Had he wanted her to be happy? Rosie didn't know.

She didn't know what to do with Patrick's ... gentility. She didn't even know how to greet him. Her whole body was tense and thrumming when she spotted his truck gliding up her driveway, and she leaned against the barn door for support when he stepped out of the cab.

"Hi," he said as he walked up to her. He stopped a step closer to her than normal, so she could feel his breath. Then he kissed her cheek.

Rosie smiled and knew things were going to be fine.

"Let's get Sunny saddled," she said.

"Yes, Ma'am."

Sunny whinnied and tossed her head when she saw Patrick and danced in the cross-ties.

Patrick laughed like someone told him a joke and patted the horse's shoulder. "You need to settle down, girl," he told Sunny, and she did.

Rosie cocked her head. "How'd you do that?"

Patrick's brushing arm froze on Sunny's shoulder. "Do what?"

"I've never seen a green horse respond like that before. I mean, Caesar sometimes knows what I mean...."

Patrick shrugged at Rosie. "I don't know anything about horses, Ma'am."

"I'm starting to wonder about you, Mister." She wagged a finger at him.

"I am the boy wonder," he said. "Lots of people wonder about me."

Rosie smiled and shook her head. "Weirdo."

Rosie and Patrick led Sunny out into the arena with the longe line.

"So, in case you hadn't realized, we longe horses before riding them to get some of the excess energy out before we put them to work. It's like sending the team to do a couple laps before practice."

"Okay."

"So." Rosie held out the longe line and the long whip. "Here you go."

"I don't know how to do this."

"Of course not. You learn by doing. I'll be right here."

Patrick took the line and whip and looked blankly at her.

She shook her head. "Fine, we'll do it this way. Pretend you're going to give me a hug."

Patrick held out his arms, and Rosie stepped toward him and then stopped.

"Oh. Maybe doing this tandem isn't such a good idea."

"I like tandem."

"Shut up. You know what I mean." She thought. "Wait here."

Rosie ran to her office behind the tack room and grabbed a puffy jacket.

Patrick laughed when he saw her. "Do you think that will help?"

"Let's find out." Rosie pulled on a pair of winter gloves and stepped between his arms, so he was behind her. She pulled his arms down so she could rest her padded hands on his.

There was a faint buzzing, but no zing.

"I can still think. This is good. Ready?" she asked him.

"Yes, Ma'am."

That was when Rosie realized that teaching Patrick this way was going to be difficult. Even though the extra layers of clothing separated their bodies, Rosie was very aware of Patrick. Plus, she could feel his breath on her ear.

Rosie sent Sunny out to the end of the line with a flick of the whip and a sharp "Walk!" The horse walked in a wide circle while the two people turned in a small circle, a dance of sorts, synchronizing their movements.

"Don't let her be the boss," she said to him. "Make Sunny do what you want her to do, not the other way around."

"Yes, Ma'am," he murmured. "Why's that, ma'am?"

"It's not a conversation," Rosie said. "Horses need to know who to follow. As a rider, it's a matter of safety."

"How so?"

Was he choosing breathy words on purpose?

"A horse's first instinct is flight, and when they run because they are frightened, their brains turn off. If they are trained to trust their rider, they'll follow your lead instead of running away with you into a ditch."

"How do you make her stop?"

"Like this." Rosie took the line and stepped toward the horse. "Whoa," she said. Sunny slowed and turned to face her.

Rosie turned and smiled at Patrick who stepped into the gap between them. "I'd follow your lead anywhere," he said and kissed her.

She might as well not have had the padded jacket on. Her body sang with his kiss.

Then she felt a muzzle shove under her elbow. Rosie laughed as Sunny looked for the horse treats she could smell in Rosie's coat pocket. Rosie pushed the horse away.

"Okay. Into the saddle, Mr. Patrick. Let's get this lesson done."

"Yes, Ma'am."

She began at the beginning: How to make contact with the horse's mouth through the bit. How to communicate with the leg. How to balance in the saddle. She knew that she really should be teaching Patrick on one of the school horses she had, even Caesar would do, instead of Sunny, but even though Patrick called her "Ma'am" in the barn, she could tell that he was completely unbendable on some things. One of those things was that he was going to ride his own horse during lessons, no matter what.

Rosie had taken Sunny out a couple times since Patrick boarded her there. Sunny was not as scary as she first thought. The horse certainly had been abused at one time and did not like a heavy, authoritarian hand. When Rosie had tried to correct Sunny, the horse planted her feet and threw her head around. When Rosie tried a softer, more persuasive hand, Sunny had been more accommodating. She wasn't about to let the horse dictate the terms of their relationship, but she was willing to negotiate a little.

So, she wasn't afraid for Patrick when he was on Sunny in the arena. He was right: he and the horse had some sort of connection. She knew that Sunny would eventually pull all the horsey tricks if Patrick didn't show leadership, but she could also tell that Sunny loved Patrick and wanted to do well for him. These were the reasons Rosie used to justify her decision to let him ride Sunny, anyway.

After an hour of walking slowly, thinking about balance and where his feet sat in the stirrups, Rosie had him dismount.

"Did we do good, Ma'am?" he asked as they walked Sunny to the cross-ties.

"Of course you did," Rosie said. "You're my star students."

"Thank you." Patrick slid his arm around her waist under her unzipped jacket.

Rosie watched as Patrick took off Sunny's tack and rubbed her down, only stepping in when she couldn't explain what needed to be done. Finally, he led his horse down the aisle and put her in her stall with a flake of new hay and an apple.

Rosie was standing at the door of the stall as he slid it shut. "Good lesson," she said when he latched the door.

"I have the best teacher," he said. He turned, leaned them against the wall kissed her.

The world swirled, but she realized that while the sensations were just as intense, she was able to ride the waves of electricity instead of feeling swamped by them. *I'm actually enjoying myself*, she thought.

"What happened to 'Ma'am'?" Rosie asked. She grinned as he kissed her neck and jaw.

"You're not my teacher right now," he muttered from her collar.

She laughed. "Not here. Come on. Let's get some dinner somewhere."

"I could eat you up," he said, but released her.

They walked out of the barn together toward her house so she could change. A little chill ran up Rosie's spine as they walked past the cowshed. It was as cold and dark as usual, but maybe something flickered nearby. She turned her head toward it just as Patrick took her bare hand in his.

As the zings shot up and down her arm, Rosie felt as if she'd walked into a blast of air so cold it took her breath away. Patrick gasped and pulled her closer.

"What the hell?" he hissed.

Rosie had the distinct feeling that something was growling. "Did you hear...?"

"No," he said. "But I felt it."

"The house. Now."

Rosie and Patrick ran the few steps to the house where Bobby was already barking next to the door. The dog was the first one in the house.

"What was that?" Patrick said after Rosie bolted the door.

"I don't know," Rosie said. "That's never happened."

"That shed was just creepy before. Now it's ... What is it?"

"I don't know." Rosie sat on a stool at her kitchen bar and found herself shaking. Patrick tried to slide an arm around her. She gripped his forearm with her fingers.

"Something growled at me."

Patrick was quiet for a beat and then said, "I felt that, too."

"When you touched me."

Bobby whined at the back door.

"Are you hungry?" Patrick asked Rosie.

"Yeah," she lied.

"Great. 'Cause I could really use a chimichanga. Let's go."

They made it through chimichangas leaned atop thick beds of shredded lettuce and a giant margarita each at Los Amigos before they were brave enough to talk about the barn.

"So, now the barn's making noises." Patrick used a pink straw to swirl the slush in the bottom of his glass.

Rosie shook her head. "If you weren't there, I would have just assumed that was another hallucination."

"Another?"

Rosie fiddled with her own straw. "Well, like last night. The shed got bigger while you were there, and then it sort of deflated." She glanced up at him and then focused on the remaining day-glow green in her glass. "I found the cow braid in there this morning."

Patrick shifted in his seat. "I popped it in after the hexing. Just thought it couldn't hurt."

"You're forgiven," she said.

"I've been thinking," he said. "Let me help you knock that thing down."

"Really? What about the sprite?"

"What about it?"

"Well, the growl? The shed changes shape. Cold air."

"I thought you didn't believe in that stuff."

"I don't. I mean, I'm started to wonder. You seem to believe the old men. But I saw it move."

Patrick took her hand from across the table. "I think the two of us can take a sprite, don't you?"

Rosie smiled at the picture in her head of Patrick in Army fatigues battling a six-inch fairy.

"Great. I'll clear my schedule and we'll demolish the blazes out of that thing next weekend," she said.

He held out his giant margarita glass and Rosie toasted with him. "Down with the shed!" he said, and they slurped the rest.

There was no question that they were going to Patrick's place after the Mexican food. His place was just around the corner, so they walked in the chilly night, his arm comfortably humming on her shoulders through her coat. They didn't talk much as they strolled from streetlamp to streetlamp. An occasional car would hiss by them, slowly bathing them in headlights as someone else headed home.

Even though there weren't many flowers up, Rosie could smell fresh-turned dirt and knew that the little old ladies were digging gardens.

"Spring is coming," she said.

"About time." She glanced up to see Patrick smiling. "It's better than the desert, but I'm tired of the rain."

"Spoken like someone who isn't native," she said. She took a deep breath and then stepped even closer to him. "Still, I'm tired of the cold."

"I have just the thing at home."

As promised, he had a bottle of bourbon at his place.

"Do you take it straight?" he asked. He set two stout glasses on the counter.

"One finger over some ice to start with," Rosie said. She was standing in front of the bookshelves admiring the horse bits again. She lifted the Russian bit and traced the curves and bends with a fingertip. It was warm to the touch, just like last time.

He handed her a drink, and she sipped it as she brought the heavy bit to eye level.

"Do you want to keep it?" Patrick asked.

"Oh, no." Rosie set it back in its place on the shelf. "It's yours. I couldn't take it."

He smiled. "It's yours if you want it." He brushed the back of her arm with his knuckles and smiled when she giggled a little.

"So, what's on the agenda now?" she asked.

"I thought we'd watch a movie," Patrick said. "I can order any movie ever made on my TV. Any requests?"

"How about something scary?" Rosie said. She settled on the couch. "You know. To psych ourselves up."

"A girl after my own heart," Patrick said. He found *The Shining* and pressed play. Then he sat next to Rosie and draped an arm around her shoulders. She shivered at his touch.

"Chilly?" He pulled an afghan blanket over the two of them.

Rosie didn't correct him because between his buzzing presence, the finger of bourbon, the giant margarita, and the warm blanket, she was feeling very, very good indeed.

The next thing Rosie knew, Patrick was gently shaking her awake.

"Oh. Hi. Did I really fall asleep during *The Shining*?" she asked as she stretched.

"Oh, you did. You were snoring away even before the hallway ran with blood."

"Did I spill my drink?"

"You were done with it by then." He touched her cheek. "Do you want to go home, now, sleepyhead?"

"You don't want to take advantage of a drunk me, either?" Rosie said, amazed at how brash she was. "What's a girl got to do to get some attention around here?"

Patrick chuckled. "Believe me, it was all I could do last time to take you home," he said. "Given half a chance tonight..."

"Stop talking," Rosie said and kissed him.

After several breathtaking minutes when her hands burned with the feel of his skin and her body vibrated with the touch of his fingers, Patrick stood and pulled her up from the couch. "Come with me."

He led her to his bedroom in the back of the house. The bed was neatly made, and the room was tidy. She had a vague feeling there were pictures on the wall and mementos on the shelves, but she lost interest in those niceties when Patrick sat her on the bed and took off his shirt. She bit her lip and looked up at his face.

"My God," she said. "You're beautiful."

"That's my line," he said, closing the gap between them and undoing her hair so it fell like a cape behind her. "How do you have all this hair?" he asked, lifting some and letting it fall over her shoulder.

"Funny thing when you stop cutting it. It keeps growing." Rosie leaned forward and rested her cheek on his belly and trembled with the flood of warmth and electricity that flooded over her.

"You know," she whispered. "I'm a little afraid."

"I won't hurt you," he said, dropping to his knees in front of her.

"I know. But, the zinging ... sensitive parts ... you know..."

He smiled. "I've never had any complaints," he said. "Anytime you feel like it, we can stop," he said. "I'm not in any hurry."

"Are you actually perfect?" Rosie asked.

"No," he said. "I'm stubborn, secretive, persistent, and pig-headed. Sometimes in a good way. Like now." He kissed her. "I can also be very, very patient. Although it's becoming more and more difficult with you sitting there looking so beautiful on my bed. Very difficult."

"Wait." She held him off with one finger. "Tell me why me again?"

Patrick regarded Rosie for a moment. "Besides being beautiful and spunky and intelligent and animals love you?" he asked. "It's because you are so you. Rosie Beaumont answers to no one. Your life is all yours. The first time I saw you, I wanted to ask you out because you were so confident. Everything around you was something that you owned or built or loved." He kissed her hands. "I live in a rented duplex.

The truck I drive I bought from my brother so he could upgrade. The only thing I love in this world besides my family is my horse. You have so much, but it is all you."

Rosie touched his hair. "I'm babbling," he said. "Sorry. Did any of that make sense?"

"We need to stop talking already," Rosie said and kissed him.

Rosie hadn't realized how dead she had been inside until she and Patrick had sex and every nerve in her body vibrated and sang with his touch. After they were done, she sank into his soft bed, pressed against his warmth, and slept, her whole being relaxed and at peace.

She awoke to Patrick gently shaking her shoulder.

"I don't know if you have a plan in place or something, but do you need to get home to take care of the horses?"

Rosie squinted at the weak morning light creeping around the drapes in his room. "I can make a call," she said.

He handed her her phone.

Rosie called her sometimes help, a girl down the road who mucked stalls on the rare occasion Rosie had to go out of town. She knew that there would be some loose lips as that girl could talk and talk, but that bothered Rosie until she hung up and Patrick pinned her shoulders to the bed again.

He kissed her. "I'm looking forward to making you breakfast," he said. "After we do this again."

"And shower."

"Oh, you want to do this two more times? Okay."

Rosie was mildly embarrassed that it was nearly noon by the time they parked Patrick's truck in her driveway. They laughed as they went into her house so she could change out of her date clothes. Bobby nearly knocked them down in his joy at their homecoming.

"Of course I brought her back," Patrick said, scrubbing Bobby's pointy ears. "She was yours first, after all."

Rosie shook her head at them. "I swear, that dog thinks he can talk to you," she called over her shoulder as she walked down the hall. She thought she heard Patrick say, "I'll tell her soon, buddy. Don't worry."

"What was that?"

"Nothing! Just talking to your dog."

"Whatever. Weirdo." Rosie closed the door to her bedroom, and wondered why she bothered. It's not like Patrick hadn't seen every bit of her already.

Rosie emerged later in jeans, turtleneck, and fleece vest. She opened the cupboard and pulled out a can of dog food when her eyes fell on the blinking light of the answering machine. Rosie had a cell phone, but all her business cards and other official stuff had her home phone number on it. She hit the button and reached for the can opener.

"That's some vintage technology," Patrick laughed when he heard the outgoing message and the beep.

"Shut up." She threw a dish rag at him.

"This message is for Rosie Beaumont. This is Kim from the Kiger Mustang rescue. We have you scheduled to accept the delivery of five horses from us on May 15th. I'm calling to tell you that due to circumstances beyond our control, we need to bump up the delivery date to April 30...two weeks from now. Have a good evening."

Rosie dropped the opened can of dog food, covering her boots and the lower counters with "gravy." Bobby appeared and began to clean up.

"What is it?" Patrick was in the kitchen. He took her arm and the little jolt made her look up at him.

"The horses. The mustangs are going to be here in two weeks. That's not enough time. Jesus." Rosie slammed her hand against the counter. "I've been farting around with this stupid cowshed, and now I don't have enough time to put up the round pen, or build a corral and a run-in shelter for them. Dammit!"

"What do you mean?"

"I can't put five wild horses into stalls in the barn. They'd kick the place apart. I need to put up a corral, a little three-sided barn so they can get out of the weather, and the round pen to train them."

"Do you need help? I'm good at helping."

"That would be great," Rosie said. "I'm going to take you up on that."

"Do you want to do that today?"

Rosie took a deep breath to calm down. "No, I need to rally the troops. Let's start tomorrow." She smiled at him. "Let's get you on your horse."

An hour later, Rosie sat at the edge of the arena on a metal folding chair watching Patrick and Sunny in amazement. Sunny had an overnight transformation from a stubborn green horse to a pliable, intuitive — dare she say it? — trustworthy mount. When the pair made a mistake, the fault was Patrick's. He still had a long way to go, but the connection he had with his horse was unmistakable.

Maybe it's the sex, Rosie thought. *Maybe that's what's clouding my judgment. No one makes this much improvement in two lessons.*

Patrick pulled Sunny up in the middle of the indoor arena and then walked Sunny over to where Rosie was sitting. "Ma'am? Can we go outside yet? It's really pretty."

Rosie looked out the door and had to agree. The cherry orchard across the road had exploded with flowers that filled the air with tiny white petals.

"Officially, I recommend against it," she said. "It's pretty risky to take a green horse outside for the first time. You'd be taking your life in your own hands."

Patrick smiled at her. "With all due respect, Ma'am, I think I've taken bigger risks in my life than riding a horse outside."

Rosie looked at him sitting atop his beautiful horse looking handsome and confident. Ben had looked that way on a horse, too. Rosie pushed that image away, determined not to dwell on the past when Patrick was around. It was time to move on.

"All right," she said. "I'm doing this under duress, but I'm sure Caesar would like to get outside, too. Let me throw a saddle on him."

Before they led the horses outside the barn, Rosie secured a beach blanket behind her saddle and clipped a lead to Sunny's bridle.

"What's the rope for?"

"Insurance," Rosie said. "We'll pony; I'll keep a long lead tied to my saddle, just in case something happens. Non-negotiable."

"Yes, Ma'am." Rosie saw a twinkle in his eyes. "That means we'll be riding really close, right?"

Rosie grinned and shook her head.

Caesar's eyes lit up when Rosie opened the gate and led him outside by the bridle. He danced a little as she swung up into the saddle, tied Sunny's pony line to Caesar's saddle, and checked the big blanket she tied behind her. She smiled and wondered if she were worried about the wrong horse.

Sunny hadn't been outside, either, because the rainy weather had saturated the pastures. Someone, Rosie or Patrick, had longed or ridden her every day, but only in the covered arena. Both horses held their heads high and sniffed and twitched their ears. Bobby trotted between the horses on the lookout for foolhardy ground squirrels to punish. Birds twittered. Rosie felt almost as good as she had the night before in Patrick's arms. The worry about the mustang's impending arrival melted from her shoulders.

They crossed the deserted road and Rosie smiled as they entered the cherry orchard. There were no cars here and very even terrain. The cherry grower had given her permission to send her boarders to ride in the orchard as long as the crop was not damaged.

"This is beautiful," Patrick said.

Riding six feet off the ground in the middle of a sea of white trees was like floating in a spice-scented cloud. Little birds hopped from branch to branch, and the air was filled with twitters and trills. The horses relaxed and swung their big heads in time to their feet, and Bobby ran through the trees snapping at falling petals.

She settled into the rhythm of Caesar's gait and turned every now and then to grin at Patrick and Sunny who was following at Caesar's hip down a row of trees. Sunny's happy horsey face seemed to echo Patrick's goofy grin.

"Almost there!" she called.

"Where?"

"You'll see."

After a few more feet, the orchard opened up around a large pond that lay hidden, nestled in a hollow surrounded by the blooming trees. The surface of the water was dotted with petals, a mosaic that was cut through with the dark trails left by the ducks and geese that had stopped on their migration to paddle and dunk in the luscious waters.

"Oh, God," Patrick said. He pulled up next to Rosie. "I had no idea this was here."

"Good. I wanted this to be a surprise."

She dismounted and pulled out the blanket. She spread it out on a dry-ish patch of ground overlooking the pond. She looped Caesar's reins on a low branch so he could munch some fresh spring grass. Patrick did the same for Sunny and joined Rosie on the blanket.

"Wow, this place is completely private, isn't it?"

"Yeah," Rosie said. "I've spent a lot of time here watching the ducks. It's nice. Hardly ever disturbed."

"So, nobody knows it's here?"

"No, the boarders know it's here, but no one is here today."

"Complete privacy, then?"

"Yeah." Rosie watched the ducks a moment, her mind returning to the screwed-up mustang schedule. Then she looked at Patrick and realized what he had been actually saying. "You're kidding."

Patrick just grinned more.

"You nut! Someone will catch us!"

"You just said no one would." He kissed her neck.

"But we'll freeze!"

"You won't have time to freeze." He laughed and untucked his shirt. "Besides, you're hot."

Rosie laughed and laughed. It felt good. "That was awful!"

"You are so sexy when you laugh," he said. Then he undid all her fasteners.

He was right again. Rosie did feel hot. She also felt like she was flying and falling and singing and laughing and she couldn't believe the noises she was making, but who was around to care? She clutched his back and arched her spine and did all those things heroines in novels did when they came, things Rosie had never understood before.

When they were done, Patrick rolled them up in the blanket like a love burrito and kissed her face. She grinned at him even though the scratchy blanket on her bare skin was driving her crazy.

Then Bobby flashed by. Rosie had forgotten all about the dog until he dove into the pond after a duck. They sat up and laughed as he swam after the bird, which tormented him by staying five feet in front of his nose. Frustrated, Bobby finally swam back to shore and ran up to them. Rosie saw what was coming but could do nothing to stop it.

"Bobby, no!" she cried as the dog stopped beside them and shook. He sprayed them with icy water and flower petals.

Rosie untangled herself from the blankets and reached for her fleece vest to dry her face. Her eyes grew wide. "Oh, shit," she said. "The horses."

"Sunny!" Patrick was on his feet.

"There!" Rosie pointed at Sunny, happily munching grass a few yards away. Next to her was Caesar, dragging his reins in the wet grass.

Before she could say anything, Patrick ran down the little hill toward the horses, Bobby hot on his heels. Naturally, this made the horses run, too. Caesar especially enjoyed the romp and did his characteristic kick/tail flip as he cantered easily away from Patrick, who was, of course, stark raving naked.

Rosie had never laughed so hard. She didn't bother to pull on clothes, either, but she did step into her boots so she could run faster through the fallen branches in the orchard.

Fortunately, the horses weren't hard to catch. Caesar made a bit of a game of it, but he was just feeling good. Sunny played the same game with Patrick, but when he stopped and then started shivering in the damp air, she turned and trotted right up to him.

Rosie used a double knot instead of a safety knot on Caesar's lead so she didn't have to worry about him while she put her clothes back on. Her jeans had been shoved off of the blanket, so they were damp, bordering on wet, and stuck to her as she pulled them on. She shivered even after she put the puffy coat back on.

"You okay?" Patrick asked.

"Just cold. I'll ride home with the blanket on my lap."

"We'd better get back, then," he said. "I don't want you getting sick."

For the ride home, Rosie chose a wider path so they could ride two abreast, Rosie still leading Sunny. Fine mist fell and petals stuck in their hair and on their clothes. Despite what Patrick had promised, Rosie's feet were very cold, and she looked forward to a mug of tea and maybe a movie cuddling on the couch with the man riding next to her.

As soon as they rode into the barnyard, though, Rosie's mood fell.

"Dammit. I'd forgotten about the cowshed," she said. She turned Caesar so they stopped in front of the building. She looked at it from atop her huge gelding and tried to remember why she had put off tearing it down before.

Patrick stopped Sunny beside them. "The offer of help still stands," he said.

She smiled at him. "Don't you have a home?"

"I don't have anything planned until work on Monday," he said. "I don't have a fish to feed or even a plant to water. I'm all yours until HP opens."

"This is the longest second date I've ever had."

"Me, too."

She turned back to the cowshed. "Why doesn't it look scary right now?"

"It's not billowing cold air for one thing," he said. He shook his head. "Maybe it looks different from the back of a horse."

"Everything is different on the back of a horse."

"Everything?"

Rosie laughed. "You are actually a fourteen-year-old boy, aren't you?"

"No, I want to try this. How do you make these things go sideways?" He wiggled in Sunny's saddle.

"Here." Rosie nudged Caesar with her calf and the horse flicked his ear and stepped to the right until Rosie and Patrick's legs were pressed together.

A breeze rustled the few brown leaves still clinging to the oak tree.

Patrick cupped Rosie's chin in one hand and kissed her, sending her down a now-familiar sinkhole of pleasure.

There was a great creaking, and a sudden blast of cold air swept over them. The door of the cowshed slammed shut. Bobby yipped and shot into the barn. Sunny spooked, tore the pony line off of Caesar's saddle horn, and ran to Rosie's newly planted vegetable garden. Even steadfast Caesar was startled enough that he spun and hopped once away from the building. Rosie collected her mount, and in three strides they caught up with Sunny. She grabbed the mare's bridle.

"What the hell?" Patrick said.

"I don't know," Rosie said. "Let's get the horses inside."

They put the horses away quickly and silently. Soon they stood inside the barn door looking across the barnyard to the cowshed that stood under its tree, door closed, looking still and dead. It still listed backward and leaned into the tree, but today the odd angles made it seem less like a benevolent leaning drunk and more surreal and sinister, like a Dali painting of elephants with giraffe legs.

Patrick took Rosie's hand, and the warm jolt from his skin made her smile a little.

"Did you see that?" Patrick asked.

"See what?"

"Watch."

Patrick released her hand and pointed at the cowshed. Then he took her hand. The air over the building waved like it was thicker.

"That. Did you see that?" he asked.

"Yeah. What was it?" Rosie's heard the quiver in her voice, so she took a deep breath.

Patrick licked his lips and didn't answer.

"Patrick? Let's go inside the house."

The sprite had followed the woman and her students on trail rides many times before, but this time, he hesitated. The new man was riding the mare and following the woman on the old horse. The sprite followed them to the edge of the orchard and watched for a moment, but then quickly caught up with them. If he was not close, he could not follow off of the ranch and would be forced to wait for their return. He could offer no protection from a distance.

The horses welcomed his company and kept up their typical horsey chatter. The mare had never been to the orchard before and was captivated by the flowers. The old horse was impressed by her bravery in the face of a new place. The sprite agreed. He preferred the quieter contemplation of a herd of cows chewing cud, but they did not explore much, and he had enjoyed exploring once.

The whole reason the sprite was here in this foreign land was because he had decided to follow his favorite cows across the sea and then follow their children across the land. He would have moved again had the cows moved, but they had simply died of age in the shed as the girl with hay in her hair grew grey and died, too.

The sprite stayed by the tied horses as the people sat by the pond. He calmed the mare when a squirrel snapped a branch. When the big old horse caught his foot in the tied reins, the sprite untangled him. The old horse, now untied, decided to nibble some grass on the other side of the pond, but the mare was tied and was afraid when she couldn't follow. The sprite loosed her as well. As long as he was there, they were safe.

But then, then the people began touching. He had become accustomed to their incidental touching, the brushes, the kisses, even, but this was different. He could feel their contact like a burr under a saddle. Like a hot needle, like a long spur. He tried being solid, but it didn't lessen the burn. He floated high above orchard, but too high and he'd lose contact with the horses and have to go back to the ranch. But he needed relief. He flew above the treetops and went home.

He fretted until he could feel them coming back from the ride an hour later. He was as ashamed as an immortal could be for abandoning his charges, and as anxious as he'd ever been. But they were back, and he met the horses at the road. They told him of the fun they'd had running from the people. Sunny reported that she had been very good and returned to the new man when he called to her because she loved him. The sprite knew of the bond between the mare and the man, and that was one reason he was confused by the man's anger.

Because the sprite was talking with the horses, he was surprised when the man and the woman stopped the horses in front of his shed and kissed. Because he was not prepared, the shock was like the sting of a whip and sent him caroming into his dark corner in a semi-solid state, which made the door bang behind him. This startled the humans and the horses and sent all of them into the barn.

It is not easy to anger a cow sprite without injuring an animal it loves. However, as the sprite cowered in his corner, he became defensive. He did not want to avoid the new man. He wanted to take care of the animals in his charge without being surprised by electric shocks.

So when the new man and the woman who loved horses stood at the door of the barn holding hands, the sprite grew angry. When they passed by, he told them he was angry.

And they ran.

Rosie felt ridiculous, but she was more than a little afraid, so she ducked her head as they dashed across the barnyard. Bobby raced ahead of them and waited for them at the door whining.

"That was weird," Rosie said once she had bolted the door. She tried to laugh, but couldn't.

Patrick peeked out of the door sidelight at the shed. "I'm liking that building less and less," he said, letting the little curtain fall back into place.

"Me, too. I wish it were gone."

"What can we do about that?"

Rosie thought. "Let me get on the phone. It'll be quicker if we can get another tractor to help. Maybe Ed can come over today. One of us can push and the other can pull."

She took out her phone and called her neighbor. She hung up a minute later.

"Ed's got a cough and Linda won't let him out of the house. She's got this fear that he's going to die of pneumonia. Let me call my dad and some other people."

A while later, Rosie hung up the phone and sighed.

"No one is available today," she said. "My dad and Alix will come over on tomorrow morning and help out."

"Alix?" Patrick and Bobby were a heap in front of the television, legs and fur in a tangle. They shared a bowl of chips. "The shaman?"

"He said that if I'm insisting on tearing it down, he wants to be here to mitigate the damage."

"Mitigate the damage? Those are some big words for Alix."

"Not really," Rosie said. "He was a defense attorney for twenty years."

"A defense attorney who knows how to hex? I'd hate to be a prosecutor in this county."

Rosie peeked out the window at the cowshed. It sat mute and still under the oak. It seemed a sad thing suddenly. A collection of dry, mossy boards.

Her stomach grumbled. She grabbed an apple and a soda from the fridge.

"So, what do you want to do until then?" Rosie asked, joining the dog pile in front of the television. She snagged the last of the chips before Bobby began licking the bowl.

"That's a dumb question," Patrick said. "Haven't you met me? I'm crazy about you."

Rosie laughed. "Besides that, I mean," she said. "How about a movie?"

"How about a bourbon and a movie?" Patrick suggested.

"Done and done. You pick the movie, and I'll make the drinks."

Rosie eventually looked up at the clock on the kitchen wall when she realized that the fifth of bourbon she had brought to the couch was gone. "Oh, man," she said. "It's almost dark out." She stretched and smiled at the way the room tilted like a top.

"Damn," Patrick said. "Time flies when you're watching a Stephen King marathon."

"Chores have to be done," Rosie said, giggling as she stood. "You'll have to help me, though. I'm a little unsteady."

"Right-o!" Patrick was swaying himself. Rosie wondered exactly how much help he was going to be, but they both put on their boots and coats and stomped out into the gathering evening, Bobby at their heels.

They laughed as they mucked out the stalls, threw hay at each other, and splashed water. They raced their wheelbarrows up and down the aisle and thought everything was funny.

"This beats doing chores alone in the dark!" Rosie said. Patrick leaned against the barn door jamb and kissed her. Then he stood next to her and looked around, his eyes falling on the bales of hay stacked in a shed on the other side of the barnyard. Then he looked at the smaller stack in the horse barn.

"How do you move all that hay?" he asked.

"Tractor."

"You can drive a tractor?"

"Of course I can," Rosie said. "I live on a ranch, don't I?"

"You're so sexy. Show me how."

"What? How to drive the tractor?"

"Yes."

Rosie giggled like a teenager. "Why not? Come on."

She led him around the corner of the barn to where the tractor stood under an overhang. She hopped on and started pointing out the controls.

"The pedals aren't quite like a car. This one is 'forward,' but this one is 'backward.' See? And this is how you control the speed."

Patrick nodded finally and said, "Seems simple enough. Move over. Let me have a go."

She laughed. "You're crazy. You'll crash."

"Not with you helping," he said. He pulled her off the machine and sat in the seat. Then he seized her around her waist and pulled her into his lap. "See? We're a team! Like Team Longeing!"

She giggled.

"You better hold on," he said and turned on the tractor.

The first thing Rosie did was switch on the light as it was damn near dark. Bobby hated the tractor and ran back inside the barn and barked at them as Patrick hit the "go" pedal and sent them lurching into the barnyard.

"You're pretty good at this!" Rosie hollered over the tractor's engine.

"I drove a lot of vehicles in the army before they decided to train me as a programmer!" he said.

"You forgot to mention that!"

"What?"

"I said, you forgot to mention that!"

They laughed as Patrick sped the tractor up and took them on a tour around the barn, around the house, around his parked truck. He pulled up to a stop next to the house. Rosie turned around so her legs gripped his waist, and he kissed her. Just above the tractor noise and the sound of his heart thrumming, she thought she heard a wail. She opened her eyes and saw thick air over the cowshed waver. They watched the air pulsate a moment.

"What is it?" Rosie asked.

"I was just thinking," Patrick said. "Why don't we just knock that piece of junk down now?"

"Now?" Her forehead crinkled. "Let's see, it's dark, it's dangerous, delicate work, and oh, yeah, we're both kind of drunk. I think it's a bad idea."

Half of Patrick's face snapped into a lopsided grin that made Rosie's insides flip. "That sounds like an adventure to me," he said.

"Really, Patrick, we should just do it in the morning."

"Are you afraid of that little sprite?" Patrick asked.

"Of course not."

"Come on," he said. "Just one push. I'll bet the whole thing goes."

"No way."

"How much you want to bet?"

"A bottle of Maker's Mark."

"You're on."

Rosie turned around. Then Patrick moved the tractor until it was a couple feet from the cowshed. In the dark, it was ominous, and cold air seeped around the tractor, making Rosie's feet freeze in their boots.

Patrick slid his hand up her neck. She turned her face toward him. "Let's piss this thing off," he said. Before she could protest, he slid his tongue into her mouth.

There was no mistaking the howl that came from the shed as anything but an indignant scream. Patrick looked up, and Rosie stared into the building.

"Patrick..."

He stomped on the pedal and the bucket loader crashed into the corner of the cowshed, making it shudder. Pieces of the roof crashed down, but with the only light coming from the tractor lamp, Rosie was unsure of how much damage they'd done.

"Patrick!" she said again. She hung on to the steering wheel for fear of falling off.

"We're finishing this thing," Patrick said. He reversed the tractor and crashed into the same corner again.

"Patrick!" she cried as they crashed a third time. "Patrick, let me off!"

A wave a panic flooded Rosie. Patrick's arms were like iron, and she couldn't get free. Suddenly, Rosie remembered the times Ben would hold her two wrists in one bear-like paw. Rosie, who could throw a 100-pound bale of hay over a fence, would writhe in his grip, unable to escape while he grinned meanly. Sometimes he would throw her to the ground or the bed, sometimes he would flick her away like a piece of trash. Rosie had hated feeling of being helpless and afraid.

Now she panted with fear as she twisted in Patrick's grip arms as the tractor attacked the shed. With a great screeching of nails pulling out of ancient wood, the cowshed finally came down, but the wailing continued after the wood was all on the ground.

"I can't let you go!" he cried. "It's not safe. Look!"

Rosie looked at the base of the tree where he was pointing and saw the trunk pulsate, the air wave, the cold move.

"What the hell?"

"I'm going to chase it away," Patrick said.

"No!"

She tried again to wriggle away, but Patrick steered the tractor toward the back of the fallen cowshed, toward the shimmer, the cold. Rosie clutched the steering wheel, not trying to drive, but only hoping, praying that she wasn't going to die.

The cold air shrieked louder as the tractor approached, and as Patrick predicted, it moved away from the bucket. Rosie watched as the shimmer moved in front of them into the darkness. Patrick escorted it to the fence line where it disappeared into the blackness of Ed and Linda's fallow oat field.

After a moment, Rosie said, "Do you think it's gone?"

"I have no fucking idea," Patrick said.

She turned to look at him and saw his face grim and surprised and frightened.

"What the hell, Patrick?" She slammed her elbow into his sternum.

Patrick blinked and looked at her, wide-eyed and white-knuckled. He let go of her waist, and she hopped to the ground and glared at him. He swallowed.

"I'm not my best when drinking bourbon," he said. "Things I saw/remembered from the Army sometimes..." He trailed off and his eyes were momentarily distant. "I'm sorry," he said when he focused on her again.

"That was unacceptable, mister," she said. She grabbed onto the tractor to steady herself. "You're, you're not allowed to ... hold me like that."

He eased himself off the tractor. "I know. You're right. I ... have no excuse, no words. I didn't mean to frighten you."

She took a step away from him. "Stay over there." The world was tipping again, in the bad way. Rosie swayed dangerously, and he stepped up and caught her elbow. "Let me go," she said and tore her arm away from him. She panted and stared at him with wild eyes for a moment. Then she blinked as if she suddenly recognized him.

He looked at her sadly. "Let's go inside," he said.

She nodded.

They left the tractor where it was, sitting sentry on the edge of Rosie's property, and walked beside the flattened cowshed into her house. Patrick opened the door, and Rosie stumbled in first and sat heavily on the couch.

Bobby immediately hid under the dining room table and peered out at them and refused to come out.

"Bobbo thinks we've lost our minds," she said, grasping for something normal.

"I know." Patrick sat at the other end of the couch and stared at the television, which was paused on a frame of the movie they'd been watching.

"What happened out there?" Rosie asked. She was still shaking from the adrenaline.

"I don't really want to talk about it," Patrick said. "But I'm pretty sure you're going to throw me out if I don't."

"You might have to leave, anyway," she said.

He nodded and took a deep breath. "Abrahim? He died trying to save his horses from a fire in the barn."

She waited.

Patrick said, "I don't usually tell people how he died. He ran into the barn to get the horses out. He didn't save all of them..."

"The stallion?"

"They died in the same stall," Patrick said.

"That's really awful," Rosie said. "I don't see how..."

Patrick shook his head.

"I went there on my day off, as usual, and found the place charred and his wife beside herself, surrounded by her family. She knew me and asked me over and over, 'Why? Why? Why?' I didn't know why. I never knew."

He glanced at her before staring at the floor. "I don't know if that thing in your shed is a sprite, but the one I saw did a shitty job taking care of the horses in Abrahim's barn. Their kind doesn't deserve respect or anything."

"You saw a sprite in Abrahim's barn?"

Patrick nodded. "It was in the stall with Abrahim and the stallion. Just standing there. Not doing anything."

"So, why the freak-out? Why wouldn't you let me go?"

He didn't look up. "I'm sorry about that. I lost control. I was, I was there again. So angry, but this time I had the tractor. I know it doesn't make sense."

Rosie's head sloshed and her eyebrows crunched across her brow. "So, you destroyed my shed to punish a fairy-tale creature on another continent?"

Patrick sniffed. "It sounds absurd when you say it like that," he said finally. "Can we just tell your dad that I was drunk?"

"I'm certainly not going to tell that other story," she said.

She went to the kitchen and picked up her emergency half-bottle of bourbon. She took a shot from the bottle and then walked back to the couch. She handed it to Patrick. "Help me finish this so I can get to sleep tonight," she said.

He met her gaze and drank from the bottle. "You're not going to throw me out?"

She shook her head. "You *are* sleeping on the couch. I have a lot to process," she said. "You're not the only one who had flashbacks tonight."

"What do you mean?"

She sat heavily on the couch next to him and took back the bottle. "My husband," she said before taking a heavy swig. She wiped her mouth and stared at Patrick's feet. "My husband," she started again. Then she looked at him.

"He hurt you?"

"Not really," she said. "But he ... he was a bully. A bully with a temper. He hurt the animals sometimes, all in the name of training, or dominance."

She handed him the bottle, and he put one finger on her hand. They froze a moment as her skin buzzed. Then she let go.

"You cannot hold me like that again," she said.

"I never will."

"You're still sleeping on the couch."

"Of course. Thanks for letting me stay. I don't trust that thing out there."

"I don't, either."

Rosie stood and walked to the hallway, Bobby close at her heels. She turned, and she was framed by the dark hall and glowed a little. "You really frightened me, Patrick," she said. "You can't do that. I've spent too much time not re-living that time over and over again..."

"I promise that will never happen again," he said.

But as she closed her bedroom door, she had a feeling that the darkness in them was not purged, and that promises that night were going to be difficult to keep.

CHAPTER FIVE

Building Projects

The man could command the steel tractor.

The sprite was not afraid of the machines, as the animals called the wagons that moved without horses or oxen. He had followed oxen wagons to this place long ago, walking among the cows. When the noisy, self-propelling "tractors" appeared, he agreed with the draft horses and oxen that it was better for a non-sensical thing that never got tired to do the work while they grazed or lazily swatted flies. In this way, tractors were good, even if they were made of steel.

The sprite knew that the tractors were strong, stronger than a team of oxen sometimes, but he had not realized that they could be used to destroy things like his shed. When the new man and the woman began driving around, their bodies so close as to annoy him, the sprite sank lower into his cool spot in the back and glowered as he watched them. When the new man drove the tractor close, the sprite told them to back off.

He was not prepared when the new man drove the tractor into his house.

For a century and a half, the sprite had lived in that spot in those timbers held together with those nails. They were an extension of him at this point, and when the nails squealed protests at being torn from their boards, the sprite shrieked. The broken timbers tore at him, and the sprite flew up into the tree and howled as they flattened his home.

When the destruction and pain ended, the sprite went into a rage. He leapt at the tractor but yelped as he bit it and flew back. It was steel, after all, a mix of metals that was dead to magic and burned the sprite's mouth. He flung himself at the new man and the woman, but the fumes of the tractor were like a poisonous shield. The sprite seethed just in front of the tractor and howled.

That's when the new man drove the tractor towards the sprite. The sprite had to move away from his house, from his tree, from his horses as the steel monster and the new man chased him, and the woman screamed. The sprite howled his frustration and fled into the fallow field on the other side of the fence until the tractor stopped, halted by the fence. He shrieked his indignation until it was apparent they wouldn't follow him, stopped by the magic of the physical fence. He stood quiet until the people left the monster and then went into the house. She was angry and afraid. He was a stew of emotions that the sprite didn't understand.

When he could feel that the people were asleep, the sprite returned to his ruined shed and mourned his lost peace. It took much energy to rebuild it, but he saved enough to return to the monster at the fence. The sprite could not touch the metal, but the parts that touched the ground were not metal at all and were softer than some flesh he'd rent before.

Rosie's alarm rang at 5:30 a.m. Despite her pounding hangover and the protestations of her warm-bodied dog lying next to her, she pulled on her barn clothes and thanked heaven once again for automatic coffee makers. She peeked into the living room to see Patrick sleeping curled on her couch. She stepped quietly into the kitchen and filled a travel mug with her own blend of witches' brew and opened her back door. She stood a moment with the mug half raised to her lips.

"Patrick!"

To his credit, Patrick was by her side instantly, vaulting over the back of the couch. He looked past her, blinking.

The cowshed was standing, real as the sunlight, next to the oak tree.

"How drunk were we last night?" she asked.

"Not that drunk," Patrick said, his skin pricking in the cold air coming in from the open door. "Look."

Rosie followed his point to find her tractor exactly where they left it by the fence, but tipped on its side. She shrank back into the house and slammed the door.

"What the fuck? What the fuck? What the fuck?" She stood shaking, waving her hands in front of her. Then she needed to sit, so she sat on the floor with a loud "whoomp." She began to hyperventilate. She waved her hand at the kitchen.

Patrick frowned at her. "What?"

She tried to say something, but the air wouldn't come, so she waved again.

Patrick went to the kitchen, and then saw a paper bag on the counter. He grabbed it, dumped its contents, and handed it to her.

She smashed the bag to her face and tried to breathe deep until she felt the panic ease out of her.

"You okay now?"

Rosie nodded. "Just, you know, surprised."

Patrick peeked out door's sidelight window.

"Is it still there?" she asked.

"The sprite or the shed? Either way, I think so," he said.

She looked out the window, too. "What are we going to do?" She realized that she was whispering as if the shed could hear her. She wasn't sure it couldn't.

The cowshed stood exactly where it had been the day before although it leaned a bit more heavily on the tree, and the one corner had distinctive tractor gashes on it.

"I don't think that thing wants to go," Patrick said.

"What is it? Why did it come back?"

"That's what I want to know."

"Shit. I hope the horses are all right."

"Of course they are." He didn't sound sure.

"I have to go check."

"Of course." He pulled on his jeans. "Just wondering, though. Are you still mad at me?"

"Shut up," she said and threw his shirt at him. "Horses first. Personal stuff later."

"Yes, Ma'am."

Bobby followed them out the front door of her house, the furthest door from the cowshed, and they circled the house, entering the horse barn from the back. The horses were grumpy about not being fed on time, but otherwise everything seemed normal. When they were done checking and re-checking the horses, Patrick and Rosie cracked the big barn door that faced the cowshed and peered out.

"If the tractor weren't over by the fence, I would swear that we dreamt knocking the shed down last night," Rosie said.

Patrick nodded. He lightly touched the back of Rosie's coat. Rosie held still. She wasn't afraid of him anymore, but she still felt wary.

He slipped his hand under her coat and fingered her shirt.

"Patrick." She leaned away, but then stopped. She felt something watching her from the shed.

Patrick pulled a corner of her shirt free from her jeans and slid a finger against her skin. She gasped a little.

Something angry moved inside the shed and the door slammed shut.

"What happened?" Rosie said.

"It hates us. Not me, not you. The two of us together."

"What do you mean? Why?"

"I think it's because of this," he said, sliding his palm across her bare back. As shivers rippled between them, the air over the shed shimmered and contorted.

"Let's not go out there." Rosie stepped away from him and slid the door shut.

He followed her into the office behind the dark, windowless tack room and stood a moment, watching Bobby curl up in his bed in the corner. Finally, Rosie said, "I think it's time you learned how to clean tack. We have time to get a couple saddles done before Dad and Alix show up to help us knock down the shed."

"Yes, Ma'am."

"Wish we'd had breakfast first," she said. She flipped on the coffee maker and went to get the saddle soap.

They shared an uncomfortable chuckle.

Lew and Alix found the two of them, sleeves rolled up to the elbows, each attacking a saddle with saddle soap and a rag.

"That's how all my second dates ended, too," Lew said, elbowing Alix in the ribs. "She's a hard woman, Patrick. 'Well mayst thou woo, and happy be thy speed/But be thou arm'd for some unhappy words.'"

Alix laughed and Rosie rolled her eyes, grateful for the change in mood. "Just keeping busy until the retired folk showed up," she said.

"I work many years so I don't have to get up at crack of dawn," Alix said. "I sleep very well, thank you."

"I wanted to ask," Lew said, helping Rosie heft a saddle onto its stand. "What happened to your tractor? It's on its side by the fence and all the tires are torn up."

"The tires are torn up?" Rosie looked at Patrick who was paler than normal.

"Hope it wasn't on its side long," said Alix. "Screws up the seals."

Lew frowned. "Wait. What happened?"

"It's a little embarrassing," Rosie began.

"We got drunk last night and knocked the shed down with the tractor," Patrick finished for her. "It was my fault. I had a bit of a flashback ... I shouldn't have let myself get out of control."

"Wait," Alix said. "You said you knocked the shed down?"

"Yessir."

"You have looked outside this morning, right?"

Rosie nodded. "That's one reason we're in here."

"So, why's the tractor all torn up?"

"We don't know," Patrick said. "We, uh, left it by the fence. Upright. With whole tires."

"Why by the fence?"

"We saw — something — come out after we knocked down the barn. We chased it off the property with the tractor and ran inside."

Alix looked grim, and Lew pulled out his empty pipe and chewed on it.

"And, you found shed like that when you got up?"

They nodded.

"Next time you call me," Alix said wagging a finger at Rosie. "I'm not prepared for all this."

"Oh, there's something else," Patrick said. "Whatever it is out there, it doesn't like it when I touch Rosie."

"What?"

"Come on, we'll show you."

They led the old men to the barn door which they slid open so they could all see the shed in the morning sunlight. Patrick said, "Watch," and took Rosie's hand.

This time, something inside the shed shook the door and howled.

Patrick dropped her hand and the howling quieted.

Alix slid the barn door shut. He contemplated his boots for a moment before looking up at Rosie. "That ist one mad sprite," he said.

"That isn't a sprite!" Rosie cried. "A sprite is a little green thing that lives in the woods! You know? Has wings? Sprinkles things with magic dust?"

"Nacht." Alix shook his head once. "That is pixie. This is sprite. Protector of animals. If you mistreat the animals, the sprite gets mad and causes bad luck. Accidents. Fires. You know." He bent to peer out of the almost-closed barn door at the shed. "This one is pissed."

"I don't abuse animals," Rosie whispered. "Look at this place! The damned horses eat better than I do!"

"And you don't have bad luck, right?"

"I don't know," Rosie said. "My husband was killed, and my house burned down. Those things didn't seem lucky."

"Maybe those things didn't happen to you. Just around you."

Rosie blinked. "Ben?" she said.

"Mebbe." Alix looked out the door again.

"Ben wasn't cruel to animals," Rosie whispered. "I never...."

"Rosie." Her father's voice froze her mid-sentence. It was the same tone he took when she threatened to run away as a teenager.

"Rosie, Ben's methods for breaking horses weren't what I would call 'kind.' Would you?"

"It was just cowboy," Rosie explained. "He just wore them out and then..." She trailed off as a memory of Ben chasing that stallion around the arena with a tire dragging behind it, hollering until the creature was so fatigued it could barely stand. She'd felt sorry for the animals, but she never spoke to Ben about it. He was absolute in his methods. There was no turning him. And he was absolute when it came to her, as well.

Rosie took a much different approach to gentling horses ... one that Ben had ridiculed. That was only one of the sticking points in their marriage, and one that stung even today as she remembered it.

But he didn't deserve to die for it.

When her eyes focused again, she saw the men in front of her watching her face. She was exhausted. "I don't understand," she said finally.

"The sprite, it is of another place," Alix said. "It came with the cows. From the old country, probably, with old country pioneers, maybe. They settled here and the sprite lived with the cows. Loved the cows. Then the cows left. Horses came instead. I don't know why, but the sprite stayed in the shed, but watched the horses." Alix looked around Rosie's barn. "Maybe there is too much metal here for the sprite. Maybe too light. Anyway, sprite lives in shed, watches Ben with horses, watches you with horses. Maybe decides you should take care of horses, not Ben."

"It killed Ben?" she whispered. She leaned against Patrick because she didn't trust her knees anymore.

Alix looked sorry, but he only shrugged.

"I don't understand why it's upset now," Patrick said.

"You knocked down its house," Alix said.

"Ben was talking about tearing it down before he died," Rosie said.

"And you've been talking about it. And leaving crowbars on the doorstep," Lew reminded her.

"Oh, shit."

"What about it getting mad when I touch Rosie?" Patrick asked.

"That is confusing," Alix said. "I will have to call my friend and ask him about that." He peered at Patrick. "You're not of...the Old World, are you?"

Patrick reddened, but said, "No, of course not."

"I see."

"I have an aunt," Patrick said. "Nan Petra."

"Old Nan is your auntie? Ah. Explains much."

"What about the shed?" Rosie asked. "What about that thing shredding the tractor and rebuilding the shed?"

Alix looked at her. "Rosie, do you really need to tear it down?"

"I don't want that ... thing around," she said. "It's dangerous. What if I have to put a horse down, and it kills me?"

"The sprite can tell you mean best thing."

"I don't trust it, Alix," she said.

"Rosie…" Alix began.

"Wait. I know you're going to tell me that the best way is to live with the damned thing, but you just said it killed my husband."

"Yah. Probably."

"I don't feel safe here, anymore." Rosie said. "And what am I going to do? Sell? Do I have to disclose that there is a demon under the cowshed, and the new owners better not beat their dog, or they could die?"

At this point, Rosie teared up. Mad at herself for getting emotional, she turned her back. The men looked at each other, worry, anger, and fear marching across their brows.

Finally, she turned around. Lew handed her a handkerchief.

"Honey," he said. "I think this thing is beyond Alix's expertise."

"Damn right," Alix muttered.

"So, now what?"

"Let him call his friends, and we'll just leave the shed alone for the time being…"

"Dad, the mustangs are coming in two weeks."

"Oh." Lew looked at his shoes. "I know that's important to you, honey, but…"

"I don't think you understand," Rosie said. "I can't send the horses back." She didn't mention that she needed the money to pay his hospital bills. She didn't need to.

"But this sprite is really dangerous, Piglet," Lew said. He touched her cheek with his cool, dry hand. "I couldn't bear it if this thing hurt you."

"Then the sooner it's gone, the better," Patrick said through a tight jaw.

Alix shook his head. "You did not read the book, did you?"

Rosie felt fourteen and caught for not doing her homework. "I opened it," she said. "But it's in another language."

"Doesn't matter," Alix said. "The part you need to read, you can read."

"Yeah, that was weird," she said. "I thought I was seeing things."

"Is always the same with people like you."

"Like me?"

"Who are always 'seeing things' but never believing them."

"Okay, fine. Let's get to the house, and I'll read the book."

They followed her out the back door of the barn into the front door of the house, each of them keeping a close eye on the shed. Patrick was careful not to even brush Rosie's sleeve until they were in the house.

Then Rosie threw stacks of horse magazines onto the couch until she found Alix's book at the bottom of the pile.

"Found it."

"Huff," Alix said. "Nice place for antique."

"I didn't know it was an antique."

"No matter." Alix took the book and flipped to a page and handed it back to her. "Read that to us."

As before, the words were foreign. "I can't read this."

"Yes, you can."

She looked at Patrick. He was watching her carefully, but tried to shrug. He couldn't pass off nonchalance.

She looked at the page again, and just like the day of the hexing, the words wavered, bubbling almost, and then resolved into English. It was written in a difficult, spidery script, but it was all English. She blinked at Alix.

"So? Read it."

So, she read aloud.

"Cow Sprites. Cow sprites are of the magical realm, put in place to care for domestic stock, especially in the cases of human neglect or cruelty. Cow sprites look after the bovines, both dairy and beef, although some specialize in particular breeds."

"So, is that thing a dairy or beef sprite?" Rosie asked.

Alix shrugged. "You have no cows, so it doesn't matter. Read more."

"It's all gobbledegook again," Rosie said.

"Skip it. You only read what's important."

"The book knows what I need to read?"

"Yes." Alix turned to her father. "Lew. Your girl!"

"Now, Alix," Lew said. "Remember, she's not familiar with ... magic books."

"And you are?" Rosie asked.

"Well, no. But I know Alix. I trust that he knows what he is doing."

The words swam for a page and then gelled with an audible "pop!"

She read again. "A cow sprite without an animal or barn to attach itself to is a piteous and frightening beast. Such creatures have been known to take revenge for enforced purgatory."

Rosie stopped reading to look at her father's grim face. He nodded, so she read on.

"However, they are easily attracted to new places. Sprites can be attracted via the building of sturdy wooden buildings of native materials. Sprites cannot pass through metal doors, so take care not to use iron reinforcements or too many nails when constructing sheds and buildings. Painting barns or sheds bright colors (especially red) can help the sprites find the buildings. The use of painted charms against evil spirits have no effect on cow sprites, but if you have a cow sprite, you will not need an evil spirit charm: the cow sprite will tolerate nothing that might endanger its livestock. Once ensconced, sprites rarely leave their buildings, even if left vacant of animals."

Rosie scanned ahead. "There's nothing here about how to get rid of a cow sprite."

"Nobody wants to get rid of a sprite except you," Alix said.

Rosie almost threw the book on the floor. "How can something magic be so effing useless?"

Alix took the book from her. "Is not useless. It's a book. All any book can do is give its contents to someone who will listen. Why don't you listen?"

"This is crazy."

"No, listen." Alix opened the book and balanced a pair of glasses on the tip of his nose. "Now, see? Sprite does not like metal. That's why it stays in wooden shed. It doesn't like to be alone, so it stays with your horses, even though they are not cows. It gets angry when it has no cows and no shelter. So, it wrecks your tractor and builds house again."

"Why doesn't it like me touching her?" Patrick asked.

Alix scanned the book. "I don't know."

"Is it because of the zing?" Rosie asked.

Lew and Alix raised their bushy eyebrows.

"I mean...." Rosie fumbled with her shirt tail.

"I have some sort of electrical charge," Patrick explained. "I zap some people. Rosie is one of them."

"Electrical charge, eh?" Alix said. "That's a new one." He returned to the book. "I don't see anything specifically about ... that kind of thing, Patrick. But I think that maybe it is sensitive to it. Humph!" Alix snapped the book shut and turned to Rosie. "Piglet. Do you really have to provoke this sprite? All it wants is to be left alone."

"If I had a bear sleeping under my porch that might have killed my husband and burned down my house and which now hates my boyfriend, would you suggest I just leave it alone?"

"Boyfriend?" Patrick said, grinning.

"I'm serious here!"

"A bear you can shoot. What are you going to shoot this with?" Lew asked.

Rosie sat on the couch and put her head in her hands.

Alix sat next to her.

"I know you are frightened. Let me call my friends. Make Patrick call his auntie Nan. We will see what we can do."

"How did this happen?" Rosie said. "I don't go to church. I don't even knock on wood. I stopped believing in the tooth fairy when I was seven!"

"I'll bet the tooth fairy stopped coming when you stopped believing, didn't she?" Alix said.

Rosie looked at him with her mouth open.

"Yes," he said, standing to go. "That's the look I see from people like you all the time."

"I don't want to leave you alone," Patrick said. He was standing in the doorway, and Rosie was behind him, shooing him out.

"You need to go home," she said. "I'm a big girl. I need to think."

"But there's a monster living fifty feet from your back door," he said.

"And you need to change clothes," she said.

"I'll go get some clothes, and then I'll be right back," he said.

"Patrick!" Rosie stamped a foot. "I will not be patronized! Go the fuck home, already!"

Patrick took her hand, but he looked like he wanted to kiss her. "I know you can take care of yourself. Who could doubt that? It would make me feel better if I could stay here with you. Otherwise, I'm going to spend the night worrying."

"You're so stubborn," she said. She pushed him out. "Take a shower before you come back!" She shut the door and allowed herself a smile. She watched him get into his truck, wave, and drive away. She thought about throwing the deadbolt for a moment, but when she tried it, the lock wouldn't work. She'd lived in the country her whole life and had never locked her door. Now it was busted. She shook her head. Figures.

The truth was that Rosie needed to process what she'd just learned, and she couldn't do that while Patrick made the air between them zing like a hive. She knew he would never leave if she was afraid, so she put on her super-brave face and threw him out. He hadn't known her long enough to call that bluff. Plus, the memory of him restraining her during the tractor ride still made her gasp a little in fear.

Also, she figured the thing probably wouldn't come out during daylight. The book said it "rarely" left its building. Last night they had chased it. It would probably just stay put during the day.

"Look at me," she said to Bobby. "Thinking about that thing like it's real. This is some crazy shit."

She sat on the couch and let Bobby press himself to her leg. She lifted the Book into her lap and re-read the passages in English.

"This isn't very helpful, Bobby."

The dog looked at her and thumped his tail.

"Maybe I need to build a teeny barn and paint it red so the damn thing will move in and I'll have room for the round pen."

She snorted.

"Now I sound like them. Next, I'll have to get a freaking cow."

She stood and Bobby whined.

"Stop that, Bobby. If Patrick isn't back in an hour, I'll be totally surprised." She patted the coward on the head and began to run hot water in the sink. She needed to at least catch up on the dishes before Patrick returned. "Not that I'm June Cleaver or Donna Reed," she explained to the dog. "I just don't expect there to be lots of time between now and tomorrow evening to get them done."

Bobby whined and looked at the door again.

Rosie sighed and pulled on a pair of yellow gloves. She loaded the dishwasher and started the cranky thing. It churned and clanked as if it were a factory full of cave dwarves. Rosie stood in front of the sink and started work on the things that were soaking, things she knew were too much for her cranky dishwasher. Cocoa mugs from a few days ago, chili bowls left to dry on the counter, even Bobby's Alpo dish. Rosie filled the sink up with bubbles and set to work, scrubbing and rinsing and drying.

The dog dish was the grossest, and once she set it into the drying rack, she looked out the kitchen window at the cowshed, which filled the panes with gray wood and lines of darkness.

She glanced at the clock. Four o'clock and the light was just beginning to hint that the day was waning. She saw a shadow move in the cowshed that was decidedly not birdlike.

Bobby whined again.

"It doesn't leave the shed," Rosie whispered. "Don't worry, Bobbo. It doesn't leave the shed."

She watched as the air above the shed shimmered and something rose into the branches of the oak tree. It solidified into a dark, hunched shape that turned and looked her in the eye.

"Eep!" Rosie backed away from the window and flew to the door, wrestled the deadbolt, but it still wouldn't latch, so she threw two dining room chairs against the door and ran to the fireplace where she grabbed a poker, still in her yellow gloves. Bobby glued himself to her calf and whimpered.

"Jesus, I wish Patrick were here!"

The sound of scratching at the door sent the two flying to the bathroom, and it was a dead heat in the race to the bathtub. Rosie might have won, but she had to close the door and lock it before she could climb in and slam shut the sliding glass shower door.

Patrick found them an hour later. When he opened the bathroom door, Rosie shrieked and clutched the poker in her gloves, and Bobby cowered in the tub behind her.

She shrieked again, eyes squeezed shut.

"Rosie! It's me!"

She dropped her poker and threw her arms around his neck. Bobby wrapped himself around Patrick's leg.

"Don't you dare leave me alone again," she said.

"All right! All right!" he said. "I promise. What's all this?"

"I saw the sprite. It was in the tree over the shed. And then we heard it scratching at the door."

Patrick frowned. "The front door's fine."

"The back door."

"Wait. The book said that it wouldn't come out of the shed."

"The book was wrong."

"Remind me to tease you about this later," he said. "Come on."

Rosie wasn't feeling brave, even with Patrick back, but she followed him to the back door. He peered out of the tiny sidelight windows, satisfied himself that there was nothing outside, and opened the door.

The outside of the door was raked with marks and the handle fell off in Patrick's hand. "Damn," he said. He looked outside at the side of the house, once left, once right, and then closed the door and banged on the deadbolt until he could lock it. He pulled Rosie into his arms. They stood and vibrated a moment.

"Can we stay at my place tonight?" he asked.

Rosie shook her head. "The horses," she said. "What if it goes after the horses?"

"It won't. It never has before."

"It's never left the cowshed before, either," she said.

"Do you think it's ever been in the horse barn?" Patrick asked.

"No," she answered.

"Let's stay in there tonight," he said. "You have some sleeping bags?"

"Yeah." Rosie frowned at him. "What makes you think the barn is a good place to sleep?"

"I have this feeling," Patrick said. "I think we'll be safe by the horses."

"Okay," she said. "Lord knows I don't feel safe here anymore."

She scurried around her house, collecting sleeping bags, pillows, and the makings of a cookout dinner which she stuffed into a backpack. She grabbed some dog food, too, and they all slipped out the front door, sneaking around the house into the back door of the stable. She felt silly the whole time because she wasn't convinced that they could escape the notice of something so obviously supernatural.

After they put their gear into the tack room, they did evening chores together, even though it wasn't dusk yet. Bobby tagged along a little more underfoot than usual, but more relaxed than he had been in the house. Rosie took this as a good sign.

They spent extra time with Sunny and Caesar because it felt good to be next to the horses' warmth and solid contentment. They were not concerned about anything, it seemed.

In the arena, far from the hay and the horses, Rosie set up a camp stove and warmed some ravioli and pork 'n beans in camp pans for dinner. She also had peaches and some green beans that they ate directly out of the can.

"You sure know how to throw a campout," Patrick said, poking a fork into the beans.

Rosie shrugged. "With food this good, who cares about the décor?"

They tried to laugh, but it was dark outside, and somehow the fluorescent tubes high above them on the arena ceiling didn't throw off enough light to make Rosie feel safe. She scooted closer to Patrick who put his arm around her shoulder.

"We'll be fine in here," he said. "I'm sure of it. Look at the horses. They aren't worried."

"They'd let us know if something was coming," she said. "Right?"

"Right."

They both glanced at Bobby who had never taken his eyes off of the big barn door. He realized that they were looking at him, so he smiled up at them and thumped his thick tail once, then went back to staring at the barn door. His dog food was untouched.

"I think it's time you told me about Ben," he said.

"That came out of left field," she said.

"Sorry. I'm just trying to change the subject."

"Why do you think we should talk about Ben?"

"Well," he said. "I got the feeling from you dad before that there's a story there that maybe I should know."

Rosie undid the end of her braid so she could unwind it and then re-braid it. "Maybe you should ask my dad, then."

"No," Patrick said. "I think I should hear this from you. Was he ... did he hit you?"

"No," Rosie said, but not defensively.

"Was he cruel?"

"He didn't think so."

"What?"

Rosie fiddled with the end of her hair until Patrick took her hands and held them until they were still. She looked up at him.

"I loved him."

"I can tell."

"I don't want to talk about this."

Patrick touched her face. "Believe me. Ghosts don't want to be talked about. They can't be sent away until they are faced."

Rosie looked around the room, checking the corners of the arena where the cobwebs collected in case there was a memory of a man caught there.

"I was being figurative," Patrick said.

"I don't believe in figurative anymore," Rosie said.

"Everything is literal now?"

"Maybe," she said. Then she sat back, stretching her legs out in front of her.

Bobby jumped into her lap.

"Ben," she said, "was always right."

"He was?"

"As far as he was concerned." She rubbed the dog's ears. "When I was young, I thought it was self-confidence. Self-assurance. Seemed sexy. But then, after we were married, he was still always right. And I was always wrong."

"You? You're so independent. I can't imagine anyone telling you that you're wrong."

She smiled at him. "It didn't happen all at once, you know," she said. "He had good ideas, usually. And he was so insistent that I just let him discover that he was wrong instead of trying to change his mind. Then, I was just agreeing to everything he said without thinking."

"I can't imagine you as a yes-man for someone else."

Rosie shrugged.

"Then Ben started going to this church," Rosie continued. "It was one of the Baptist churches in town. The big one. I went to a Lutheran church with my dad and mom for a while when I was little, but as a teenager, I preferred not getting out of bed on Sunday. Ben wasn't having that. As soon as he joined that congregation, he announced that I was going, too. When I said no, he insisted that I try it out by going to the Wednesday night choir sing. Have you been to one of those?" she asked him.

"No."

"It was the first time I had witnessed anyone speaking in tongues. People I knew from around town my whole life would sing out of tune grinning and enjoying themselves, and then, when the song had ended, the music would go on, and these happy people would moan, they'd raise their arms, and they'd start spouting gibberish. They'd twitch and lurch around like zombies with their eyes closed. Worse, Ben was doing it, too."

Patrick nodded.

"No, I mean, it was the second time he'd ever gone. He was so competitive, so intent on being right that he had to speak in tongues right away, too."

"You mean he was faking it?"

"Of course he was faking it." She scowled. "Worse, he was angry with me that I didn't even try it."

"I thought that speaking in tongues was supposed to be a spontaneous sort of thing. Like the Holy Spirit is supposed to seize you or something."

"Right."

"So, if you hadn't been to church in years..."

"Yeah, how was I supposed to suddenly be inspired, taken by the Ghost?"

"Doesn't seem fair."

"It wasn't," she said with a sigh. "Years later, I realized that. But at the time, newly married, I was still afraid he'd leave. So I tried. I was in that church for years."

"Years?"

Rosie nodded. "I still see them around town, and sometimes they ask me when I will come back, but I won't go back. They are nice enough people, but I'm not the same as them."

"How?"

"Well, I have trouble accepting things on faith." She smiled at him sadly. "You haven't noticed?"

"Yeah, I noticed. Faith is one of those things religion kind of requires."

"So, years of a church I didn't like with ... Ben. Who was never wrong even once, just like his faith. It wasn't just church, though. He went from one training regimen to the next, in search of the perfect method."

"And he wasn't kind to the horses?"

"He'd wear them out with endless longeing, or put a tire around the neck of an unbroken horse and let him run around until he was exhausted. Ben was all about submission."

Rosie rubbed Bobby's ears and looked at the dark ceiling of the arena. "I felt so bad. I should have stood up to him about the horses. The only horse I kept from him was Caesar. I just said that I wanted to train my own horse for competition. That was a nasty fight, but I won."

Patrick stroked her loose ponytail so he didn't have to look her in the eye. "Do you want to tell me about the day he died?"

"No," she said. "I don't like thinking about it. About how surprised I was when his horse came home without him. About riding Caesar bareback through the orchard and the woods until I found him in a ditch in the back acres. About having to leave him there to ride back to the ranch because I forgot my phone in my panic." She stopped. "I don't like thinking about it."

"I know," he whispered. "It was a terrible thing. I'm sorry for you."

"Me, too." She tried to force the lump back down her throat and smiled bravely at him. "Now you know."

He put his arm around her shoulders, and she let herself fall into him. "Can we change the subject now?"

"Of course. More beans?"

"Oh, yes. Please. Bean me."

"I plan to, later."

"You're pretty confident." She gave him some side-eye.

He shrugged. "I might be wrong," he said. "It takes two to tango."

"Oh." She smiled.

Later, they put out the camp stove and walked back to the semi-secret office door in the back of the tack room. Rosie hesitated a moment on the edge of the arena and then left the lights on.

They spread the two sleeping bags out on the floor of the office. Rosie turned on the computer and they tried to amuse themselves watching videos online, but the internet connection was on the fritz, as usual. Eventually, they just turned on the radio, sat on the ratty couch, and talked.

Rosie leaned on Patrick. He might have had an episode where he had frightened her, but after talking about Ben, she was reminded that Ben did not have episodes: he was always controlling and frightening. Rosie realized that she was not only used to the buzzing that touching Patrick created, but that she liked it. It was reassuring to feel his presence to acutely. Also, she was no longer instantly sexually aroused by his touch. Instead, she found that she felt invincible when he was next to her and very vulnerable when he was away.

"Patrick," she said. "I feel like the story about the sprite you saw in Iraq isn't finished."

He was quiet a moment. "The horse sprite?"

"Yeah. At Abrahim's."

"I didn't get there until long after the fire was out and Abrahim had been taken away. All I saw were smoldering remains of the stable and the horses. The stink was terrible. But I saw the sprite. It was just cowering in a corner, near that stallion's stall. It shimmered black and silvery, like the heat rising off of the hot coals, but it was there. It was hiding. The coward. It didn't even try to save them. The fucking thing!"

He was rigid and Rosie held her breath, instinctively hiding from such fury. But she felt him relax a moment later.

"Can you imagine watching a barn full of horses burn and just stand there after?"

"That would be awful," she said. "Maybe it was hurting. You know, grieving."

"What?"

"I mean, if it loved the horses the way this sprite loves cows ... the way Alix thinks it loves cows, maybe it was grieving the horses that died."

"Grieving? You really want to give it emotions?" he asked.

"No," she said, stiffening. "But maybe it's not ... I don't know. I do know how I'd feel if my whole barn burned." She shuddered. "I'd be immobile, too." She shook her head and grumbled. "I can't deal with any of this magic shit. I just want to take care of my horses and give a good home to some mustangs."

"I know you do," Patrick said. "I know."

Eventually, Rosie had an attack of the yawns, which quickly spread to both Patrick and Bobby. They threw the couch cushions on the floor, and they did what they could to make a bed. Rosie sat on her desk chair and took off her boots. She shivered, so she leaned over and turned up the space heater and warmed her hands for a moment. When she looked up, she saw Patrick leering at her.

"What?" she asked giving him a quizzical look.

"You are so sexy."

She rolled her eyes. "You must be joking," she said.

He shook his head, but kept his eyes on her. "Nope."

"My hair's a mess, I'm wearing dirt-covered jeans and a barn coat that hasn't been washed in months. How can I be sexy?"

"You're naked under your clothes, and your hair looks like you just got out of bed," he said. "Totally hot."

"Patrick," she said. "There's a monster outside, it's freezing in here, and my nerves are so jangled I can't tell which way is up."

He knelt by her chair and took her cold hands in his warm, electrical ones.

Very naughty thoughts raced through Rosie's head, and she blushed. This made his grin even bigger.

"But that thing hates it when we touch. Won't we piss it off if we ... have full-body contact ... out here in the barn?"

"I'm pretty sure we're safe here."

Rosie looked at him carefully. "You're a risk-taker, aren't you?"

He shrugged. "Making love in a locked barn seems less risky than lots of other things I've done in the past. Even if there is a monster at the door."

"I'm not much of a risk-taker," she said.

"I'm a sure thing," he said. Then he kissed her. "Sleep with me tonight."

She smiled ... and then hesitated.

"I'm not Ben," he reminded her. "We can take it slow if you want. I'll sleep on this couch, too, if that would make you feel better."

"Nah," she said. "That's not necessary."

"Well, don't get all excited," he said. "You don't need to smother me with your enthusiasm."

Rosie laughed and then shuddered. "It's cold in here."

"Then, let's get into the bag," he said. "Here. I'll warm it up for you." With that, he stripped naked and dove into his bag. Then he wiggled around. "Hell, yeah! That is co-old!"

"Ok. Here I go!"

She took a huge breath and then stripped, flinging clothes everywhere. She plucked a sock off of the heater before she dove into the sleeping bag with Patrick. The contrast between the cold, slick nylon and his searing skin made her shake, not shiver. He pulled her close and threw a leg over her hip and rolled her over so he was blanketing her and she was on his warm spot. Soon the shaking stopped.

"Much better," she said.

"Still not much room to maneuver," he said. He reached over to her sleeping bag and dragged it over them. Between the two of them, they were finally able to zip the bags together without freezing.

"Much better," she said. "Now we can move."

"My favorite part," he muttered, and then kissed every part of her body.

Outside, the cowshed shook. The sprite paced as only a creature that is mostly air can.

The two humans were joining mere feet away, but the sprite couldn't tell exactly where. All it could sense was that they were coupling nearby. The very air crackled with their combined energy.

It made its four feet solid and put them onto the ground. It had to find the people and make them stop.

The night was cold and clear. The sprite stood in the shed doorway and lifted its snout into the air and sniffed. Alas, still no scent of cow nearby. Off in the distance, on the next farm, there were beef cows grazing, but they lived in a steel barn. Sometimes the sprite would visit those animals, but they weren't the right kind of cows and talked funny. Plus, they were nearly all marked for market which made the sprite sad. They were fat and content, however, so it left them and their caretakers alone.

It crunched across the gravel to the house and climbed onto the back porch. It could feel the humans were still coupling, and they might be inside. The sprite was confused by the sparks caused by the humans joining, so it growled. The back door showed the gashes where it had half-heartedly tried to open it earlier to let the stupid dog escape. This time, the sprite simply pushed it open, so it fell flat on the floor inside the house. It tore at the doorjambs until the opening was wide enough for it to enter. It could have entered in its formless state, but it was grumpy.

The house reeked of both humans and the dog so much that the sprite could not tell if any of them were still actually there. It swept its great head right and left and crashed through the dining room, shoving furniture out of its way as it smelled its way around. When it arrived at the living room, it tore at the couches because they were soft and smelled like people. Mostly like her, although, he could tell the man had been there the whole night before.

The hallway to the bedrooms was too narrow for its solid state, but her scent was strongest at the end. The sprite didn't think they were there now, but it decided it had to go see, so it pushed through the flimsy walls, making room for its bulk as it went to the bedroom. It tore the bed apart with its black claws, digging in the mattress in frustration. Then it went to the bathroom where it could smell her fear and the dog's, but found nothing even after it tore the tub out of the wall.

The air still sparked when the sprite emerged from the house, so it circled the trucks in the driveway. One of them smelled more like the man, so the sprite tore the door off by hooking a claw into the window so it didn't touch the steel. Then it chewed the seats until they only smelled like cowsprite spittle.

Her truck didn't smell like him at all, so the sprite didn't bother with it. Instead, it prowled around the property, sniffing and sensing, but never finding exactly where the two people were.

Finally, the sparking stopped. The sprite waited for a while, and when the sparking didn't begin again, it returned to the cowshed and sank into the cool spot by the roots of its oak tree. It was good to rest again.

Patrick curled his arm around Rosie who yawned happily and snuggled deeper into the now warm sleeping bags.

"Tell me something fantastic about yourself," she said. "Something that would explain how you are so wonderful."

Patrick chuckled into her hair which was everywhere because he had unbraided it. "Let's see ... if you go back far enough in my family tree, you'll hit royalty."

"No shit?"

"Yup. Danish, I think."

"You don't look like a Danish prince," Rosie said. "But I'll buy it."

He laughed. "Okay, maybe not royalty. Certainly nobility. We had a couple crazies in the family."

"Oh? Do tell."

"Ahhh. There was Sven Svenson who made his living as an alchemist who would tell anyone in earshot that he'd changed lead to gold."

"That would be handy."

"And Arno Svenson who, according to family legend, killed the last dragon in Europe."

"Dragons? That's reaching back a ways, isn't it?"

"I suppose."

"Any other family kooks?"

"Oh, plenty. My own Auntie Nan is a witch."

"Really?"

"Yeah. She still dresses up in a black hat with a broom stick for Halloween, not that any kids ever go up to her door. I think that makes her sad."

Rosie frowned. "What kind of witch?"

"The kind that casts spells and makes potions," Patrick said. "It's a side business. Her husband used to insist that she called it 'herbal medicine,' but we all know what she does."

Rosie sat up and instantly regretted it as a blast of cold air surged into the sleeping bag. She flopped back down and looked Patrick in the eye. "You never mentioned that you had a witch as an aunt."

"It's not normally something you bring up the first week you know someone," he said.

"A witch aunt," Rosie said. "A week ago, I would have laughed."

Patrick's face moved in a wave of emotions.

"What else aren't you telling me?" Rosie asked.

"Auntie Nan showed me some stuff. She thought I might have some talent..."

Rosie groaned. "That's why it hates you," she said.

Patrick nodded. "I think so, too."

"Why didn't you tell me?"

"Not first date material," he said softly. "You really want to know?"

Rosie nodded.

"Okay. Aside from making your skin tingle, I can ... talk to animals."

"Talk to animals?"

Patrick's chin lifted just a bit.

"Of course you can talk to animals." She looked at her dog who smiled happily at her and thumped his tail. "My boyfriend can talk to animals, Bobby," she said. "But you already knew that, didn't you?"

"Rosie..."

"Hush," she said, lifting a hand. "If there weren't a fucking monster outside, I'd go take a walk. So, you just have to be quiet for a minute."

"Yes, ma'am."

Rosie lay on her belly, her hands twined in her hair, holding her head up as she thought. Finally, she said, "Can you talk to the sprite?"

"No," he said. "I don't think it talks."

"But you talk to animals?"

"In a manner," he said. "Mostly they aren't conversationalists. Bobby won't shut up, of course."

The dog thumped his tail from his dog bed near the heater.

"The horses?"

He swallowed before talking. "They love you so much. They were why I asked you out."

"What?"

"Caesar told me he loved you and wished you were happy. He didn't like Ben, but he knew you missed having a mate ... husb- ... man around. He recommended you very highly."

Rosie smiled in spite of herself. "That sounds like Caesar. He's always taken care of me." She thought a moment. "Sunny?"

His face broke into a smile. "She sings to me."

"The stallion?"

"He was the noblest soul I've ever met. Wisest, too."

"Bobby?"

Patrick smiled. "Dog stuff. Smells, bones, scratches, toys. Plus, even though you think he's a coward, he'd go to hell and back for you."

Rosie nodded. She couldn't dispute any of what Patrick said, not just because it was impossible to do so, but also because she knew it all to be true.

"So, you're a wizard," she said.

"Do I look like a wizard?" he asked.

"No, but Alix doesn't look like a shaman, either." She sighed. "Do you have any idea what we need to do now?"

"No," he said. "I called my aunt when I was at home today, and she's supposed to call back tomorrow." He kissed her cheek. "Do you forgive me?"

"For what? Not telling me that you're magic? After I spent all that time at the hexing talking about how stupid I thought magic was?" She shook her head. "I have no idea why you asked me out at all after that."

"Maybe I like a challenge."

"Well, you found one," she said. "I'm a work in progress."

"Me, too," he said.

"So, what did he say to you?" Rosie asked.

"Who?"

"The stallion."

"Well, at first, I was just chatting with the mares and foals. They started it. I stopped and this mare walked up to the fence and asked for a date."

"A date?" Rosie laughed.

"She meant a fruit. I guess dates are more common that apples in Iraq."

"Did you give her one?"

"I didn't have a date. I gave her a sugar packet."

"That must have been popular."

"Yup. One reason Abrahim came out was because all the horses ran to the fence when I came by. He said it looked like I was preaching to them. He wondered what all the commotion was."

"I see." Rosie chewed on a strand of hair. "I guess I don't really understand. What do the horses say to you?"

"It's not like cartoons," he said. "They don't talk like people. They mostly say things like, 'Hey, I like apples.' Or, 'You're nice.' 'That horse over there is mean to me.' Shit like that. Like a 2-year-old would say."

"So, that's what Sunny and the stallion said to you?"

Patrick thought a moment. "They are different. They both speak — this sounds really cheesy. They both speak to my inside self. Kind of like you." He smiled at her.

"You're right. That's cheesy."

She kissed him, but didn't let him off the hook. "Go on. Explain. What about the stallion? Sunny?"

"Taj...that was the stallion's name. Abrahim took me on a tour of the barn, and there was this magnificent animal at the end of the stable, swinging his head over the stall door. Abrahim warned me, 'Stay away. That horse is crazy.' So, I walked up and stood out of reach and said, 'Hey, man. What's wrong?' And he stopped swinging his head and looked at me."

"I'll be Abrahim shit a brick."

Patrick smiled. "Yeah. He did. Taj said, 'My mouth hurts.' So I go up to him and open his mouth. There's a rotten tooth in the back. I mean, I'm not a dentist, but I can see this swollen jaw. I call Abrahim over and tell him about the tooth and fetches the most wicked pair of pliers I've ever seen and has me hold Taj while he yanks the tooth."

"And the horse just let you do it?"

Patrick nodded. "Like I said, Taj spoke to me. There was an instant connection. I told him, 'This might hurt, but it will make your mouth feel better.' So he said he'd stand still."

"You could rent yourself out as a vet assistant," Rosie said.

"That's what my auntie and my parents were aiming me at. I don't want to live that way. It's hard to explain, but I'd rather not let my talent define how I live."

"So, you're the piano virtuoso who refuses to practice because you'd rather answer phones for a living?"

He shrugged. "I just don't want to be a Dr. Doolittle, you know?"

"You'd look cute in a top hat."

They laughed.

"So, what does Sunny tell you?" Rosie asked a moment later.

"Let me ask you. What does Caesar tell you?"

"Caesar doesn't talk to me."

"Sure, he does," Patrick said. "I hear it as words when he talks. You hear it in other ways."

She chewed her lip as she thought. "He's my friend," she said. "He's careful with me, takes care of me. When we were competing, he was my biggest cheerleader. He never let me feel sorry for myself."

"I get that from Sunny."

"Is it because you saved her?" Rosie asked. "I mean, you helped Taj and he seemed grateful. Does Sunny know you saved her?"

"Maybe," Patrick said. "It's more than indebtedness, though."

"It really is cool that you hear animals talk," Rosie said. "But you really can't hear the sprite talk?"

"No," he said.

"Rats."

"Hey!" Patrick laughed because Bobby was diving into the sleeping bag. "A little warning next time, Buddy!"

"I don't think he's sorry," Rosie said. "Bobby, stop licking my feet!"

They made a warm pile in the cold, un-insulated, steel-clad office.

CHAPTER SIX

Auntie Nan

It was very difficult to leave their makeshift bed in the morning, but Rosie had set an alarm to make sure they didn't oversleep. She had lessons coming, and, someday, Patrick had to go back to work. The alarm woke them at six, and, groaning, Rosie pulled the clothes she could reach on while still in the sleeping bag. She tossed Patrick his clothes and turned on the coffee maker and space heater.

"It will never be my favorite room," she said, "but last night was way better than some camping trips I've been on."

"They company was way better than my last deployment," Patrick said.

"And somewhat hairier, I imagine." Bobby refused to leave the sleeping bag.

"Well, the sooner we get the chores done, the sooner we can take a shower."

"You smell great," Patrick said, pushing his face into her hair.

"I smell like horses and sex," she said. She wound her hair into quick braid and tied the resulting rope into a knot.

"Like I said. You smell great."

She shook her head and led the way out to the barn. Bobby emerged from the warm office only when Patrick said, "Really, Bobbo. We're doing chores now."

Rosie shook her head. "This talking to animals thing is going to take some getting used to."

He nodded. "Well, let's put it to good use."

They spent chore time discussing the things that the horses had told Patrick and applying them to what Rosie knew was best for them.

"It's nice to know that Princess prefers the Equine Senior feed," Rosie said, "but she's too chubby a pony as it is."

Patrick pouted. "This is what her face would look like if she were a person."

Rosie laughed. "Okay. I'll make sure she has some as a treat now and then."

After they had mucked the stalls and fed the horses, Rosie opened the barn door, looked across the barnyard, and staggered backwards. Patrick caught her on the way down, but he was weak-kneed, too, when he saw the door torn off of her house and his truck's upholstery strewn across the driveway.

He sat Rosie down against a stall door. He looked out the door for a moment and then pulled his phone out of his pocket.

"Who are you calling?" asked Rosie.

"My aunt Nan."

"The witch?"

"The witch."

"I thought you were joking last night," Rosie said.

"I know you did. But I wasn't." He held up a hand and Rosie heard a woman's voice on the tinny cell phone speaker. "Hello, Nan. I have a problem."

Rosie watched Patrick talk on the phone. His end of the conversation didn't make sense, but she wasn't listening, anyway. The door to her house had been torn off its hinges. What the hell might have happened if they had decided to sleep in her bed instead of the barn?

A few minutes later, Patrick hung up the phone with shaky fingers and sat next to Rosie. Bobby wedged himself in between them, panting.

"What's your aunt say?" Rosie asked.

"You need to get the truck, and we need to bug out. Then we'll get everyone—Alix, Nan, whoever—and make a plan."

"She wants me to do what?"

"Auntie Nan thinks that it is too dangerous for me to go out in the yard, and that we need to get out of here. She said you need to go get your truck and drive it to the back door so we can leave."

"Your aunt is nuts if she thinks I'm going out there after what that thing did to my house!"

"I know," Patrick said. "But look, I really think it hates me because, you know, the magic. It doesn't seem to mind you. Hell, you didn't even know it was there..."

"Until we tried to knock down the shed," she said. "You don't think it's mad at me, too?"

"Well, your truck wasn't damaged. I've never been in your truck, so that shows it was looking for me, not you."

"Or maybe it got bored after it shredded your truck."

"Ok. Let's try an experiment." Patrick stepped up to the door and opened it. "Watch," he said. He took a big step out of the building.

The cowshed did nothing for a long moment, and then the door creaked open. Patrick leapt back and slammed the barn door shut.

"Right," Rosie said from the corner. Bobby was doing his best to crawl into her jacket. "We've already established that it hates us."

"No, it hates me. Here, you try."

"No way."

"Please?"

"Fuck this," Rosie said, pulling out her cell phone. "I'm calling my dad."

She punched in the number and waited for the phone to ring. She shook the phone and held it to her ear again. She peered at the screen and then sighed. "Do you have any bars in here?" she asked Patrick.

He handed her his phone and she dialed. "Dad!" she cried. "We're in a lot of trouble over here. Can you come get us? We're in the barn." Patrick waved at her. "Oh, come to the back door of the stable."

Minutes later, they watched through the cracked barn door as Lew charged up the driveway in his truck, then slowed to a crawl as he passed the house and Patrick's ruined rig. He came through the back door as instructed.

"What the hell happened here?" He grabbed Rosie in a bear hug and looked at Patrick with wide eyes.

"We'll tell you on the way," Patrick said.

As Patrick climbed into the truck cab, he could hear something groan.

"Shit," he said, slamming the door.

They tore out of the barnyard and around the house. Rosie saw that the windows had been blown out of both bedrooms and the curtains were floating on the outside.

"Oh, no," she breathed.

"We have bigger problems, honey," Patrick said. He was looking out the back window at the cowshed.

"Shit," Lew said. He was looking in the rearview mirror.

Rosie turned to see a darkness rising above the cowshed. She gasped and clutched at Patrick. As soon as she felt the sparks, she knew she'd done the wrong thing. The darkness darkened and then moved towards them with surprising speed.

"Drive faster," Patrick said.

"Am doing," Lew said. "Hold on."

The truck hit the paved road at the end of the driveway at terrifying speed, and Lew had to hang on tight to the wheel to keep them from flipping. Then he stomped on the gas.

"Update?" he called.

"It made it to the end of the driveway and stopped," Patrick said.

"Good," said Lew, but he didn't lift his foot. "We're going to my place. Alix is going to meet us there."

Alix was waiting in Lew's living room. Molly, Lew's wife, was there, too, as big and burly as Lew was tall and willowy. She hugged her step-daughter and then handed her a cup of coffee. "Have you eaten?" she asked.

"No."

Molly dragged them all to the kitchen table and began heaping scrambled eggs in front of Rosie and Patrick.

"So, you're the new young man I've heard about," she said to Patrick.

"Guilty as charged," Patrick said, mouth full.

"What's been going on at the ranch?" Molly asked. "I've been hearing all sorts of stories from Lew and Alix, but I learned a long time ago not to believe anything those sons of guns say."

Rosie put her fork down. "It seems I have a monster living under my cowshed."

"Monster?" Molly's fork froze in midair. "Is that what you were talking about, Alix? Is this 'monster' the sprite?"

Rosie looked at Alix who shrugged. "Tomato—to-mah-to," he said. "Either way, it's mad because they knocked the cowshed down with a tractor, and it hates Patrick."

"Who could hate such a sweet face?"

"I'm a ... well, I come from a family of ... magic people."

Molly frowned. "You mean like Alix?"

"I don't know," Patrick said, turning to Alix. "Are there witches in your family?"

Alix drew himself up. "No," he said. "We do our hexes and charms through medicinal methods."

"Oh," Patrick said, sitting back a little. "Because I have this aunt who is a wit- ... an herbalist."

Rosie glanced at Molly, who noticed.

"What is it, Rosie?" she asked.

"Just that, you're okay with all of this. I thought..."

"You thought that a church lady like me wouldn't want any part of this supernatural excitement?"

"Well, yeah."

Molly took a sip of her water. "My dear, the Lord works in mysterious ways, as does the devil."

"You think it's devil?" Alix said. "That's backward and wrong!"

"I didn't say it was a devil," said Molly. "Now sit down, Alix. Silly man, getting all worked up."

"We're lucky it's not a devil or a demon," he said. "Then we'd need someone from the church."

"I'm a little outside the church," said Patrick. "Sorry, Ma'am," he said to Molly.

"No matter," she said. "You're only a potluck away from joining up." She grinned.

"Just ignore her," Rosie said. "I haven't gone to a potluck in ages."

"Maybe your auntie could conjure up a hot dish," said Lew, winking.

Alix leaned against the counter. "Oh, my family, we wish that we had the magic, religious or otherwise. Makes all the difference when you have difficult troubles like the sprite."

Patrick said, "My aunt is going to help us."

"I'm going to help you," Alix said.

"I hope both of you are going to help them," said Molly. "Call your aunt when you're done eating, Patrick."

Patrick shoved the food in his face, and then called Auntie Nan. Rosie couldn't make out what they were saying since Patrick was mostly just nodding and saying, "Uh huh." Finally, he handed the phone to Alix.

"Nan wants to talk to you."

"Oh?" Alix took the phone and after a couple words, he stomped into the next room and began yelling into the phone.

"Are you going to let him yell at your aunt like that?" Rosie asked.

Patrick shook his head. "Nan can stand up for herself. I think the two of them together will come up with a plan."

Eventually, Alix stomped back into the kitchen and handed Patrick his phone.

"Your aunt is one crazy," he said. "She has that shop on Sixth street. Charges too much."

"Did you come up with a way to get rid of the sprite?" Rosie asked.

He glanced at her and then looked at his hands. "We have a couple ... ah ... strategies that might work," he said.

"Like what?"

Alix shifted a little and leaned back up against the counter. "Well," he started. "You could take vacation. Or sell the ranch."

"Not an option," Rosie said.

Lew put his hand on her shoulder. "Now, listen to what Alix and Nan say, Piglet," he said. "The sprite didn't bother you until ... well, until Patrick showed up, right?"

"No, it killed Ben, Daddy," she said. "And it burned my house. How am I supposed to forget that?"

Lew squeezed her shoulder and said nothing.

"What are the other options?" she asked Alix.

"Is the cow tail braid still there?" he asked.

"Yes," said Patrick.

Alix nodded. "By itself, the braid isn't doing much good, but we can build on it."

"What do you mean?"

"We can build more charms on it. Maybe drive sprite away. Maybe trick it to think there are cows around. Are you sure you don't want to buy a cow?" Alix asked, his eye lighting up.

"I don't want to placate the thing," Rosie said. "I want it to go away."

"Yes, of course." Alix sat at the table and fiddled with a fork a moment before he looked up at Patrick. "That leaves you and your magic."

"My magic is pretty useless," Patrick said. "All I can do is talk to animals."

Molly dropped her knife with a clatter and gaped at Patrick.

"You can what?" asked Lew.

"Your auntie thinks you have enough of magic," Alix said. "She says you have quite a lot of talent. Especially when combined with more talent."

"Patrick and Nan are going to battle the sprite?" Rosie asked.

"No, you two are."

"What?" Rosie said. "You said Patrick needed someone else with talent. I don't have any magic."

"It seems to Auntie Nan that you have an amplifying effect on her nephew."

"The sparks," Rosie said. She looked at Patrick who was watching her. "You knew."

He nodded. "Again, not exactly a first date discussion topic."

"I feel kind of dizzy," she said and sat down. She looked at Lew. "Does any of this make sense to you, Dad?"

Lew scratched his head. "There was a story about a great-aunt of mine who was a water-witch, and some distant cousin who could predict an earthquake or thunderstorm. Nothing magic about them, I reckon."

"No, no," Alix said. "Those are talents."

"What do we have to do?" Patrick said, taking Rosie's hand.

"You don't have to help me," Rosie said. "This sounds dangerous. We've only known each other..."

"I'm just going to cut you off there," Patrick said, kissing the back of her hand so she could feel it in her cheeks. "I'm in this with you. What do we do?" he asked Alix.

Rosie looked at Alix carefully. "Are you blushing?" she asked.

"Best way to drive out sprite is to amplify your magic together," he said.

"How do we do that?" asked Patrick.

"Close contact."

"How close?"

"As close as possible."

"Wait," Rosie said. "Is he saying what I think he's saying?"

"We have to have sex in the cowshed," Patrick said.

"My dad is right here," Rosie hissed.

"I sure as hell am," Lew said, his face inscrutable.

"Calm down, Lew," Molly said. "It's not like Rosie is some virgin."

"She's my little Piglet, and always will be," Lew said. Then he winked.

"Doesn't matter," Rosie said. "I never want to go within fifty feet of that shed. No way I'm getting naked and walking in to its lair. Did you tell them what it did to my house?"

"Rosie, I don't think you understand. The only way that thing is leaving is if we use magic. My magic isn't strong enough without you. And I know enough about magic to tell you that it's strongest during the most intense parts of life ... like sex."

Lew snickered.

"Lew, hush," Molly said.

"The sprite's going to tear us to shreds before we get to the shed," she said.

"Not if we're together," he said. "Together, we're safe."

Despite her protests, Rosie found herself shivering next to her ruined house with a white sheet wound around herself, standing next to Patrick. She was careful not to touch him as she leaned over to whisper, "Are the togas really necessary?"

"The 'drapes of white' are required," said Auntie Nan. She made a little adjustment to Patrick's robe—actually one of Rosie's spare flat sheets. It had tiny roses on it, but they were so faded that Nan decided the sprite wouldn't see them. "If we are going to do this, we should do it right."

Nan re-consulted Alix's book. As much disdain as the little woman with long white hair seemed to harbor for the "Old-world Shaman" as she called him, she did not quibble with his literature. "No, it says the couple must be wrapped in white clothes of the purist origins."

"I'm not sure these will do..." Rosie started.

Nan shushed her with a wave of a thin hand. "No matter, dear. Texts often exaggerate those kinds of things. The purity of virgins and the like." Auntie Nan gave Rosie a look that made the younger woman feel enraged and ashamed at the same time.

"Nan. Stop that."

At Patrick's word, the older woman sighed and looked away. "I could tell you all sorts of things..."

"Don't want to know it your way."

"Fine. Let's get this started, then."

Rosie was completely confused by this exchange. Auntie Nan had insisted on assisting in the "ceremony," and Rosie later deemed it the most awkward meeting of family she had ever been a part of. This was not only because the Nan who showed up was about as different as possible from the witch Rosie had pictured in her head. Nan arrived driving a blue Prius, and while she was suitably old and wizened, she was dressed more as an old hippy than a practitioner of the black arts. Her flowered sundress and long, white, loose hair startled Rosie. Nan didn't even seem to have a broomstick or a pentagram.

Then Nan insisted that Rosie strip naked and wrap herself in a sheet. Yeah. Definitely the most awkward meeting ever.

Rosie decided she could only deal with one thing at a time, so she glanced around the corner at the cowshed. It was quiet and glowed warmly in the sunset.

"How do you feel?" Lew asked her, standing close.

"I'm scared shitless," she said.

"The first time is always daunting, Piglet," Lew said. "You'll be fine."

The first time?

Rosie tried to choke down her laugh, but it bubbled out, anyway.

The only good part about this plan was that her Dad was going to be sitting in the truck with the motor running for their quick getaway. Or, was that the super-freaking awkward part? Rosie was losing track.

Alix was watching the sun, and once it touched the horizon, he said, "Okay. It is time. Go."

Rosie looked at Patrick, and he gave her a thumbs-up. She felt her stomach drop to her shoes, but she took a deep breath and stepped around the corner.

She listened and watched the barn as their shoes crunched across the gravel driveway. She heard her father start the truck and was reassured a little by its idling. She desperately wanted to clutch Patrick's hand, but they weren't supposed to touch until they were in the barn. They were hoping to sneak up on the sprite.

That didn't happen. The cowshed began to waver when they passed Patrick's ruined truck and were walking the last fifty feet of open space to the door.

"Patrick," Rosie said, reaching for him.

Patrick leapt away. "Hold it together, Rosie," he said. "We can do this. Come on," he said, jogging the rest of the distance.

Rosie had no choice but to follow him. She pushed open the door, according to the plan, and the wave of cold, wet air hit her like a soaking wool blanket. She took a step back, but Patrick stepped inside. He looked at her and waved her in.

Rosie shook her head once, frozen in place. Despite the glowing sunset flooding the shed with light, the darkness in the corner was solid and menacing. She couldn't take her eyes off of it. It was terrible.

Patrick snatched her hand and dragged her inside. As soon as she was inside, the door slammed shut and the sprite began wailing. Patrick clutched Rosie, and she could feel his heart leaping around his chest. The sheets were thin enough that Rosie felt the sparks up and down her entire body, and they warmed her despite the fierce cold that accosted the rest of her. She squeezed her eyes closed, and hot tears streamed down her cheeks.

"I don't want to die," she sobbed.

"You won't," Patrick said. He sounded convincing, but she could feel his knees knocking.

"Let's go," she pleaded.

"We'll be fine," he said.

He touched her cheek and then kissed her which increased the wailing. He kissed her harder. Then he stopped. He hugged her to his chest.

"We have to go," he said.

"Why? What's going on?"

"I'm, I'm, I can't..." Patrick said. "Let's go."

They ran out of the cowshed. Rosie could see her Dad's, Nan's and Alix's faces in the back window of the truck, but they looked so far away. They ran and then leaped into the back of the truck. Patrick hollered, "Go!" and Lew stomped on the gas.

Rosie watched the cowshed as they sped away. The noise was like a tuning orchestra in is volume and dissonance, and the black fog looked noxious. They were not followed this time.

After a couple miles, Lew pulled over and let Patrick and Rosie into the cab where they squeezed into the back seat. They drove back to Lew's house silently. Alix and Nan watched the couple, too, as best they could with the mirrors. Nobody asked any direct questions.

Rosie could tell that Molly, who had waited at home, knew something had gone wrong, too, but Molly just ushered Rosie and Patrick into the spare bedroom and bathroom to change back into their clothes.

When Rosie stepped out of the bedroom, Patrick was waiting for her in the hall. He pulled her to him and whispered, "I'm sorry," into her ear.

"It's okay," she said. "It wasn't your fault."

"It was my ... fault," he said. "I couldn't..."

"Hush," Rosie said. "It was a dumb idea. So much of this is a dumb idea."

"But, if we — I could have pulled it off..."

"We didn't." Rosie touched the corner of Patrick's eye where worry had crinkled the corner. "It's okay. On to the next thing."

He smiled.

"Rosie? Are you guys hungry?" Molly called.

"She doesn't actually think we want to eat?" said Patrick.

"No. That's code for: 'Come out and tell us what happened.'"

"Oh. Ready?"

Rosie took his hand. Why did it feel like they were going to the inquisition?

When they stepped into the room, Rosie cleared her throat. "We couldn't do it," she said. "I was too scared."

Patrick looked at her gratefully.

Alix and Lew sighed. Nan shook her head.

"Surely there's a plan B?" Rosie asked.

"Not one that will work altogether," Alix said.

"Well, what if we did a lot of them all at once?" Rosie asked. "I mean, the thing didn't chase us or harm us this time even though we couldn't … you know."

Alix nodded. "If you guys were together while we did the other charms, it would make them work better."

"Like a shotgun," Lew said. "We hit it with lots of little pellets instead of one big bullet."

"You have more ingredients for charms, right?" Alix asked Nan.

"I'm sure I do, but I don't really think they'll work. The sprite has been there over a century. It has more claim to this place than she has. Rosie should really make her peace with it."

"I'm sorry," Molly said. "Who are you exactly?"

Nan drew herself up to her full 5'2". "I'm Patrick's aunt, Nan Petra. I own the herbalist natural food shop in town."

"She's a witch," Patrick said. "I mean, a real one."

Molly just nodded.

"That's all, Molly?" Rosie asked. "No reaction to a witch in your house?"

Molly shrugged. "After a monster under your barn and a boyfriend who talks to animals, a witch seems pretty mundane." She pointed to Alix. "Plus, I've known this guy for years."

"Right, right. All of this seems pretty straightforward if you look at it that way." Rosie rubbed her temples. "If you guys don't need me, I'm going to take a shower. I have a headache."

"I can give you something for that," Nan said.

"I think I'm just going to take an aspirin and go to bed."

Later, Patrick tapped on the guest room door and peeked in.

"Rosie?"

"Come in," she said, sitting up. "I'm awake."

"How are you feeling?"

"Not too bad." He sat next to her and took her hand. "Better now."

He smiled. "Why don't you come home with me tonight? I'd feel better if I knew you were safe."

"No, I'm exhausted," she said. "I'll stay here in the spare room with Bobby. Go home. I'm fine."

"Really? It's not because of ... what happened in the shed?"

She laughed. "No. I've seen your gear work. I'm not concerned. I'm just really tired."

He kissed her, and the sparks were comforting, like a shared power.

His talons gripped the top of the shed, his outline wavering. The people had run away, but they had obviously meant to provoke him.

Did they not understand that they caused him pain? That the man's hate was amplified by their combined energy?

He felt them moving away rapidly, and soon their scent and the crackle in the ether dwindled. When dawn eased into the sky, the sprite made his rounds again because his shed still trembled, and he couldn't rest there until the ether settled.

At the door, he greeted a darkly speckled barn cat who purred a hello. But she had a warning. She'd been told by the hawks that a newcomer, a great cat, was on the move through the territory.

The sprite thanked her. He was too shaken to detect any distant predator, but he promised to watch for any intrusion.

By then, a truck was creeping down the drive, headed for the back door of the barn. His shed still vibrated, so the sprite settled outside the barn door. He longed for the company of the horses because they would make him feel better. He was in luck because the people left to door open while they did morning chores.

It was just light the next morning when Rosie and Lew arrived at the back door of the stable to do chores. Bobby leaped from the truck first only because Rosie pushed him off her lap so she could get out.

He had been "Velcro Dog" all day, clinging to her leg so devoutly that he annoyed her. She was surprised that he wanted to come along this morning, but he was in the cab of the truck as soon as she opened the door.

Once he figured out where they were headed, he whined and fidgeted. "Oh, you are such a coward," Rosie said. She hugged him, though. She knew now what he'd always known:

that thing in the cowshed was very dangerous: a thing to be feared.

It was obvious to all of them that Patrick should not go back to the ranch until they were ready to drive the sprite away, so Lew had offered to help with morning chores.

Rosie and Lew opened the back door of the stable, and Bobby raced inside and stood cowering by Caesar's stall. The big red horse put his head over the door and watched the dog, amused.

"I wonder what they're saying," Rosie said.

Caesar looked at her and blinked.

"He is wondering what's up," Lew said. "You don't usually come in this door."

Rosie stared at her dad.

"What? I can't make obvious statements, too?" He laughed.

"Daddy!" Rosie's anxiety waned a little with her father's familiar teasing.

They went to work, clearing the stalls and feeding the horses. They dumped their wheelbarrows on the manure pile outside the back door.

Rosie kept a careful watch on the door closest to the cowshed. Every unfamiliar rattle on that side of the barn made her jump, and every shadow under the door made her freeze. Bobby stayed by her heels the whole time and kept careful watch on the door, too.

Lew dropped a bale of hay just as Rosie stepped into the aisle, and she cried "Eek!," and flattened against a wall.

"Relax, Piglet," Lew said, putting a hand on her shoulder. "We're nearly done."

"I know," she said. "I'm just..."

"Of course. Let's finish up and get out of here."

The last stall, the one closest to the front door, belonged to the pony Princess. The little mare couldn't see over the stall door unless she stood on her hind legs and put her front feet on the door. Even so, Rosie could still hear the pony's impatience.

"We're coming, Princess," she called.

They stepped in, and Rosie mucked out the stall as Lew stuffed hay into the feeder and rinsed the waterer out. Bobby stood outside the stall door and watched them, whining.

"Quiet, Bobby. We're almost done," Lew said. He grabbed the other pitchfork and made short work of the last bit of soiled bedding. Then they tossed their tools into the wheelbarrow and stepped out of the stall.

Bobby yodeled with concern and cowered behind Rosie's leg. "What is it?" she asked, looking at the door.

The sun was just lightening the sky, so there really wasn't enough light to make a shadow, but there it was, blackness seeping at the bottom edges of the door. "Daddy," she whispered.

"I see it," Lew said. He was sliding the stall door back quietly, gently clicking the latch shut. "Let's just leave the barrow where it is."

Rosie nodded, and they backed up the aisle toward the truck.

The shadow moved, too. Something was moving back and forth along the doorway but didn't touch it. Finally, a solid shape appeared beneath the door, far too large to fit under, but Rosie heard a familiar sound: sniffing.

"It's smelling us," she said.

"Move," Lew said.

They all turned and ran to the back door, which, Rosie realized with sudden dread, they had left wide open while they dumped manure outside. When they ran, the snuffling under the door stopped, and a shadow appeared at the back door, blocking the dawn completely.

Lew grabbed her and pulled her and the dog inside a stall and slammed the door shut. "On the ground!" he ordered. "Get behind the horse!"

Rosie picked Bobby up and ducked behind the horse as Lew peeked out between the bars on the stall door. "Shi-it." He ducked down and scooted behind the horse, too. "I think it's coming," he said.

The horse was Rocky, a giant paint with feet the size of dinner plates. He was old, maybe thirty, and was ridden by a little old lady who adored him. Rocky had seen some shit in his day, Rosie was sure, but she was astounded at how unconcerned he was by the two fearful people and cowardly dog that now crouched behind him. He swished his tail and looked at them as if he wondered what treats they might have.

"Why aren't the horses spooked?" Rosie said.

"I don't know," Lew said. "Next time you see Patrick ask him."

"If there is a next time," Rosie said.

"Hush," her father said. "None of that."

They fell silent then, listening to the horses munch their breakfast and not hearing anything else. Rosie strained to hear more sniffing, or shrieking, or the sound of a horse being dismembered, but there was nothing. No sound. Nothing.

"Daddy, what's going on?" she asked finally.

Lew shook his head. He moved to the front of the stall and peeked out. "Nothing out there," he said. He stood taller and peeked around the corner. "Nothing out here," he said. He stood and slid the stall door open and took a cautious step out. "Come on."

Rosie put Bobby down. They left and latched the stall behind them. None of the horses behaved as if this were anything but a normal breakfast. Caesar wrinkled his kind eye at Rosie in concern because he could tell she was upset. She rubbed his nose as they moved to the door and felt calmer because of his calmness.

At the back door, Lew again made sure the coast was clear before he stepped out into the quiet, thin morning and walked to the front of the truck. As soon as Lew opened the truck door, he cried, "Rosie! Inside!"

Rosie froze at the barn door and heard Bobby barking. She turned. There was the sprite, huge and dark, amorphous and solid at the same time, looming in the bed of Lew's truck where she and Patrick had lain as they made their escape the night before. It was swinging its huge head back and forth between the spot where she and Patrick had been and where Lew was running toward the orchard. The bed liner was in shreds. On the ground below was Bobby, barking frantically at the monster which ignored him.

"Bobby!" Rosie screamed. "Bobby! Come!"

The dog gave her a pained look and barked at her once. Then he resumed his vigil pestering the monster.

Rosie hated feeling helpless. The sprite took one claw and tore another welt in the bed liner and then lumbered off in the direction of the orchard. Bobby followed, barking. Rosie dropped to one knee and picked up the largest stone in reach, only about the size of an apple. She stepped back and pitched it at the monster.

It pinged on its back like a pebble, but incredibly, the rock dropped through the sprite like he was made of water and fell on the ground.

The huge head swung toward her. Nostrils as big as water buckets snuffled, and it turned around. That's when Rosie realized it had no eyes.

"Bobby!" she shrieked.

Bobby looked over his shoulder at her at exactly the wrong time, and the sprite swiped the dog out of its way like it was brushing a spider off its sleeve. Bobby didn't make a sound when he landed twenty feet away.

"Bobby!"

He didn't move. Rosie ran two steps toward her fallen friend, but she saw the sprite move toward her. It moved so fast that Rosie only had time to slam the barn door shut and lock it. She leaned against the door a moment.

"What do I do?"

Suddenly, her ankles were cold through her chore boots. She looked down to see something like a claw made of mist seeping around her feet.

She raced to Caesar's stall and leaped over the door. She climbed on her old friend's back. She sat there, fingers wound in his mane, listening for the sounds of the creature tearing the barn apart, shredding it like her father's truck. But she didn't even hear sniffing under the door again.

The image of Bobby trying to protect them and his limp body outside tormented Rosie. She had to get to him.

She slid off of Caesar and lead him out into the aisle by cupping her hand under his chin. Then she climbed back on. She and Caesar used to compete in Dressage, so steering him with her legs was no problem. They walked to the barn door, and Rosie leaned over and unlatched it. She took a deep breath and tried to reassure herself that since Caesar wasn't worried, they were safe.

She slid open the door.

The day was brighter. There was no sign of the sprite. Rosie urged Caesar to a walk, and they went the few feet to where Bobby was lying. She gathered him up in her arms. The dog was breathing, but he was cold.

Caesar sniffed the two of them. He pricked his ears, curious.

"It was the sprite," she whispered.

The horse flicked his ears.

"Yes, really," she said. She pulled her coat over Bobby's body.

"Rosie!"

She looked up to see her father emerge from the orchard.

"Am I glad to see you!" he said.

"Me, too," she said. "But we have to go to the vet's."

Lew took one look at Rosie and Bobby and said, "Of course. What about Caesar?"

"Put him in the stall. I'll get into the truck."

As Caesar and Lew went back to the barn, Rosie climbed carefully into her father's truck. She tried not to look at the damage and hoped it still drove okay. She settled Bobby on the seat and cradled his head in her lap.

"I'm so sorry, Bobbo," she said and stroked his ears. "I'm sorry for every time I called you a coward. I'm so sorry about being wrong about the sprite. I'm so sorry."

She couldn't be sure, but she thought she heard his tail thump once, but it might have just been her father closing the barn door.

Because Lew called ahead on his cell, the vet met them at the door of the clinic. Dr. Cody Arden was an old friend — actually, he had once been more than a friend to Rosie and was now Meg's husband — and he knew Bobby well. He took one look at the limp animal in Rosie's arms and said, "Oh, hell."

Rosie carried Bobby inside and laid him gently on an exam table. Dr. Arden went to work, checking heartbeat and breathing, feeling for breaks along the bones.

"What happened?" he asked.

Rosie and Lew glanced at each other. "Car hit him," Lew said.

"Poor blighter," Dr. Arden said. "There's probably some internal injuries, but he's in no condition for surgery. Damn." He ran his hand through his hair. "I'll get him on some IV fluids and a painkiller, but honestly, he's going to have to wake up before I'm going in. Anesthesia will kill him if we try it now."

Rosie broke down. She'd been holding it together, being strong for Bobby, but now she collapsed into Cody's arms. She felt her father close the hug. "Can't you help him, Cody?" she sobbed. "He saved me."

He stroked her hair. "You know I'll move heaven and earth for Bobby, Rosie," he said. After a moment he said, "Saved you from what?"

"It wasn't a car, Cody," said Lew. "There's a monster or something on Rosie's ranch. It got Bobby when he was trying to keep it from getting us."

Dr. Arden frowned. "A monster? You mean a cougar?"

Lew shook his head. "No, we mean something supernatural. A cowsprite in the cowshed."

Dr. Arden held Rosie at arm's length so he could look her in the eye. "A sprite?"

She nodded.

"I didn't think you bought that stuff."

"I hadn't seen one before."

Cody put his hand on the dog's shoulder and the creature stirred a little. "Well, I'll double my efforts for the brave little man, then."

"Wait, you believe us?" Lew asked.

Cody shrugged. "'There are stranger things on heaven and earth than are dreamt of in your philosophy,'" he said, quoting Lew's favorite play. "One thing I've learned over the years is to not discount folk legends. If you say you've got an angry cowsprite, I'm not one to argue."

"You don't know anything about cowsprites, do you?" asked Rosie.

He shook his head. "I know lots about cows, but not about sprites," he said. "We sort of skipped that part in vet school."

"Well, if you think of anything that might help us get rid of it, let us know," said Lew.

Dr. Arden nodded. "Why don't you go home, and I'll call you if there's any change?"

"Call her cell phone. No one in their right mind will be at her ranch."

They met Patrick at a breakfast joint since they were in town, anyway. As soon as they stepped in the café, Patrick appeared and hugged Rosie. "I'm so glad you're okay."

"Thanks," she said.

"How's Bobby?" Patrick asked as they sat at a table.

"It's pretty bad," Lew said. "Possible internal injuries, some broken bones. Doc won't be able to do much until he wakes up."

"Oh," Patrick said.

"He was protecting me," Rosie said.

"He was?"

"From the sprite. He was barking at it and harassing it so it wouldn't go after dad or me." She swallowed hard. "It's the bravest thing he's ever done."

Patrick covered Rosie's hands with his own. "I know he'll pull through."

Breakfast was somber and tasteless in the mouths of the three people sick with worry.

"You know?" Rosie said dropping her fork. "I'm done. I'm just done. This thing has cost me two houses, a husband, and now maybe my dog. It's stronger than I am. It wins. I'm never going back there."

Patrick shook his head. "You can't give up on this, Rosie," he said.

"Watch me."

"No, you can't leave the horses. You can't leave the ranch. You've put too much into it."

"Yes, I can," she said. "It's just a house and a barn. Only one of the horses is mine. The others can find somewhere else to live. Maybe I can just crash at Dad's place for a little bit while I find a new place."

"What about the mustangs?" Lew asked.

The picture of the beautiful striped-legged Kiger mustangs sprang into her mind. "I'd lose them," she said. Her voice caught in her throat. "I'd probably not get another chance of adopting Kigers for years."

She looked up at the people next to her. "But if that thing takes one of you, I would never forgive myself. Horses, a ranch, those things are just things."

"Horses aren't things," Patrick said.

"They aren't people, either," she said. "I can't lose you. Either of you."

"I'm sorry, Piglet," Lew said.

But Patrick set his jaw. "I'm sorry," he said. "I'm not giving up. That thing has got to go."

"Patrick, we can't get rid of it."

"Did you see what it did to the bed of my truck?" Lew said.

"And it nearly killed Bobby just by brushing him aside."

"And it could have killed either of you, but it didn't," Patrick said. "Why not?"

"It didn't care about me," Lew said.

"I ran into the barn, but it never came in," Rosie said.

"It was only interested in the bed of the truck."

"It sounds like it was looking for me again," Patrick said. "But why doesn't it go into the barn?"

Rosie shrugged.

"I've got a funny idea," Lew said. "Maybe Patrick should talk to the horses. Ask them what's going on."

"I can do that," Patrick said.

"Wait, he can't go back to the ranch," Rosie said.

"Okay," Lew said. "We'll hitch the trailer up and bring one of them to him."

"Caesar and Sunny," Patrick and Rosie said together.

"What about Meg's horse, Talent?" Rosie said.

Lew shook his head. "I can do a two-horse trailer. I can't back one of those huge ones anymore."

Rosie looked at Alix who shook his head. "I can do small trailer only."

"Okay. The horses seem safe. Maybe Meg will be okay with leaving Talent."

"Right," Lew said. "I'll go get them after breakfast."

"You can't go alone," Rosie said. "I'm coming with you."

"No," Lew said. "I have a feeling that one person, me, without any scent of Patrick, going alone and staying on the far side of the barn, I think that will make the least trouble."

"Dad, are you sure?"

"Honey, I'll be in and out of there so fast, that thing won't know what's happened."

"Alix should go with you," Patrick said.

"All right. Alix will go with me."

The sprite watched as the two old men slowly drove up the driveway in Alix's truck slowly, making an effort not to disturb the gravel too much or otherwise call attention to themselves. They pulled in front of Rosie's trailer and sat in the cab a few moments watching the cowshed. All was still. The sprite shimmered atop the oak tree, but the old men didn't look up there.

They hitched up the trailer and scooted back into the cab. They watched the cowshed. Then they backed the trailer to the back door of the barn.

The sprite floated over to sit in one of the trees in the orchard where he could watch.

Shaman sat in the truck and the tall man moved swiftly to Caesar's stall and opened the door. The horse rumbled in recognition.

"Let's go for a ride," he said, slipping on Caesar's halter. "Come on."

He led the big gelding to the yard, and Caesar's ears pricked up. The horse swished his tail and stepped into the trailer.

The tall man ran back to get Sunny who did not know him except from breakfast. The sprite could feel Sunny resist the tall man. The sprite's feet formed claws as it gripped the tree branches. If the horse was scared, the sprite wanted to help her.

However, the tall man spoke to the horse and calmed her. The horse relaxed; the sprite relaxed, and its claws dissolved again. It settled to the ground near the trailer.

As they stepped out of the stall, there was a tentative "beep" from the truck. The tall man trotted the horse out the door and up the ramp. He didn't bother to tie the horses in, but slammed the door closed and raced to the cab.

"Let's go!"

The Shaman pulled out faster than was wise with two horses in a trailer and rounded the driveway curve in a just-barely controlled maneuver. The sprite floated over the orchard and watched them leave. Then it moved back to the oak tree to continue its conversation with the spring spirit about the cows a century ago.

When they pulled up to Lew's trailer on the alpaca ranch, Meg, the owner, and Dr. Arden, her husband, were standing with Rosie, Patrick, Molly, and Auntie Nan next to a makeshift paddock made of gate panels. The alpacas were lined up two rows deep against the fence to watch the excitement, their big eyes watching with a mix of alarm and curiosity. It was nearing shearing season, so they were all covered with thick fleece. Rosie always thought that they looked like impossibly fluffy baby giraffes or cute aliens.

Alix and Lew pulled up next to the paddock and joined the group.

"How'd it go?" asked Patrick as Rosie and Dr. Arden opened the trailer and led the horses out.

"No hitches," Lew said.

"I could feel the thing's colds, so we left fast," Alix said.

"Caesar and Sunny seem to have made the trip fine," Dr. Arden said and turned them loose in the little paddock.

"What are you doing here?" Lew asked, shaking the vet's hand. "And how's our boy doing?"

"Bobby is awake and comfortable. I'm encouraged," the vet said. "Meg called because was everyone here setting up a pen, so I came by. Did you know that this guy here can talk to animals? And that she's a witch?" he asked Alix as he pointed at Nan.

"Yes," said Alix.

Dr. Arden chuckled. "The things happening on your ranch, Rosie. Can I stick around and watch?"

"Of course," said Rosie. "I'll probably need your help."

"You should talk to the horses, now," said Nan. Caesar turned to look at her, and Nan took a big step backward and crossed her arms.

"They are all yours, Patrick," Lew said.

"Geesh. I don't usually do this with an audience," he said. He took the lead from Rosie and rubbed Caesar's nose. The horse rumbled and bumped him in the chest with his big head.

"They are happy to be here," Patrick said. "Caesar likes the look of the fresh grass."

"Can't have too much of that," warned the vet. "He'll founder."

"He thinks you're a grump," Patrick said, and they all laughed.

"Patrick, can you ask them why they aren't freaked out by the sprite?" Rosie said.

Patrick was quiet a moment and then shook his head and tried again. "They don't know what you mean," he said finally.

"Caesar says that there isn't any danger out there. Sunny says that they are very safe in the barn."

"Ask if they are safe outside the barn."

"Yes," Patrick said. "Safe outside."

"What about Sunny in the cowshed?" Alix asked.

Patrick rubbed Sunny's nose. "She says that she shouldn't have been in the shed. She's not a cow." He looked at Rosie. "Even so, she's not afraid, inside or outside, either."

"Do they know that the sprite is in the shed?" Lew asked.

"Yes."

They all stared at the horses who stood swishing their tails and eyeing the grass.

"He says that the sprite is there to keep them safe. He's confused why we would be afraid of it."

"Ask him," Rosie choked. "Ask him if he remembers Ben."

"Yes."

"Ask him if he remembers how Ben died."

"He remembers that the young stallion threw him."

"Does he remember why the stallion threw Ben?"

The horse turned to look at Rosie with his soft, kind eye and rumbled deep in his chest.

"He says now he understands why you are frightened," Patrick said.

Rosie felt like the ground moved below her, but she resolved not to cry. She felt the horse's nose on her shoulder, and she wrapped her arms around his head and squeezed her eyes shut.

"Rosie," Patrick said. "Rosie, Caesar says he can help."

"How?"

"Caesar says that he knows something about the sprite. He says that the sprite can't ... uh ... see in the stable."

"It doesn't have eyes," Rosie said.

"It doesn't? Wow. But it's more than that," Patrick said. "Caesar says that sprites can't live in metal. No, they can't touch metal."

"So, we're shielded in the stable? It can't see us, and it can't come inside?"

"That's what he said."

"That explains a lot," Lew said.

"It's in the book," Alix said in his sharp, foreign voice. "Why don't you read the book?"

"We have, Alix," said Nan. "The book only tells us what it wants us to know."

"That's true," Alix said. "Damned book is borderline useless if it's in a bad mood."

"I told you about the metal and the fae, too," Nan said to Patrick.

"I'm dying to make a 'from the horse's mouth' joke here," Lew said. "I can't think of one that fits."

"Can they tell us anything else?" Rosie asked.

"Caesar says he'll think about it. He's not used to thinking, so he might be a while."

Cody put a hand on Patrick's arm. "Do you want a job?" he asked.

Patrick laughed. "Thanks, but I already have one."

"Can you consult, then? Please?"

"I doubt I'll be able to avoid that, anymore," Patrick said, smiling.

Lew brought out a twelve-pack of beer, and they sat in puffy jackets in a ring of lawn chairs in front of the pen where Caesar and Sunny stood chewing new grass and ignoring the hay. The horses hadn't said anything new according to

Patrick, other than to claim this grass was even sweeter than at home. Caesar and Sunny also thought the alpacas lined up at the fence were hilarious.

"The alpacas are pretty sure the horses are going to eat them," Patrick said.

"They're afraid of the barn cat and of the bunny rabbits," Meg said. "They can be pretty clever, but they are really, really skittish." Meg took a swig of beer, and then said, "Say, do they speak in a Spanish accent? I've always wondered. Dawn over there is a Chilean import."

Patrick laughed. "It doesn't work that way."

Alix cleared his throat. "This is fun," he said. "But I think we should have a plan before sunset."

The group grew somber. Evening chores loomed, and no one wanted to venture onto the ranch.

"At least we know that once we get into the stable, we're safe," Patrick said. "Someone can at least go feed the horses tonight."

"I wish we could just get this whole thing over with," Rosie said. "I'm tired of being scared."

Patrick put his arm around her, and she leaned into him, vibrating pleasantly.

"Well, I talked with my friend in the old country," Alix said. "He gave me a spell to try. It's supposed to get rid of unwanted spirits."

"Is a sprite a spirit?" Lew asked.

"No. It's a kind of fairy," Nan said. She was draped on a lawn chair like a girl in a 1920's beer advertisement with her long white hair flowing. Rosie was getting used to Nan's incongruity.

"That thing is a fairy?" Rosie asked. "I thought fairies were tiny naked girls with wings and wands."

"Nah." Alix snorted. "That's what they sell to little girls."

"'Thou speak'st aright; I am that merry wanderer of the night,'" Lew said.

"Ya," Alix said. "Real fairies can be nasty things. It's a name used sometimes to call lots of supernatural beasties."

"Will a spirit charm work on a sprite?" asked Patrick.

"Maybe. Depends on the charm. It will certainly annoy it," Nan said. "I still think you should get a cow and be done with it."

"I'm not getting a cow," Rosie said. "I can't see a reason to get a cow."

"Well, I can," said Alix. "If we have a cow while we're doing charm, it might follow cow."

"So, could we put the cow in a trailer and lead the sprite off the ranch?" Rosie asked.

"Maybe," said Nan. "I doubt it."

"Do we know someone with a wooden barn that cows live in who might want to adopt a cowsprite?" Alix asked.

"I think I can help with that," said the vet. "I'll go to the clinic and make a couple calls. I can check on Bobby while I'm there, too."

"Okay, let's assume we can get a cow. Did you have any other suggestions?" Rosie asked.

"I have a potion that we can use on the doors and windows of the shed," said Nan. "It's a repellant. You need to tear the barn down."

"We tried that already," Rosie said. "Remember? Not only did it wreck my tractor, but it resurrected the shed."

"True," she said. "But you didn't really finish the job. You just knocked it down. You really need to dismantle it. Possibly even disperse the boards."

"No matter," Alix Said. "Sprite can live in fairy house made of leaves."

"There seem to be a lot of steps to this," Rosie said. She sighed and finished her beer. "I don't think we're doing this today before the sun goes down."

"No, we have to do it at sunset or sunrise," Alix said. "That's when it's weakest."

"Why?" Rosie asked.

"I don't know. Something about the changing light. You ask so many question!"

Caesar had come over to the fence during the discussion and stood with his head over the panel. Rosie wondered if he were listening. "Can he understand us?" she asked Patrick.

"Not really," Patrick said. "He understands some words, but it would be like if you were plopped into some foreign country with a phrasebook of a hundred words."

"Does he have anything to say?" Lew asked.

Patrick looked at the horse who swished his tail.

"He's wondering if we're worried about the tree or the spring, too."

"Which tree?" Rosie asked.

"The tree has a spirit, too?" Alix asked.

"Apparently," Patrick said. "And, the wet spot is a spring, with its own spirit."

"My, my," Nan said. "Who knew your place was such a supernatural hot spot?"

Rosie groaned.

"Caesar says that we shouldn't be worried about the tree or the spring. He was just wondering."

"Where are the ghostbusters when you need them?" Lew chuckled.

"Maybe you can look for them when we get the horses back to the ranch," Rosie said. She squinted at the sinking sun. "We had better scoot if we want to make it before it gets dark."

"Grab your toothbrush," said Molly. "I'm not letting you stay there tonight."

"Right. You can stay with me." Patrick took her hand.

Rosie squeezed it, but she said, "This place is closer to the ranch. I'm staying here. You can go home. Go to work. We'll be fine."

Patrick's face contorted and then settled into some hard lines. "Yes, Ma'am," he said.

"Don't be like that. I'm fine here. You can't be on the ranch ... not yet, anyway."

"I don't like feeling helpless."

Rosie shrugged. "Sometimes all you can do is wait."

"You can meet her on the ranch with me in the morning," Nan said.

Rosie looked at the little witch. "Why are you going to my place in the morning?"

"Why, to meet your cow, of course."

"Oh, right." Rosie sighed silently. She had already forgotten about the cow.

CHAPTER SEVEN

Kua Fe

Rosie couldn't believe she was at a dairy in the drizzly rain, but there she was.

She stood at the edge of a football-field sized structure of steel and concrete. The stench was astounding, and even she, a woman of fortitude who was around livestock every day, was nearly overwhelmed. She hadn't spent much time at a confinement dairy.

Still, she was glad Patrick decided to go home to shower. Rosie guessed that the stench and the chatter from the 200 cows would have permanently put him off of working with a vet.

Cody had spent time at this kind of place, however. He stood a few feet away chatting with the dairy farmer. Dan

Wick was thin, wiry, short, and sixty. Even though it was drizzling cold April rain, he didn't even wear a ball cap on his bald head. Sometimes he blinked when a raindrop hit his eye, so Rosie knew he did actually have feelings.

The discussion was over a skinny cow whose hipbones jutted from her sides like icebergs. She was a Holstein, black and white, with a pair of curved horns that were blunted at the ends. There were hollows in her flanks, and her enormous udder hung loose beneath her. The only upsides Rosie could see about the beast was that her ribs weren't prominently showing, and there was a certain brightness about her look.

"Tell me why she wants a broken cow again?" Dan asked Cody.

"She needs a cow to help one of the horses," Cody lied. "It was raised on a ranch, and we think it misses cows."

"Stupid horses," Dan said. "Never had a use for 'em."

Rosie tried to look interested in the cow and not insulted that Dan wouldn't give her the time of day. *I should be used to it*, Rosie thought. It wasn't the first time she'd been ignored in favor of whatever man was in her company. Ranching was still a man's business, even though things were changing. They just weren't changing fast enough for Rosie.

"Well, you can have Bossy if you want 'er," Dan said. "She don't milk anymore, not since that last calf wrecked her."

"That why I thought of her," Cody said. "I remembered that uterine infection. I hoped you had kept her around."

"Yeah. Well." Dan kicked an imaginary rock in the barnyard. "Kept her until she was done milking. Then, never got around to getting rid of her." He stepped over to the cow and rubbed her head. "Some of 'em, you know. She's a nice one."

"You get attached." Cody let Bossy sniff his hand. "I understand."

Rosie watched the old man rub his cow behind the ear and let her opinion of him soften. He said, "If Rosie here'll give Bossy a nice place to live, I'll be happy for her. Better future than what I have to offer."

"Great!" Cody said and shook Dan's hand. "Rosie, meet your new cow."

"Hello, old girl." Rosie held her hand out to be snuffled. "Want to come live with me with a bunch of horses?"

The old man laughed. "She's never seen a horse, Rosie. Bossy here's not been off of the farm for years. Heck, today's the first time in years she's even been outside in the rain."

"Wow, really?" Rosie scratched the cow's face. "Then a shed under a tree with grass to eat will be like cow heaven, won't it?"

She saw Dan Wicks swell a little before he said, "I treat my girls right fine, Missy."

"I didn't mean anything," Rosie said.

"Nah, s'pose you didn't," he said. He looked at his gigantic barn and sighed. "It's not the way my daddy did it," he said. "But times change, and you can't hardly make a living selling milk anymore. Everything's automated and shit now."

He rubbed Bossy again and said, "Need help getting her into the trailer? Not sure she's ever been in one before."

As Rosie arrived home towing the cow in a trailer, she saw Patrick and Nan in his truck — with a plastic window and blanket upholstery — waiting her. They had parked near her front lawn, in sight of the cowshed.

Everyone was nervous about Patrick returning to the ranch, but Nan insisted it would be fine. "Between me, the cow, and Rosie, the sprite won't care about you," Nan said.

"Especially if you can control yourself and not touch your girlfriend."

Patrick bristled at the remark but kept his mouth shut.

"How'd it go?" Patrick asked. He held the door for Rosie as she hopped out. Rosie saw that he could tell there was a cow in the trailer. His smile was tight, though. Nervous. She couldn't help touching his chin with her fingertips.

"Fine," she said. "Bossy's in the back."

"Why are cows called 'Bossy'?" Patrick wondered aloud as they walked to open the trailer door.

"Bosporus," Nan said as if this word answered his question.

"What?" Patrick asked.

"Bosporus. The strait between the Asian and European parts of Istanbul? You were in that part of the world, Patrick. Didn't you pick up any of the language?"

"Not that part," he said. He banged on the latch of Rosie's old trailer.

"That's forever getting stuck," Rosie said.

"Bosporus," Nan announced, "means 'cow crossing' in Greek. 'Bos' is cow, and 'porus' means through."

"Oh, so 'Bossy' is just Greek for cow," Rosie said through her teeth as she put her shoulder into the latch. "Why didn't you say so?"

"I thought I just did," Nan said and crossed her arms.

"Dammit!" Rosie kicked the trailer, and Bossy mooed. "Sorry. I should get a new trailer."

"Or some axle grease." Patrick jogged to his truck and came back with a jar of ooze which he slathered on the frozen latch. It slid open at his touch.

"Aren't you smart?" Rosie said as she opened the door. She caught the cow and clipped a lead onto her halter.

Naturally, the cow, whites of her eyes showing, planted all four feet and refused to move.

"Here," Rosie said to Patrick. "Work your magic."

"I wish you wouldn't call it that."

"Seriously?"

"Oh, all right," he said. He stepped into the trailer, taking the rope from Rosie. "Hiya, Bossy. I'm Patrick. You should really step out of this metal box. There's actual grass over there."

Bossy blinked at him. He rubbed her between the horns.

"Yes, I'm serious. Come on out and see."

Bossy stepped to the edge of the trailer and peeked out. As soon as she saw the grass in front of Rosie's house, she lurched out of the trailer and dragged Patrick there.

Auntie Nan looked across the gravel driveway at the cowshed.

It started to rain again, so Rosie and Patrick pulled up the hoods of their jackets, but Nan simply stood in the downpour, little rivers coursing down the crannies in her face. Her high heels sank into the wet lawn and her flowered spring dress was soggy.

"What's she doing?" Rosie asked.

"I don't know," Patrick said.

"I'm just watching the shed," Nan said, turning. She sighed and walked over to them. "There's not much going on over there."

Rosie peered at the shed. It leaned in the gray light as always. Rosie would feel safer if they could put the cow in the barn, but there seemed little use for the cow if she were in a metal building where the sprite couldn't see her.

Patrick rubbed the cow's nose.

"What's Bossy say?" Nan asked.

"She's happy there's a sprite over there."

Auntie Nan asked, "What else does she say?"

Patrick scratched the cow between the ears, and she blinked at him. "Bossy says she likes it here. She wants to stay."

"She does realize there aren't any other cows here, right?" Rosie said. "And there won't be any more cows," she added crossing her arms.

"She's sad about that, but she can't have babies or give milk anymore, so she's just content to hang out with the sprite and the horses." He put his hands over her ears comically. "I think she knows what happens to cows that can't give milk, and she likes this alternative better."

"I don't believe this," Rosie said. "She's only here until we get this sprite thing figure out. She can't stay. I keep horses. See?" She swept her arm across the ranch. "Horses. Neigh. Not moo."

The cow sneezed. "You're hurting her feelings," Patrick said.

"You should get used to cows, Rosie," Nan said, squeezing rain out of her long white hair. "If you want to live peacefully with the sprite from now on, you're going to need a cow around."

"I don't want the sprite here!" Rosie cried. "My life is so surreal! I'm having an argument with my magic boyfriend's witch of an aunt who is telling me to keep a cow so a supernatural creature will live next to my house without killing me!"

"Oh, you're an official couple now?" Auntie Nan said.

Rosie glared at them and turned her back muttering, "Unbelievable. As bad as my dad."

"Is she usually this temperamental?" Nan asked.

"She's under a lot of stress," Patrick said. "Are you sure there isn't any way to get the sprite off of the property? I mean, it must have come here with the cows. Isn't there a way to lure it off to another place with cows?"

Nan shook her head. "As I understand it, if the barn falls of its own accord, the sprite will move on, or possibly dissipates into the ether."

"But removing the barn just makes it mad."

"Right." Nan looked over her shoulder at the shed next to the tree.

"What does it say?" she asked.

"What do you mean?"

"What did it say when you talked to it?"

Patrick stopped petting the cow and frowned. "It can't talk, Auntie," he said coldly. "And if it could, I couldn't talk to it. It's not an animal."

Auntie Nan rolled her eyes. "You mean you wouldn't talk to it."

Patrick scowled. "It's one of those creatures, Nan," he said. "Its brother stood by and watched those horses die. They are evil."

"Prejudice will always get in the way, Patrick," Nan said. "You never understood what happened in Iraq because you never spoke to that sprite. These creatures protect animals. They don't destroy them. How many horses died in that fire?" she demanded.

"Four."

"And how many survived?"

Patrick blinked. "Fifty maybe?"

"Do you think that those fifty surviving was an accident?"

"I, uh..."

She shook her head. "You go over there and make nice to that thing and see what it wants."

"But..." His face twisted, but he turned toward the shed.

"Go on," she said.

"You'll be killed," Rosie said and gripped his arm. He put his hand over hers, but kept looking at the shed.

"No, he won't. He's just going over to talk." Nan glanced at Rosie's worried face and said, "I won't let anything happen to him. Promise."

"Take the cow," Rosie said to Patrick. "Maybe it will be in a better mood with the cow around."

"Good idea," Nan said.

"Okay," he said.

Patrick walked Bossy to the shed. Rosie braided the tail end of her hair again and again. Cow and man stood by the shed for a moment. Nothing happened.

The cow began chewing her cud.

"Maybe it's asleep?" he said to the cow.

Bossy blinked at him and swallowed.

The air above the shed shimmered and waved gently. Rosie's heart stopped.

"Patrick," she whispered.

"Hush," Nan hissed.

He cleared his throat. "Nice place you have here," he said aloud.

Bossy hit him with her head. "Okay, okay. Let me start again."

"O, cow sprite, please tell me what you want."

The cow brought up more cud, unconcerned, so he stood still and waited.

The cow blinked at him.

"No, I didn't hear it," he said to her. "Why? Can you?"

Rosie and Nan watched Patrick and the cow as they stood in front of the shed.

"What's going on?" Rosie asked.

"They're talking," Nan said.

"Who's talking?"

Nan shook her head. "I thought the cow would protect Patrick from the sprite, but I think...I think the cow is translating for him."

"For the sprite?"

"I don't know why I didn't think of it before," Nan said. "Of course, the cow can understand the sprite."

"Oh. And Patrick can talk to the cow." Rosie was quiet a moment. "I didn't think the sprite could talk."

Nan nodded. "Your ignorance is excusable," Nan said. "Patrick's isn't. He knows better than to assume anything concerning the supernatural. Had he left his anger and prejudice when he encountered this sprite..." She glanced at Rosie's bedroom window where the curtain still fluttered outside. "We might have prevented some of this ... damage."

Patrick tied the cow to the tree, and she began to graze. After standing a moment scratching her on the back, Patrick turned and walked back to them, stopping a few feet away, thoughtful.

"Well?" Nan asked.

"Well." Patrick blinked and looked at them each. Then he rubbed his eyes. "It talks."

"I knew that," Nan snapped. "What does it say?"

He rubbed his head a moment. "It was mostly talking to the cow. It loves this cow."

"Was it mad at you?" Rosie asked.

He looked at her finally. "No. It didn't seem to even notice me. All I heard from Bossy was how happy the sprite is that she is here."

"What's its name?" Nan asked.

"Bossy calls it 'Kua Fe.'"

"Kua Fe?" Rosie felt a little light-headed. The sprite had a name.

"Seems like the cow was a good idea, after all," Nan said.

The smell of smug coming off of her incised Rosie. "It can't stay."

"But it's so happy and peaceful," Nan said. "As long as it has a cow, it will be placated. It will protect your farm."

"It's a ranch," Rosie corrected. "And it can't stay. This is the creature that killed my husband, and you want me to let it live here and keep a pet cow?"

"Don't get angry," Nan said.

"But I don't want to have that ... killer living with me!"

"It's not leaving," Nan said.

"What if we tore down the shed again?" Patrick said and stepped closer to her. She noticed he was still careful not to touch her this close to the sprite.

"No, Alix was right. It could live in a fairy house made of fallen leaves," Nan said.

"Aren't there other charms or spells we could use?" he asked.

"Child, I don't think you understand what a treasure you have here."

"Treasure?" Rosie said.

Nan sighed. "Patrick, make sure the cow is happy. We need to go someplace warm and have a drink."

If Rosie felt weird about sitting at the bar at noon on a weekday and sipping a bourbon, she decided it was the least weird thing that had happened to her in a week. Even though the bar was one of her former haunts, she didn't know the afternoon bartender. Just as well. She took comfort in the long wooden bar — the owner's pride and joy — and the splashes of light coming through the stained-glass windows of the old building. She had forgotten about the stained glass since the last several times she'd been there it had been dark outside. The windows reminded her of the church her mother had taken her to when she was little. Rosie decided that the drinks were better at the bar than the church.

The bourbon warmed her insides and took the jagged edges off of her anger. Still, the whole idea of appeasing the demon in that shed under her tree was ... well ... ridiculous.

She said so.

Nan sighed. "It isn't ridiculous, dear," she explained again. "It is reasonable. There are some battles you'll never win, my dear, and this is one of them. That creature has lived under that tree for a century at least. Its only purpose in the world is to protect cows. It was content to live without cows and talk to your horses until your husband — Ben, right? — until Kua Fe observed Ben's methods at breaking horses and found them to be cruel."

"And killed him," Rosie said. "How am I supposed to live with a creature that killed my husband?"

"You could try forgiving it," Nan said.

"You're serious," Rosie said.

Patrick took her hand.

Nan drew herself up. She was still tiny. "I don't believe that Kua Fe killed your husband."

"How do you know?" Rosie demanded.

"I know sprites. When they intentionally kill people, you'd never mistake it as a riding accident. They do not bother masking their work."

Patrick nodded slowly. "They aren't subtle creatures."

"Well, what about my house burning down? Wouldn't that count as bad luck like Alix was talking about? Isn't that the sprite's fault?"

"Again," Nan said. "Unless you can connect it directly with some drastic case of animal abuse, I don't think Kua Fe was involved."

"Stop using its name like it's a person," Rosie said.

"Why? It's probably eons old. It may be the only one of its kind in this state. I think it deserves the modicum of respect we can offer by using its name."

Rosie glared at her drink, anger returning despite the warm fuzz in her brain from the bourbon. "So, the death of my husband, the fire that destroyed my house, the monster under my cowshed ... all these are coincidence?"

Patrick squeezed her hand, but Rosie pulled it away.

Then she had a thought. "What, what about me?" she said. "What if I have to put a horse down because it's sick, or I have to give it some painful treatment to save its life? How do I know that ... Kua Fe won't kill me in my sleep or cause another 'accident'? How can I feel safe at my own house with that thing out there?"

"You felt safe before," Nan began.

"You said it: 'Before.'"

"There are ways to keep the sprite away from your house," she said. "Honestly, though, I don't believe your sprite is interested in hurting you. He's had ample opportunity. Years, in fact. Years when you probably have had to put a horse down or deliver unpleasant treatments. Nothing happened during those times, did it?"

"No."

Patrick ordered another round of drinks and the afternoon bartender, bored with cutting limes, delivered them quickly. They waited until he resumed his chore on the other side of the bar before they spoke again.

"You said that the sprite was a treasure," Patrick said to his aunt.

"Indeed." Nan wound her long white hair into a rope as she organized her thoughts, and Rosie thought again that she looked more like an aging hippie than a witch. "Here's the thing: Sprites are a dying breed."

"Except for Kua Fe who insists on existing in my yard."

"Don't interrupt, dear, or I'll pull out the attention spell I had to use on young Patrick." She took a long pull off of her Long Island Iced Tea.

"It's the pole barns, of course. Once it was cheaper to build outbuildings out of steel sheets than wood, the sprites were homeless. They can't stand iron or steel, you see."

"Then why didn't he leave when we knocked down the shed?"

"Well, how did you knock it down? Did you tear it to pieces and then cart away the debris? Did you pour a concrete floor and put up a steel building?"

"No."

"What you have is a special sprite," Nan said. "Not only is he strong enough to rebuild his home, but he is married to your place more than most."

"Caesar and Sunny said that there is a tree spirit and a spring spirit on that spot, too," Patrick said.

"That's right," she said. "There is something special, sacred about that place, Rosie. It's worth protecting."

Rosie groaned. "I'm not drunk enough to be having this conversation," she said. "If you start spouting New Age-y shit about the holiness of space, I'm going to need a whole bottle of Maker's Mark."

Nan puffed up a little. "If you studied that 'New Age-y shit' a little, young lady, it might answer some of your questions."

"I'm sorry," Rosie said. "I get bitchy when I'm not in control. I hate being at the mercy of this thing."

"Negotiation is not being at something's mercy," Nan said. "There are ways of limiting Kua Fe's movements and his influence. We can keep him content and happy in his shed if the cow is nearby. You know, sprites aren't very smart."

"Neither are bears," Rosie said. "They still cause lots of damage."

Nan swirled the straw in her drink. "You know," she said. "Your ranch is wasted on you."

"Excuse me?"

"I think what Nan means is that you don't appreciate how special your land is," Patrick said.

"I don't understand," Rosie said.

"Not many places are inhabited by so many spirits." Nan still stirred her drink.

"Haunted, you mean."

"Exactly," she said. "Haunted places are very, very special. Full of magic and possibility."

"Possibility for what?" Rosie said.

"Well, magic people like magic places."

Rosie crinkled her brow.

"Magic people might pay to visit a magic place. Like yours."

"You want me to open a zoo for witches and warlocks to come visit my sprite and tree spirit?"

"Well, the spring spirit is probably the most powerful of the three, but you've got the idea."

"You mean like that place over in Cooperton? The one with the sinkhole spirit and private hot tubs?" Patrick asked.

"Exactly." Nan beamed.

"Wait, you have seen my place," Rosie said. "It's not exactly a spa."

"Oh, that won't take much to fix," Nan said. "I have a builder friend who can fix the damage. We could spin it as a dude ranch for magic people!"

"I need another drink," Rosie said. "I've gone from a perfectly happy person living alone with my horses to actually having a discussion about opening a magic dude ranch."

"It will be fine," Nan said. "Plus, it will be very lucrative."

"It will?"

"Yes," Nan said. "Three spirits in one spot? And a chance to ride horses? It will be a great vacation spot. Say." She looked at Patrick. "Do you think we could get a unicorn?"

Patrick shrugged. "I can ask around."

"A real unicorn?" Rosie's eyes sparkled like a five-year-old's. "I shouldn't be surprised that unicorns are real," she said. "But, really? A unicorn?"

"If we could convince one to live here. They are a bit picky," he said.

Rosie shook her head.

"Listen," she said. "None of that matters. Even though I'd give my right arm just to see a unicorn, I do not want to get into the magic dude ranch business. I just want to go back to my old life!"

Nan sat back and looked at Rosie with pursed lips and a schoolteacher's frown on her face. Finally, she said, "I can't take you back in time, which is what you are asking for. However, I can buy the ranch from you."

"Buy my ranch?" Rosie blinked.

"I'll figure out how to make the place a destination for magic folk."

"Do you know anything about horses?" Rosie asked.

"Heavens, no!" Auntie Nan fanned herself. "I can barely stand the cat familiar that hangs around me. He stays outside. I'd hire someone to run the place for me."

"I don't know," Rosie said. She looked at Patrick.

"I don't know, either," he said.

"Think about it," Nan said. "We'll just call it a standing offer for now."

Patrick glanced at his watch. "I hate to be a party pooper, but I kind of said I'd go to work today."

Rosie looked at her watch. It was noon. How was it only noon?

Patrick stood and kissed Rosie on the forehead, and she smiled when the tingles came.

"Listen to Nan," he whispered. "She knows this stuff way better than I do."

"Maybe."

After the door swung shut behind him, Nan drained her drink and said, "Well, you'd better come to the shop with me. Let's see if we can't keep your sprite inside his shed."

Rosie followed Nan to her herbal shop in a historic building in the middle of town. One customer stood at the door, waiting for Nan to open it. It was Al, a Sheriff's deputy Rosie knew from high school.

"What's up, Al?" she asked.

"Just waiting for Nan," he said. "Only place in town to get fenuric. You know Melissa had a baby girl, right?"

"Congratulations!" Rosie said.

"Fenuric is good for lactating mothers," Nan explained as she turned the key in the lock. "Al's wife needs it." She pushed open the door.

The smell of the place was overwhelming. Patchouli, sage, potpourri, cinnamon all accosted Rosie's nose so fiercely that she began sneezing.

"Goddess bless you," Nan said. She plucked a bottle from a shelf near the front. "Is this all for you, Al?"

"Yes, ma'am." He smiled and handed her his debit card.

Rosie sneezed again.

"Tell Melissa to make some tea out of the contents of the caplets. Just taking the pills doesn't work as well."

"Will do." With a sheepish wave, he left.

Nan swung her arms over her head, and the smells went away so suddenly that Rosie thought she had broken something in her nose. "The smell is just about atmosphere for the hippies that come in here. The rest of the store is for people like me who make potions."

She led Rosie through a beaded curtain she hadn't noticed and into a room that was so huge it was impossible that it actually fit inside the building. Rows and rows of shelves were stacked with five-gallon glass jars bursting with green and gold and fleshy things that Rosie couldn't begin to identify. She stood, mouth agape, at the entrance until Nan touched her arm.

"It's a little cramped in here, don't you think?" Nan said. Rosie stared. "I'd love to expand but business is a little slow since the economic downturn."

"Are all herbal stores like this?" Rosie asked.

"No, some are run by non-magical people, but they don't usually last very long. It's hard to make a living selling chamomile tea and fenuric. The real money is in pickled frog eyes and bat tongues. Oh, and vanilla orchids. You'd be surprised how difficult it is to get the actual flowers. They are a key ingredient for love potions, you know."

"If you say so."

"Well, think about it," Nan said. "The best perfumes all based have a vanilla base, right?"

"You mean perfumes are ... are spells?"

"Well, potions, technically. And pretty weak ones, too, but yes, they all have their bases in love potions. That's why the best ones are so expensive. It takes real skill to make a love potion be potent long enough to be bottled."

"I see." Rosie touched a nearby jar filled with green buds that glistened with oil. "What's this?"

"Cannabis," Nan said rummaging through a sheaf of papers. "Where did I put that protection spell?"

"Isn't cannabis marijuana?"

"That's the common name for it, yes."

Rosie didn't mean to side-eye Nan, but the witch saw her.

Nan put down her papers and smiled at her. "Aren't you adorable?" she said. Then she opened a book and began searching again. "It's legal in this state both medically and recreationally, but it's not like I sell it to teenagers who want to get high," she said. "Well, not knowingly."

Rosie put her hands behind her back. She felt a sudden trepidation about the things in the shop and its owner.

"Here's a protection spell," Nan said, handing Rosie a photocopy of an old, jagged-edged page. "And, here's a perimeter spell. These should keep Kua Fe in his place and keep you safe in case he gets grumpy again."

"These should make me feel better," Rosie said. "Right?"

Nan smiled at her. "Did you ever carry a rabbit's foot?"

"When I was nine. It was dyed green. Ed keeps trying to give me a new one. "

"Did the one you had as a kid make you feel better?"

"Actually, it did. My dad gave it to me. He said to rub it whenever I felt sad. It helped a little. "

"I'll make you another," Nan said. "This one will have a better protection spell on it than your original," she said. She opened a jar and selected a furry white foot.

"Why do I feel like I've just been dropped onto another planet?"

Nan shrugged. "It's like when someone is born again into Christianity," she said. "At first, it's a whole new world."

Rosie wondered if Ben felt this way when he started at his new church.

"Wait," she said. "There are Christian witches?"

"Of course," Nan said. "What do you think a faith healer is?"

Ben definitely wouldn't have liked the idea that his favorite TV Evangelists striking demons from people were actually witches. She smiled.

Rosie fingered her new rabbit's foot. She took it from her pocket as she drove, but she was thinking of using a chain she could loop it on so she could wear it around her neck. Despite what Nan said about the protection spell she was going to cast on the house, Rosie liked having something tangible on her, so she felt safe.

That evening, Patrick came to her place straight from work. As he parked, Nan arrived at Rosie's holding a small black pot in her lap and another in the back seat. When Rosie asked earlier in the day where the giant black cauldron was, Nan laughed. "My grandmother had one of those," she said. "Now I use my food processor and microwave. The iron pot is just to mask the potion from the sprites and spirits."

Nan steered the Prius gingerly onto the gravel drive and parked beside Patrick's truck. He stepped out of his truck still in shirtsleeves and shoved the blanket back onto the seat. The sun was still shining weakly from behind the evening clouds, but it was strong enough to throw blond highlights into Patrick's cropped hair.

"Not strictly necessary," Nan said when Patrick opened her door and took the pot from her. "I can get out myself." Still, she used both hands and heaved herself onto the drive. "It's not like I'm two hundred years old."

"How old are you?" Rosie asked without thinking. "Oh, I'm sorry. That was rude."

Nan laughed. "I'm only 102," she said. "Patrick here is 59. There are benefits to being of magic stock."

"Nan!" Patrick had turned white.

"Fifty-nine?" She stared. Hadn't he said 36 before?

"I was going to tell you," he said.

"A baby, really," Nan said and patted his cheek. "Let's get your house taken care of, Rosie. Oh, here's Richard."

Rosie saw a huge black Cadillac turn down her drive. It parked next to them and a very fat, very tall man climbed out and slammed the door. "Nan!" he thundered. "Good to see you!" He embraced the little woman in a huge hug.

"Richard. Good to see you." Nan's voice was barely audible from the hug.

"Pat!" He shook Patrick's hand and then said, "You must be Rosie!" He pumped her hand and laughed. "I see that sprite really tore up the place. He must have been pissed off." He peeked in a window, shielding his eyes with his hands. "Yup, tore up."

"Who is this?" Rosie whispered to Patrick.

"Oh, Richard is an old friend," Nan answered. "Contractor. He'll clean up your house, and later we can talk about a boarding facility for the dude ranch. Oh, there he goes."

Rosie watched as the giant man began stomping around the outside of her house, counting his steps so loudly she could hear him on the other side. When he returned to his starting point, he raised his bear-like arms and hollered, "RESTORATION!"

There was a clap of thunder, and Rosie felt a "whump" of air like she was too close to the business end of a jet engine, and it threw her into Patrick. When she opened her eyes, new landscaping with bright orange mulch and young trees had appeared in her yard. She saw that the windows had been replaced and — she rubbed her eyes and looked again — yes, the whole exterior had been repainted a calming shade of blue.

"There you go, Little Lady!" the huge man shouted. "Go on inside and make sure I didn't miss anything."

Rosie glanced at Nan who nodded. Rosie ran up her porch steps and nearly wept to see the furniture repaired and even the dirty dishes washed and put away.

She went back outside wiping her eyes. "How can I repay you?" she began.

Richard waved a huge paw at her. "Nan here has saved my butt I don't know how many times," he shouted. Rosie realized that he must always shout. "This one's on the house. Get it?" He laughed exactly the way Rosie imagined a bear would laugh.

"Anyway," he said. "I'll make you a deal on the bunk house. I wanted to make sure you were comfortable, though." She was surprised at how gently he patted her back. "An angry sprite is enough to ruin anyone's day." With that, he clambered back into his car and was gone.

"I'm beginning to like magic people," Rosie said.

"I would have thought that Patrick was the person to make you like magic people," Nan said winking and nudging Rosie with an elbow.

Rosie blushed.

"Ninety-nine percent of that is Patrick," Nan said. "But I'll bet he has a 1% enhancement spell operating," Nan said. "Usually it's in the aftershave."

"Nan!" Patrick said.

Rosie took Patrick's arm. "She's worse than my dad," she said.

Patrick groaned. "Can we stop talking about this? Please?"

"Oh, all right. Spoil sport," Nan said. "Let's get this place protected, then enchant the heck out of Kua Fe's house."

Nan picked up her black pot gave it to Patrick, then handed Rosie a small device.

"What's this? A magic amulet?"

"It's a compass, silly," Nan said, flipping open the top for her. "I need to put the potion on the four points of the compass."

"Oh."

The older-than-she-looked woman took out a very beat-up ladle, checked the compass in Rosie's hand, and dished out a spoonful of potion. She said, "*De Chalet*, I say," three times and then poured the potion on the roots of one of the new trees in a planting group.

"Come on." Nan led them to another side of the house and repeated the spell.

On the fourth side, Rosie said, "It wasn't luck that those four new trees just happened to be just where you needed to pour the potion, was it?"

Nan smiled. "No, but I did ask Richard to plant the trees in a cluster so the exact trees wouldn't be obvious. That's why I needed the compass. Now, let's go make it more difficult for Kua Fe to get out of his house."

She retrieved the other pot from the back seat of her Prius and gave it to Patrick.

"I feel like a pack animal," Patrick said.

"At least you're useful," Nan said.

Then they all walked to the cowshed, Nan wobbling on the gravel in her sensible beige pumps.

"Should I get Bossy some hay and water first?" Rosie asked.

"Oh, good idea," said Nan. "Happy cow, happy sprite."

Rosie trotted to the barn and slid open the door. Inside, she was greeted by a chorus of whinnies and rumbles from the horses.

"I know you guys are bored. I'm doing my best to resolve the sprite situation," she said, feeling less silly today talking to the horses than she did a week ago. She talked to them before, but she hadn't known that they basically understood her.

She went to the stack of hay bales and pulled off a flake for the cow, then filled a pail of water. She closed the barn up behind her to the protests of the horses and brought the food to the shed.

Bossy was ecstatic and plunged her head into the bucket for a long drink.

"She says thanks," Patrick relayed.

"You are going for a 'Captain Obvious' award, aren't you?" said Nan. Rosie wasn't sure if Nan was teasing or not. She understood better why a teenaged Patrick had rebelled against her wishes.

"All right. I'm ready," Nan said. "Are you?"

"I guess so," Rosie said.

"Bossy is as happy as a cow can be," said Patrick.

Rosie looked at the cowshed. She hadn't been this close to the shed in a while, and it struck her as a little sad. She felt an urge to paint it ... red. "What do we do now?"

"Hold this." Nan lifted the lid from the pot Patrick held and handed it to Rosie. Then she took out a huge paintbrush. She dipped the brush into the liquid.

"Put the lid back," Nan said. "And for goodness sake, be careful not to touch him!"

Rosie replaced the lid gingerly. Then Nan began painting the shed and chanting under her breath.

"What are you doing?"

Nan shook her head and continued painting and chanting.

"What's she doing?" she asked Patrick.

"Hell if I know," he said. Rosie could see that he was still grating from Nan's earlier jibes. She rubbed the edge of the pot close to his hand with one finger, and he gave her a quick smile. "Sorry. I really don't know."

Rosie nodded and just lifted the pot lid each time Nan came back to re-load the brush.

When Nan had painted all of the house she could reach with the clear liquid, she turned and beckoned them to follow her. When they got to the lawn, Nan loosed her hair from the informal bun at the nape of her neck and raised her arms to a wind that suddenly rose to lift her hair and send her skirt behind her like a standard. She held this pose for a moment, and then lowered her arms. The wind abated, and Nan turned to Rosie and smiled.

"That should do it," she said.

"What did you do?"

"Well, we painted the house with a pretty strong impetus spell ... that means that the creature within will continue to do what it is doing ... it takes a lot to break impetus." She wound her hair into a bun again and pinned it in place with a pencil. "Then I asked the wind to sing to Bossy and Kua Fe each night to make sure they were happy."

"The wind does your bidding?" Rosie asked.

"Hardly," Nan said. "But it loves to sing and will sing to anyone who asks. Some houses ask, so every time there is any wind, it whistles and sighs throughout the house."

"That makes sense," Patrick said. "Explains all sorts of haunted houses and things."

"One last thing." Nan took Patrick's hand and purposefully placed it on Rosie's shoulder. Rosie gasped in horror and looked up at the shed ... which did nothing.

"Oh!" Rosie said.

"Good," Nan said. "Spell's working."

"What would we have done if it hadn't worked, Nan?" Patrick said.

"Run." Nan lightly spun and gathered her pot and brushes.

Rosie still watched the cow and cowshed. "So, what is Kua Fe doing now?"

Nan looked at Patrick who shook his head. "Bossy is too busy eating to talk."

"He's at rest," Nan said. "He'll stay that way unless something very dramatic happens. I think you'd have to torture a cow in front of him to get him to move now. I wouldn't try that, though."

"Don't worry about that," Rosie said. "Bossy is about the luckiest cow in the world."

Rosie decided that it was about time to catch up on chores, but Nan was still on Rosie's porch swing next to Patrick, asking questions about the ranch, in no hurry to go. Finally, Rosie stepped from the porch and said, "I'm sorry, Nan, but I really have to get chores done. I am so behind."

"Oh, of course." Nan hopped off the swing and stood next to Rosie. "What do we do first?"

Rosie couldn't help glance at Nan's high heels and flowered skirt. They were dry from the rain this morning, but the barnyard was a minefield of puddles and ... well, manure. She looked at Patrick who just barely rolled his eyes.

"Are you sure you want to do that?" Patrick said.

"How else am I going to learn?" Nan said.

Rosie was tired, so she tried the direct route. "I'm going to go shovel some shit, Nan. I don't think you're dressed for it."

Nan looked at her shoes. "Oh, I'm just going to watch," she said. "Don't worry about me."

Rosie tried to smile as she turned toward the barn. Instead of Bobby at her heels, she had a witch. It wasn't the same. She missed her dog. He was doing better, but Cody said he needed a couple more days of fluids and painkillers before he'd be ready to go home. At least Patrick strode next to her, holding her hand.

"Aren't you two cute?"

Patrick squeezed her hand and Rosie bit her lip. Nan was losing her charm, and while Rosie was grateful for her help, she was getting tired of her snideness.

As Rosie and Patrick mucked out the stalls and lugged bales of hay around, Nan puttered behind, constantly asking questions.

"What's that thingy for?"

"Why do you use that kind of salve?"

"How much do horses eat each day?"

"How much does your water bill come to?"

"Nan, I appreciate your ... help," Rosie said as she cleaned an automatic waterer. "But I'm really busy. I still have to longe the horses and..."

"Oh, I can help with that!"

"No, you can't," Rosie said.

"Of course, I can. I have a spell..."

"No, I didn't mean that you weren't able to," Rosie said. "I said that you can't. I won't let you. I don't want you hurt."

"Well, how am I supposed to learn?"

"Learn what? Why do you want to learn?"

"Well, if I buy this ranch, I'd have people to do this for me, but I should know how to do it at least, right?"

Rosie put her palms to her temples and squeezed until she could hear her arm muscles quiver.

"Rosie." Patrick sounded worried, but he was across the aisle in a stall.

"Nan. I am not going to sell my ranch. To you. To anyone. Ever." She let go of her head and watched the stunned Nan swim and then focus. "I think you should go wait in the house or go home now," Rosie said. "I need to get my work done."

Nan lifted her chin. "I suppose I should go home."

"Fine."

Rosie flung her rag in the aisle of the barn and walked directly to Nan's Prius, Patrick at her heels. She tried not to kick the tires.

"The nerve of that woman!" she hissed at Patrick.

"She didn't mean ... I mean ... I know." He stood just out of Rosie's reach, as if he were afraid of her. That suited Rosie just fine. Her fury made her feel powerful for once. But she cooled as she stood there, and her eyes fell on the cow shed.

A moment later, she heard Nan's steps crunch on the gravel. She opened the passenger side door and set her pots on the floor.

Rosie swallowed the anger and the pride and said, "I do appreciate all you've done for me, Nan. I'm really tired. I didn't mean to snap at you."

"Apology accepted," Nan said.

"But I'm not going to sell my place."

"I see that now."

"It's all I have."

"I understand, child," Nan said. She shut the door carefully. "I think it's foolish of you. I could really make something of it. You? I think you'll just waste it."

"Well, I'll be dead in fifty years. You can have it then."

"That's a possibility."

"I was joking."

"Of course you were." Nan smiled in a way that made Rosie's insides twist a little. Then she climbed into her car and drove away.

Rosie and Patrick watched Nan turn onto the paved road and drive toward town. Even though they had lots more work to do, the two of them sat on her porch step for a moment.

"I'm sorry," Patrick said.

"For what? You can't pick your relatives," Rosie said.

"I know, but ... I know what she's like. Jesus, she can turn me into a surly teenager faster than anyone."

"I know the feeling." Rosie leaned into Patrick and gazed at the cowshed and the oak.

"Hey," she said, sitting up. "What we were saying before about, about haunted places..."

"Yeah?"

"Are all the places kids think are haunted ... are they all haunted? You know, the old Presbyterian church, the house where the first mayor and his fifteen children lived, that old tannery."

Patrick looked away.

"They are, aren't they?"

"Not with ghosts, exactly," he said. "I don't understand the whole dead people thing, but spirits occupy lots of places, and most people can at least feel their presence."

"So, if there are spirits here, if a unicorn could be convinced to live here, where are the griffins and trolls? Is every fairy tale true?"

Patrick shook his head. "Not all of them. But lots more than you'd think."

Rosie put her head on her knees a moment and tried to breathe slowly until she felt better. Patrick rubbed her back in large circles. When she sat up, her eyes fell on the bark of the huge tree next to the shed. The oak was just beginning to leaf out, and a pair of kind eyes blinked at her from the bark.

"I can't believe this is the new normal," Rosie said. But she stood and waved to the eyes which blinked at her. Then Patrick followed her back to the barn.

The cow was awake, so Kua Fe was with her, even at this late hour. She was telling him of her life at the confinement dairy where she and a thousand other cows lived under a metal awning and never walked on the grass. She described her daily routine of eating, being milked, and jostling for a spot near the gate where she could feel the sun and look outside.

It was all so strange to the sprite. Cows standing on hard floors and eating dry hay and corn even during the summer? Bossy didn't know why cows were kept this way, but she knew they weren't the only ones. New cows would join the herd and tell the same stories of concrete floors and steel roofs.

He was almost used to the horse woman and the magic man now that they had reclaimed the house. Bossy had told him to ignore them, even if their coupling bothered him. They had brought the cow to him, so he left them alone.

He was pondering Bossy's description of the milking machine when they both heard the car crunch the gravel almost silently down the driveway. Bossy looked at the car and remarked that it was that "quiet" car the witch drove. Kua Fe receded into his house. The witch made Kua Fe nervous. The spell she had put on his house made him feel sluggish. Bossy didn't like her, either.

The witch parked her car near the cow and cow shed, but instead of going into the house as almost all humans did, she opened her car doors and worked next to it.

Bossy told Kua Fe that the witch removed a battered, top-opening bag and a small cage containing a rabbit from the back seat of the car. She set both of these on the ground just inside the wedge of light spilling from the car doors.

Bossy mooed, "Good evening. What are you doing?"

Nan glared at her. When Bossy mooed again, Nan picked up a rock from the driveway and chucked it, hitting the cow in the soft part of her belly behind her ribs. Bossy squealed and hustled sideways until she was behind the oak tree. She peeked around the trunk and mooed at the witch again.

"Stupid cow," Nan said.

Kua Fe swelled out of his house but didn't materialize, a huge, angry shimmer in the dark. The witch had intentionally hurt his cow. He growled a first, dark warning.

The witch didn't seem to notice or care. She opened her bag. He could smell several items she set on the ground: packets of herbs and flowers, a little jar of lard. He couldn't smell the ominously long, curved knife, but Bossy worried about it, so he knew it was there.

"Now, you weak-willed little bitch," Nan muttered. "Let's make this sprite so strong you'll have to leave." She opened the cage and held up the black and white rabbit by the scruff so she could look it in the face. "That girl wouldn't know an opportunity if it ran up and bit her in the ass."

The bunny twitched its nose at her and then lashed out with its big feet, twisting and writhing, but it couldn't escape her grip.

Bossy mooed again, "Hey, you're hurting him!" and strode toward Nan to the end of her rope, stopping several feet away.

"Stop mooing. You'll wake everyone," Nan scolded.

She tucked the rabbit firmly under her arm and proceeded to mix the herbs, flowers and fat together with her free hand. She stood and smeared the mix in a cross shape on the upper door jamb of the shed. Kua Fe growled, but again, she ignored him.

Then she smudged some on the bunny's head.

"Spirit!" she cried, holding the rabbit high. It started kicking again, so she lowered it, smacked it on the head so it was stunned, and then held it aloft again. "Spirit!" she began again. "Spirit, show yourself unto me!"

Kua Fe growled darkly, louder, but didn't solidify. She was harming a rabbit. Kua Fe's teeth and talons shone, and his mane bristled.

Nan repeated herself. "Spirit! I compel you to show yourself to me!"

The rumble thrummed louder and the air thickened. Kua Fe appeared, perched atop his house like a salivating gargoyle.

Nan stepped closer to the sprite. This put her close enough to Bossy for the cow to bang her with her big, horned head. Nan brought her elbow down on the cow's soft nose, sending her bellowing behind the tree again.

Kua Fe grew bigger and growled louder. He no longer cared what the witch was up to. He had warned her.

"Sprite!" she commanded. "Accept this blood offering! Be strong! Defend yourself from this threat!"

Nan drew out her long blade and held it to the rabbit's throat and started slicing. The bunny screamed as only a dying rabbit can and kicked so much that Nan had to adjust her grip. She looked up as she sliced again in time to see Kua Fe's face an inch from hers. She probably never saw his huge claw swipe her belly. She dropped the rabbit and the knife and hit the ground screaming. Kua Fe put his huge foot on her face and leaned until he felt a crunch.

Kua Fe sniffed her thoroughly. She was dead. Usually, Kua Fe was frightening enough to scare predators like cougars and coyotes away from animals in his charge, but during his long life, he had dispatched several threats that had not yielded. They had also been warned.

Then Kua Fe found the rabbit, bleeding, a couple feet away. After sniffing it carefully, he licked the blood off of the little thing with an enormous black tongue. The rabbit shook from shock, but soon calmed as its wound closed. After a moment, it hopped into the shed and went to sleep.

Finally, he went to Bossy and snuffled her, too, until he was satisfied she was fine. He nuzzled her bruised ribs and sore nose, and she thanked him. With a last snort over what was left of the witch, the sprite dissolved into his house.

Bossy yawned and thought, *Nothing like this ever happened at the dairy.* She went to sleep standing at the edge of the wedge of yellow light cast by the Prius's open back door.

CHAPTER EIGHT

Care and Feeding of a Cow Sprite

"Patrick?" Rosie stood looking out the kitchen window the next morning, coffee mug in hand. She pulled her sweater closed at her throat that against the surge of panic she felt at the sight of Nan's Prius parked outside. "Patrick? Is Nan coming today?" she asked.

He stepped out of the bathroom where he had been scrubbing cold water into his cheeks to help wake him up. "No. Why?"

"Because her car is out there. By the shed."

Patrick stood by her and looked out the window. "Damn. What does she want? Let me get some pants on."

Soon, they stepped out on the porch, Patrick hopping to put on his second boot.

"Hey, Nan!" he called. "Why are you here so early?"

There was no answer, and the two people glanced at each other. They started across the yard.

"Bossy! Where's Nan?" he called.

The cow blinked at him and mooed, just as they walked around the front of the car.

"What do you mean she's here? I don't see..." Then he did see, and so did Rosie.

Rosie shrank back against the car, grasping at it to keep from falling down. Patrick stood rigid, as if transfixed, but he began breathing far too fast.

"Oh, God. Patrick. That's Nan, right?" Rosie whispered finally.

Patrick shook his head, but Rosie knew he was trying to deny what he was seeing.

"Patrick. Breathe, Patrick," she said. She touched his arm, and he swung around and pulled her into his arms. Energy surged between them, lighting Rosie's skin and brain afire, and she clung to him because she felt even stronger with him than on her own.

"What happened?" she whispered when his breathing was slower.

"I don't know," he said.

Rosie peeked over his shoulder. She could see Nan's ridiculous pumps, but that was all. "What did Bossy say?"

Patrick held his breath a moment. Then he said, "Bossy just said that Nan was by the car."

"Ask her what happened. Or, you know, if we should run."

Patrick nodded, and then steered them so the car was between them and the body and the cowshed.

"Bossy? What happened to Nan?"

The cow lowed and swished her tail. Then a rabbit came out of the barn and hopped over to them and sat on Patrick's feet. He picked up the bunny and stroked it thoughtfully.

"Well?" Rosie said.

He looked at her as if he'd forgotten she were there. He handed her the rabbit. "This is Buster."

"Hi, Buster," Rosie said. "What did Bossy say, Patrick?"

"Nan was performing some sort of ritual that involved beating Bossy and cutting Buster's throat. Bossy said that Kua Fe warned the witch three times, and then when she hurt the bunny, he killed her."

"Ritual?" Rosie said. "What for?"

Patrick was staring at the cow shed, his look becoming darker and darker.

"Patrick? Are you all right?"

"That damned thing has killed my aunt," he hissed. "Do I look all right?"

"Stop it," she shot back. "When we thought it killed my husband you were okay with it."

"It was never 'okay' with me," he snarled. "I've always hated these things. This is the last straw, though."

"Wait," she said. "Let's calm down. We're not mad at each other. What do we do? Call the police?"

Patrick snapped his head around to look at her. "Not the police. Not yet. We have to clean up here, first."

"Clean up?"

"Yeah. We need to get her magic stuffs out of here." He bent and picked up a wax paper packet with a tiny amount of green leaves in the corner. "It's magic people protocol. Regular police aren't supposed to be exposed to this kind of evidence. They wouldn't know what to make of it, anyway."

Rosie clutched the rabbit to her and stepped around the back of the car to the open side door. Patrick's words stung her, and she noticed that he hadn't echoed her truce attempt. It was like he'd finally come to her way of seeing the sprite, but his anger — hatred really — was uncontrolled. Rosie knew this much about herself: she reacted to anger with anger, only — weirdly, this time — she was angry with Patrick, not Kua Fe.

Rosie stopped when she could just see Nan around the open back door because the sight made her stomach turn. The poor woman was hardly more than a pile of gore except for her incongruous beige pumps. The sight shocked her out of her anger and made her glance at the shed which sat impassive and inert. She didn't even feel like she was being watched anymore. She wondered if Kua Fe was hiding in shame, or if that was even an emotion he had. She snuck a look at Nan's body and wondered if he had any emotions.

The bunny squirmed in her arms, surprising her because she'd been so lost in her thoughts that she'd forgotten she was holding him. She set him down, and he hopped to Bossy's side and began munching the grass next to her. She wondered what she'd need to take care of a bunny. Then she wondered what other animals she'd end up taking care of before this ordeal ended.

"You okay?" Patrick said. His look had softened as if he were calming down, too.

"Yeah."

She hugged herself a moment, then Rosie turned her focus from the dead witch to picking up the pots and containers. Patrick did the same, and soon they had all of it gathered up and stowed under a tarp on the far side of the barn.

When he was satisfied, he pulled out his cell phone and called the police himself.

Several hours later, Patrick wrapped an arm around Rosie, and they watched the county coroner's van pull away down the driveway with his Auntie Nan in the back. It made Nan's death even more real to Rosie to see the police swarming over her place. But she still wondered why Nan was there in the first place.

The Sheriff was wondering that, himself, aloud.

Rosie shook her head. "I don't know why she was here in the middle of the night," she said.

"What about you?" he asked Patrick.

He shook his head and wiped his eyes with the cuff of his jacket and recited from the script he had devised before the police arrived. "She was helping us with the cougar problem ... you know, with organic, natural deterrents. I don't know why she came in the dark without telling us, though."

"Uh-huh."

The Sheriff looked like he knew they were holding something back, but Rosie hoped he could also sense that they were genuinely surprised that Nan was at Rosie's ranch and was dead because they were.

Then the Sheriff scuffed a bit of drying bunny blood with the toe of his shoe that was a little away from the main pool of Nan's.

"Any idea what this is from?"

Rosie began to sniffle again.

The sheriff sighed. "You guys can go back inside," he said. "We've got a little more work out here to do, then we'll talk again, okay?"

"Let us know if you want to move the cow," Patrick said.

"Gotcha."

Inside, Patrick and Rosie sat on the couch with Buster, staring at the blank television. It didn't occur to them to turn it on. Rosie did and didn't want to talk about why Patrick was so rigid. Of course, he was angry, she knew that. Ben used to get angry, too, and stiffen and harden. That was when he would get mean. Rosie didn't know if Patrick could get mean, but she also didn't want to find out, so she stroked the bunny and didn't say anything as he glared at the blank television.

Finally, she took his hand. "Patrick?"

He blinked and then said, "Yeah?"

"I'm sorry about your aunt."

He surprised her by taking in a huge shuddering breath, as if he'd been underwater for a long time and had just resurfaced for air. He slid an arm around her and pulled her closer. "I know," he said. "She was an old witch, but she was my old witch."

Then his arm tensed so Rosie squirmed. "Patrick," she said. "What is it?"

"That thing under your barn has to go."

"What?"

"That thing. That thing that killed my aunt has to go."

A day ago, Rosie would have agreed with him. Today, though, she said, "But..."

The savage look Patrick flung at Rosie frightened her and brought back memories of Ben and his wicked words. She cringed.

Patrick did not seem to notice her fear. He stood and strode to the kitchen. "What do you mean 'but'? There is no 'but'! That thing is a killer. I thought you wanted it gone?"

"I do," Rosie stood. "I did. I mean, this time, it was protecting Bossy and Buster. Nan would have been fine if she weren't hurting them. Bossy told you so, right?"

"So?"

"Well, it proves the point that Nan and Alix were trying to make. It only seems to lash out when its animals are in danger."

"It killed my aunt." Patrick's voice and look were darker than she'd ever seen them. "It has to go."

Rosie pulled herself to her full diminutive height. "It's my farm. I think Kua Fe can stay."

"I don't believe this!" Patrick rushed back at her and glowered at her. "Don't use its name!" he shouted.

Rosie stood stunned a moment, then the lines on her face hardened. "Don't you ever shout at me again," she said, her voice steadier than her knees. "You need to leave now."

Anger, panic, regret, shame all flashed across Patrick's face, but he finally turned on his heel and stomped to the door, grabbing his jacket as he went. He stood, hand on the handle, and turned, as if he were going to say something when they heard a new car on the driveway.

The last of the police were leaving as the new car approached. Rosie looked out the door over Patrick's shoulder and watched a blue sedan pull up next to Patrick's truck. A tall man with olive skin and closely cropped dark hair stepped out and shut the door of the car.

Patrick glanced back at her with a bit of trepidation in his eyes. The anger was gone for the moment. "That's the guy I've been expecting."

Rosie was confused, but she nodded. They went out to meet the man.

"Rosie?" he called. Then, "Hey! Patrick? What are you doing here?"

"Al?" Patrick shook his hand. "Rosie, this is Al. We were in the service together."

"Hi, Al." She shook his hand, too.

"You two know each other?"

"Yeah. North High School. Go Tigers, right?" Al said.

"And I saw you at Nan's. You were buying fenuric for your wife."

"Right." He looked at Patrick. "So, um, she knows?" Al asked.

Patrick nodded. "We've been dating for a little bit. Plus, she gets the tingles from me, so, yeah. She knows."

"About magic?" Rosie asked.

"Yeah." Al looked around. "Nice place you have here." He pointed at the cow shed. "I didn't know you had cows."

"Just the one," Rosie said. "Why does it matter if I know about magic?"

Al flipped open his notebook. "Well, the sergeant transferred this case to me when we realized Nan was ... involved."

Rosie looked blank.

"Because she's a witch." Al said.

Rosie blinked. "There's a department in the police that handles witches?"

"My department handles all magic around here," Al said with a bit of pride. "We're not big enough to specialize in witches or fae or anything. We're not as big as Portland or Seattle. Wouldn't that be nice?"

"Are you?"

"Magic? Nah. I just learned from weirdoes like this guy." He slapped Patrick on the shoulder in that affectionate manly way that Rosie never understood. "I would give my left you-know-what to have some clairvoyance, though, you know? Really helpful in my line of work."

"You couldn't tell a rainstorm was coming if your face was wet," Patrick said. They all laughed, and then were quiet.

"So, um, your aunt," Al began. "I'm really sorry, man. Nan gave us a freebie spell for morning sickness when Melissa was really spent. I liked her."

"Thanks." Patrick looked at his boots a moment.

Al fanned the pages of his notebook. "So, um, cougar didn't get her, did it?"

Rosie and Patrick shook their heads.

"Mind telling me what did?"

"Cow sprite," said Patrick.

Rosie shot him a look, but he ignored her.

Al blinked. "Really? I thought those were extinct around here."

"No." Patrick said. "This one is far from extinct."

"What made it so mad?"

"I think she was doing some blood rite or something, and it upset the sprite before she could finish."

"I see." Al made a note in his book. "Why was she doing that?"

"I don't know," Rosie said.

"I have a guess," Patrick said. "She wanted Rosie to sell the ranch to her, and Rosie said no."

"She was going to use Kua Fe to scare me away?" Rosie's blinked as this sank in. "Oh, my God."

"Kua Fe?"

"The sprite," Patrick said.

"You can talk to it?" Al frowned. "I thought you talked to animals."

"I use the cow to translate."

"Okay. Let's go."

"You want to interview a sprite?" Rosie asked.

"It's a first for me," Al said. "But if it's the prime suspect, I need to get a statement from it if possible." He stopped. "So, where is it? The sprite?"

Patrick glanced at Rosie and the pointed at the shed next to the cow.

Al squinted at the shed. "What's weird about that building?" he asked.

Rosie squinted, too, looking carefully at the shed. "Huh. Maybe when the sprite rebuilt it after we tore it down, he kind of mixed the boards up or something. The boards haven't weathered evenly."

Al blinked at her. "The sprite rebuilt the shed?"

"Yeah. It also shredded my tractor tires."

"You tore down the shed and the sprite rebuilt it."

"Yes." She frowned at him. "Nan said that was something sprites did."

Al shook his head. "I don't know. I've never met a sprite. But that's weird." He scribbled something in his book. "Have you talked to it today?" he asked.

"Oh, no," Patrick said.

"Think it's mad?"

"I would be," Rosie said.

"Well, let's not invade his space any more than we need to. Can you talk to the cow from here?" Al asked.

"Yeah."

"Go for it."

"Hey, Bossy."

The cow looked up at him and blinked.

"Wait!" Rosie said. "What will happen to Kua Fe?"

"What do you mean?" Al said.

"If he killed Nan? Then what?"

Al frowned a little. "Well, it's within its rights to protect itself and the creatures in its care, but this is a little extreme."

"What might happen to him?"

"If it killed her, it might be spellbound or exiled."

Rosie relaxed a little. "Not killed?"

"Oh, if it's fae, it's immortal," Al said. "But an eternity floating in space or rooted to one spot would be..."

"Torture."

"Ma'am, if this creature has killed a person, it can't go loose." Al said this in his best "it's for the best" police voice.

Rosie looked at Patrick with wide eyes. Kua Fe was a killer. But, what kind of killer was he? Somehow, she didn't want Kua Fe's fate to belong to some system. So she shook her head at Patrick.

Patrick turned away.

"Can we get on with this now?" Al said. "So, what do you do?"

"I just talk to the cow, and she interprets for me."

"So, ask her to ask it what happened and why."

Patrick glanced at Rosie and then turned to Bossy. "Hey, girl. Ask Kua Fe to tell us what happened."

Bossy mooed and then began chewing her cud.

"Well?" Al asked after several moments of cud-chewing.

"Patrick," Rosie said. When he looked at her, she gave him a pleading look. His eyes hardened.

"Everything okay?" Al asked.

"Sure," Patrick said.

"Well, ask the cow what killed Nan."

Patrick took a deep breath. "Bossy says Nan ... Nan threw rocks at her and then was slitting the bunny's throat when Kua Fe appeared and saved the bunny's life ... by crushing my aunt's skull."

Rosie felt faint. What was Patrick doing?

"This blood is the rabbit's. You can test it. I also have all her magic stuff over by the barn if you want to look at it."

Al was scribbling furiously. "Yeah, I'll want to look at that in a minute," he said. "This is what the cow is saying, right? Not the sprite?"

Patrick paused. "Yeah."

Rosie grabbed Al's arm. "Kua Fe was doing what he was supposed to, right? He was protecting the bunny and the cow. Isn't that justifiable or something?"

"Ma'am," Al said, sliding her hand from his jacket sleeve. "That's not my department. I'm just here to get the information." His brow crinkled. "Aren't you worried about this thing on your ranch? It seems dangerous to me."

"No. Not anymore. It's just doing its job, I think."

"It's a worthless killer, just like all of its kind," Patrick said.

"Well, it's my worthless killer, then," she shot back. "And I'd thank you to get off of my property and stop harassing my animals."

Patrick blinked in surprise, and then glared back at her.

Al stepped between them. "I don't know what's going on between the two of you, but I do know that I need to get the sprite's version, if possible, and then see Nan's things. I need to write a report."

"Please don't," Rosie said to Al, but she was looking at Patrick.

"I'm sorry," Al said. "I have to. Come on, Patrick. Show me Nan's things."

He started toward the barn. Patrick, with a final strained look on his face, followed him.

Rosie watched them walk to the other side of the barn. Then she felt a nudge on the small of her back. She looped her arm around Bossy's neck and looked at the shed. "What are we going to do, Bossy?" she asked the cow.

Bossy flicked her ears and watched Patrick, too. Then she pushed Rosie forward, hard. Rosie looked back at the cow who was watching the men walk away. Then she lowered her head and scraped the ground like a bull.

"Really? You want me to make them leave?"

Bossy snorted and mooed, "Meahh!"

Rosie scratched Bossy between the horns. "And here I didn't think I liked cows," she said. Then she ran after the men.

"Wait!"

Patrick and Al turned, all raised eyebrows. "What is it?" Patrick said.

It was the tone of his voice more than anything, Rosie decided. That tone of impatience, of being interrupted, of being entitled. "Here's the thing," she said. "Al doesn't have a warrant. You have pissed me off. You both have to leave, NOW."

"Ma'am," Al started again patiently, but Rosie cut him off.

"Don't 'ma'am' me, Al," she said. "Go get your warrant. Come back pissed off, I don't care. I don't want you here now, so you have to leave."

"Rosie, be reasonable," Patrick said.

Rosie spun to face him, eyes flashing. "I don't need a reason to make you leave," she said. "If you don't, I'm sure Al will be willing to escort you off the premises."

"But..."

"But nothing. This is my place. You get your magic and other shit off of my land until you both learn something about manners and how to treat a woman who doesn't need either of you."

Back at the shed, Bossy gave a high-pitched moo. Rosie had never seen Patrick look more surprised.

Al looked pissed, but he closed his notebook and stuffed it in his jacket pocket. "I'm sorry you feel that way, Ma'am ... Rosie. I'll go back to the office and complete the paperwork. I'll be back later today." He stepped toward his car. "Patrick, perhaps you'll accompany me to the office, and we can continue our conversation?"

Patrick was still staring at the angry cow. He blinked and then said, "Yeah, sure, Al." He stepped around Rosie without really looking at her and got into his truck. He followed Al's car down the long driveway, and they turned onto the road and were gone.

Rosie watched them drive away, gravel crunching under the tires of the two vehicles. She suddenly missed Bobby very much. She turned and walked the rest of the way to the barn so angry and worried that she felt numb.

Had she really just thrown a cop off of her land? Oh, sweet Jesus.

Caesar put his head over his stall door and nickered. Chores that morning had been cursory at best, and Caesar looked like he felt neglected. Rosie grabbed several carrots from the tack room on the way to his stall. She broke off a piece and gave it to him, then shut the stall door behind her and sat in the sawdust in the corner.

Caesar pricked his ears as he chewed and watched her. He gave her a look of "What's wrong?"

Her eyes welled and she sniffled. "Damn. I'm so jealous of Patrick right now." Caesar lowered his great head and sniffed her hair. She broke off another carrot for him. "I'd give anything to talk to you right now."

The horse chuffed at her. Rosie could have sworn he lifted an eyebrow at her.

"Well, I meant I wish you would talk back to me," she said. "I could use some advice."

Caesar chewed expectantly.

"I don't know what to do," she said. "I've thrown a cop and Patrick off the ranch. I think I've messed everything up."

The horse bilked and flicked an ear.

"I was mad at Patrick because he's mad at Kua Fe for killing Nan." She looked at Caesar who did not look surprised. "You aren't worried about that, are you? You know the sprite killed Nan to protect us, don't you?"

Caesar blinked and the stole a whole carrot from her lap. Rosie didn't mind.

"He protected all of us. How are we going to protect him?"

The horse shook his head, flinging orange carrot juice onto the walls of his stall.

She sighed. "I need help," she said. "But Patrick is gone, maybe for good. Who can help me now?"

This time Rosie was sure Caesar rolled his eyes.

"What are you implying?" she said. "Who else do I know who understands the sprite? Magic?"

The horse sighed.

"Oh, of course," she said. "Alix! My dad and Alix! Why didn't I call them before?" She pulled out her phone and fumbled to select her dad's number with shaking fingers. He picked up on the second ring.

"Hey, Piglet. How's things?"

"Bad, Dad. Can you and Alix get here right away?"

"Oh, is the sprite acting up again?"

"You have no idea."

Rosie walked to meet her dad and Alix at their car in the driveway. AS soon as he opened the door, her dad said, "Jesus, Piglet! What's up with all the police tape?"

"Seriously? You don't know?" Rosie looked at her watch. It was barely 11 AM. That morning felt like it had lasted a year.

Alix was staring. "Is Nan here?" He pointed to her car, which was draped in yellow tape.

"No." Rosie looked blankly at the car.

"Good. I don't really like her. Always meddling with the magic."

"She's dead, Alix," Rosie said.

"Oh."

"Jesus, Piglet!" Lew said again. "Why didn't you say so on the phone?"

"I don't know. I mean, the police have already been here. They were here until just before I called you."

Lew strode over to the car. "How did it happen?" he said as he walked. "Did she have a heart attack?"

"Dad! Wait!" Rosie called, but it was too late.

"Shit," he said in a way that made Alix scurry over to look, too. For once, Alix didn't say anything.

"You need to tell us what happened," Lew said.

"Come on inside," Rosie said. "I've already made coffee."

For the next hour, Rosie retold the story of finding Nan, the police coming, the fight with Patrick, and the throwing of boyfriend and magic-policeman off of her property.

When she was done, Lew sat holding his cold mug of coffee. He'd picked it up and forgotten to take a drink the whole time.

"So," he said slowly. "So, now, now that the sprite has killed a person, now you want to protect it?"

"I know it sounds crazy," she began.

"Just a little."

"I know, but Kua Fe was protecting the bunny. He was protecting the cow. Ultimately, he protected me, whether he meant to or not." Rosie stood up and walked to the window where she looked out at the cow shed. "If Nan had succeeded in whatever she was doing, she might have made Kua Fe truly dangerous."

"Aye," Alix said. Rosie spun to look at him because he hadn't said anything for so long. He looked up at her. "She was probably doing a blood rite. That usually involves killing something like a rabbit. It's a way to kind-of feed something supernatural, but it makes them ... darker."

"Wait, so you two are saying she deserved to die?" Lew said.

"No," Alix said. "But she should have expected it. Blood rites were out of her league. She was a spell-maker, not a demon-conjurer." He shook his head. "Plus, she was ambitious. And sloppy. And entitled. Did I mention that I didn't like her?"

For the first time that day, Rosie smiled.

"The point is, Dad, that Kua Fe was acting the way he is supposed to. He isn't a random killer. And, he kind-of saved me from Nan."

Lew looked from Rosie and Alix. "Well, if you are convinced, so am I." He glanced at his cold coffee and set it on the table. "So, what do you need us for, Piglet?"

She came back and sat at the table. "It's Patrick and Al. Patrick is still convinced that Kua Fe is an indiscriminate killer."

"Understandable since it killed his aunt," said Lew.

"Right. But he won't listen to me, and he's bent on getting Al and whatever magic authority there is to punish Kua Fe."

"Punish it?"

"A banishment or a fixation," muttered Alix. "Makes the sprite immobile or inert and totally useless." He looked up at Rosie. "We need to save him."

"Right. How?"

"Don't know." Alix sat back in his chair and stared at the table. "Don't know. Where is my book of Lucks?"

Rosie stood next to her father on her porch as Alix walked toward the cowshed, an empty soup can with a few dried beans in it gripped in one hand and the friendliest of her barn cats tucked under his other arm, purring. The spell was supposed to change the little cat into a looking like a big one. Alix thought a picture of a cougar might help show Kua Fe was innocent.

"Do you think this is going to work?" Lew asked her.

Rosie shrugged. "I'm done trying to predict anything to do with magic," she said. "None of this makes any sense, so I've given up trying to make sense of it."

Alix stopped ten feet in front of the cowshed, carefully avoiding the mashed grass where Nan had fallen. Bossy lowed at him, so he rubbed her head with the bean can in greeting. Then he stepped away and shook the rattle.

"Kua Fe!" he called. Bossy bumped him with her head, so he had to stop and scratch her again.

"Maybe you should move away from the cow," Lew called.

"No. She's fine," Alix called. "Leave me be, *große Kuh*," he muttered. Bossy shook her ears but did not bump him again.

"Kua Fe!" he began again. "*Form in große Katze verwandeln.*" He sang softly at first, repeating the phrase and shaking the rattle. The cat squirmed in his arms, and he paused to rub its head with the soup can until she resumed purring. Then he rattled and repeated, getting gradually louder until he was shouting.

Without warning, he dropped the cat and the can, which struck sparks when it hit the ground. The cat flicked her tail and blinked before leisurely walking to the cow and rubbing against her legs. Alix shuddered and fell to his knees. Rosie and Lew ran to his side.

"Are you okay?" Rosie said as she skidded to his side and dropped to her knees.

"Ach. Yes. Just, that cat got heavy." He looked up at the dark tortoiseshell as she wound her way between Bossy's legs. "That one is a familiar."

"A familiar?" Lew put his hands on his friend's arm and helped him stand.

"Like, witch's friend. Only, no witch. Anyway," he said, brushing off his pants. "That did not work."

"Oh." Disappointment slid like a cold rock down Rosie's back. "How can you tell?"

"Because, if it had worked, there would be a cougar in the cowshed. And there's not."

Lew walked slowly to the door of the shed and peeked in. "No cat, unless it's a black panther hiding in the shadows."

"Oh, let me see," Alix said, hopeful.

Rosie followed Alix and looked in the shed, too, but the shadow was empty of cats, big or little, black or tawny.

"Damn." Alix kicked the dirt. "That's all I can do." He looked woebegone and seemed to droop like an under-watered begonia. "I am sorry, Piglet."

"It's okay, Alix," Rosie said. She hugged him, then she hugged her dad. "We'll figure something out."

Lew and Alix didn't want to leave Rosie alone that afternoon on the ranch, but she insisted.

"I'm fine. I have lived here for years all by myself." Her argument was not strengthened by the police's flatbed impound truck that had arrived to cart Nan's Prius away.

"That was before the sprite murdered a woman in your back yard."

"It was in my barnyard, but I know. I'll be fine. You know I will."

"I'm only leaving if you let Ed come over and check on you before bedtime," Lew said, hands on his narrow hips.

Rosie smiled and hugged him. "All right. I'll give you a ring before I turn in, too, Daddy."

At eight o'clock, Ed rapped on her door. "Jesus, Rosie," he said when he stepped into the house. "Is what your dad said true? Did someone really kill Nan?"

Rosie nodded, unsure what Lew had actually told Ed. "Yeah. It's been awful."

"Where's that boyfriend of yours?"

"We had a fight."

"Rotten timing," he said. "But you're all good here, right? Good. I'm going back. No offense, but your place is giving me the willies."

"Right. See you, Ed." Rosie watched as the old farmer walked back to his place, giving the cowshed a very wide berth.

She picked up the phone at nine and called her dad. "I'm fine. I'm going to bed."

"Are you sure you're okay, honey?" he said. "I can come back and sleep on your couch, or you could stay with me and Molly."

"I'm fine. I'm going to bed. Goodnight." But she smiled as she hung up the phone. *His worry seems less silly today than it normally did, but it was still endearing.*

Rosie poured herself a stiff drink and then stood at the window, bourbon in hand. She watched the cowshed, which did nothing, and Bossy, who had laid down and was sleeping with her head folded against her side. That position had always reminded Rosie of the way that birds tuck their heads under their wings to sleep, and she smiled at a mental picture of a dairy cow with wings, feathers, and udders flapping in the wind.

As she was turning, she thought she saw the air waver in front of the tree, and she whipped back around to stare. It was the tree. It was smiling at her again, and then it wasn't. Rosie rubbed her eyes a little and then looked at her drink. A month ago, she would have blamed the liquor, but not today. She didn't know the etiquette for responding to a tree's smile. She decided she'd see if the book of spells would deign to tell her tomorrow.

She knocked back the rest of her drink and then went to bed.

"Good night, Buster," she said to the bunny curled up in a laundry basket at the foot of her bed. "Never thought I'd have a rabbit."

Never thought I'd sleep inside a house, thought Buster.

The next morning, Lew called first thing, so early that Rosie was still standing at the window, staring at the cow shed before she went out to do chores.

"Just checking in," Lew said.

"I'm fine, Dad. Thanks."

"Nothing happened last night?"

"Not that I can tell," she said.

"Sleep well?"

"Not a wink." They laughed together.

"Well, let me know if you want help," he said. "Your old Dad worries, you know."

"Worry is bad for your heart," Rosie said. "So, stop it."

"Stop giving me things to worry about."

"Fair enough. Love you, Dad."

"Take care, Piglet."

She took a deep breath and stepped out into the early morning air. Buster hopped out of the door and toward her shaggy lawn, but nothing happened other than Bossy mooed at her. A stray strip of crime scene tape flapped in the early breeze. The farmer in Rosie noted with pleasure that it was going to be a fine spring day and that the mud had dried up for the most part. If yesterday hadn't happened, Rosie would have turned the horses out that morning for couple hours and a first taste of spring grass.

But yesterday did happen, and Rosie was watching the inert cowshed remain inert until she hitched up her overalls and tried to stride confidently to the barn. She didn't think she was fooling anyone, but she wondered whom she was trying to fool. Probably herself.

As soon as she opened the barn door, she realized that the horses knew how nice it was outside, too. Caesar poked his head over his stall door and give a shrill whinny, and he was quickly joined by the other horses. Rosie put a hand on his neck.

"I know. It's nice out, isn't it?"

Caesar threw his head up and down and then pawed his forefoot in the pine shavings.

"Maybe," she said. "I've got to do chores first, and then, we'll see."

Sunny snorted from across the aisle. Rosie looked at her sadly. The sight of the bright chestnut mare reminded Rosie of Patrick, and her chest constricted. She gave his horse an extra ration of grain as if she had to atone herself to his horse as well.

"I'll be back later," she promised all the horses when she left. "If it's still nice later, we'll go outside for a spell."

One of them banged its stall impatiently, but Rosie needed to do so many things before she could let them out. She made a mental list: check the turn-out pen's fences, make sure the fence charger was working, double check that the ground was dry enough, pick all of their feet again...

Then, Rosie's cell phone rang with the call she had been waiting for.

"I think Bobby is ready to come home," said Cody. "Do you want to come get him today?"

"Do I!" cried Rosie. She had her keys in her hand before she even hung up the phone.

Soon she was sitting in the familiar vet's exam room, practically vibrating in anticipation. She was only a little disappointed when Cody stepped in alone.

"Hey, Rosie," he said. He shut the door and flipped through Bobby's chart. "So, even though Bobby has several broken ribs and is bruised everywhere, I think he'll do better recovering at home."

"Oh, thank you," Rosie said, smiling. She wiped her eyes. "I can't tell you how much I've missed him."

"Not as much as he's missed you," Cody said, smiling back. He hesitated a moment and then said, "So, is everything all right at the ranch now?"

Rosie's face fell, and she examined Cody's shoes. *Don't cry,* she commanded herself.

"I'll take that as a 'no.'" He sat next to her on the other chair. "What's up, Piglet?"

She put her head on his shoulder, and he put an arm around her. "It's a mess. Did you hear about Nan?"

"The witch? What about her?"

Rosie shook her head a little. "Kua Fe killed her."

"He what?"

"She was doing some blood rite, maybe to make him stronger so I'd be scared into selling her the ranch. The sprite didn't want her to kill the bunny she brought, so it killed her."

Cody squeezed her shoulders. "Shit."

Rosie suddenly teared up and her words tumbled out. "Yeah, shit. Nan's dead, there are cops crawling all over my place, including magic cops. Did you know there are magic cops? I didn't. And then Patrick and I had a fight, and Kua Fe is going to be exiled or something, and I think I'm in love with Patrick, but I hate him because he sold out the sprite, and now I'm alone and..."

Cody squeezed harder as she sobbed. "Damn," he said when she was out of tears. "Do you need anything? You could stay with me and Meg at our place."

"No," she said. "Seriously, I'm pretty sure Kua Fe won't hurt me. I'm not sure about what the magic police will do to him, though. And Patrick." She sat up and looked at Cody with bright eyes. "What am I going to do about him?"

Cody shook his head. "It seems to me that Patrick has some shit he has to deal with. The stuff he told me about Iraq doesn't have anything to do with you."

Rosie considered this a moment. "Maybe. But if that's true, then he's got to 'deal with it' differently. The next time he shouts and charges at me like that, I'm going to gut him with a fish knife."

Cody nodded somberly. "He's a fool if he doesn't believe that you'll do that," he said. "And you're a fool if you do."

Rosie half chuckled and shook her head.

"How about if I bring you your dog?"

"That would be the best thing that happens today."

Bobby was ecstatic to see her in the way only a dog that has stayed at the vet's can be, practically squirming out of his skin in his excitement despite his healing ribs. Rosie carefully loaded the blanket-wrapped dog into the front seat of her truck, and he wiggled with joy on the ride home. That is, until he began whining pitifully when they started up the driveway to her house.

"It's okay, Bobby," she said. "Kua Fe won't hurt you anymore."

She glanced at Bobby who was staring at her.

"I know," she said. "I can't believe those words came out of my mouth, either." She patted his head. "Let's just say that things are safer now."

Bobby thumped his tail twice and looked out the window dubiously eyeing the cow shed as it came into view.

After they parked, Rosie gently carried him into the house and set him on the couch. She fetched herself a coffee and settled in next to him, flicking through the channels until she found a documentary about wolves. "Just 'cause you're sick," she said. Bobby smiled at her.

She let herself sink into the couch, very tired. Rosie had spent the previous night at her own place sans canine companionship without incident. Sort of. Being alone had been nerve-wracking. She woke up to some snapping twig or creaking gate every few minutes. She panted in fear each time before calming down enough to doze again. Even though Rosie was pretty sure that Kua Fe wouldn't hurt her, part of her was still paranoid that the sprite was going to come for her again. But then, until a couple weeks ago, she didn't even know that sprites existed. Now she had three of them. And a cow. And a bunny. And a feline familiar.

But now she had Bobby back. Even in his broken state, she felt better for having him home. She hadn't realized how much he filled up her life until she was knocking around her empty house without either him or Patrick underfoot. She realized that she would probably sleep even less with Bobby in her bedroom because he had better hearing, and he was jumpy after his encounter with the sprite, too. He had saved her life, though, and she knew that he would do it again if he had to. She brought him a bowl of vanilla ice cream on the couch and rubbed his ears as he gobbled it down.

"We'll be okay," she said. "You and I. Together, we'll be okay."

After lunch, Rosie looked wistfully out the window. The day was becoming more and more beautiful, and the temperature threatened to reach 60 degrees. Sunshine poured through the living room windows and warmed Rosie's shoulders as she sat on the couch with Bobby. Rosie wasn't one who could sit still for long, even if she had a drowsy dog's head on her lap. She slid Bobby off of her thigh and stood despite his protests.

"Sorry, Bobby. I'm just itching to get outside." She peeked out the window at the cowshed. Bossy was sunning herself and swishing imaginary flies off her back. The oak tree blushed green. It may have winked at her.

"If I put you in the wagon, would you stay quiet while I fix the fences so the horses can go out?" she asked Bobby. He thumped his tail twice. "I'll take that as a yes."

Rosie fixed the wagon she used to tote tools and hay bales with a spare dog bed and a worn horse blanket. Then she gathered Bobby up in her arms and settle him in.

"Now, *stay*," she commanded.

She pulled the wagon, and Bobby, in true cow dog fashion, followed her orders as she took him the long way past the barn and to the turn-out pastures, avoiding the cowshed as much as possible.

He whimpered just a bit when the shed came into view, but Rosie hushed him.

"None of that, now," she said. "A lot's happened since you were here, Bobby. Right now, we're trying to be brave around the sprite."

He whimpered again. Rosie looked up and chuckled.

"Yes. That's a rabbit. His name is Buster. I'd advise you to leave him alone. He's got a very big friend."

Bobby still whined, but he stopped when the shed slid out of view behind the barn.

It was good to work outside. Rosie decided exercise and a problem to solve were exactly what she needed that day. She eventually worked up a sweat, and she peeled off her barn coat and hung it on a fence post. The sun felt hot through her shirt and that relaxed her. She smiled when she finally got the electric fence working properly.

"See? Nothing to it," she said to Bobby.

He thumped his tail twice. Then he threw his nose up into the air and sniffed urgently. A low growl rumbled in his throat.

Rosie looked over her shoulder in the direction of the cowshed. "There's nothing over there," she said, maybe trying to convince herself as much as her dog. She squinted. "No, nothing's moving. We're fine."

Bobby laid his ears back in disagreement.

"No, we're fine, Bobby. I'll go get the horses. You *stay*, okay?"

She could feel Bobby watching her walk to the barn, so she turned and repeated "Stay, Bobby!" when she got to the door. Still, she worked quickly, haltering Caesar and Sunny first because they were closest to the door and leading them out into the sunshine. Bobby remained in the wagon, sniffing the air first in one direction, then in another.

"Good dog!" she said when they got close. Bobby glanced at her but continued to smell the air.

Rosie put Caesar in the inner turnout and Sunny in the one on the edge because the grass seemed greener. The instant she unclipped the lead, the horses ran to the grass, and after eating a bite, they began to roll, flinging their feet into the air and rumbling in pleasure.

Rosie laughed. "That never gets old, does it, Bobo?"

Bobby thumped his tail and smiled at her. Then he resumed his air-scenting.

Rosie shrugged and went back to the barn to let the rest of the horses out into the sunshine.

When Al returned to the ranch with the search warrant, Rosie had moved on to fixing a water pump for the outside stock tanks which had frozen over the winter and busted. She heard the crunch of tires on gravel at the same time Bobby did and smiled when he started barking, on the job even from his wagon. She shushed him and stood, stretching until she recognized Al's sedan. She crossed her arms when she realized that there were two people in the front of the car. One of them was Patrick.

When Patrick stepped out of the car, Bobby began whining hysterically and struggling to stand up. Rosie knelt next to him and said, "Bobby, you need to stay, Bobby. Quiet down, honey, you'll hurt yourself."

But before she could grab his collar, Bobby launched himself from the wagon and, yelping in pain, tried to run to Patrick who stood dumbfounded next to the car's open door.

"Bobby? Bobby!" he cried. He ran to the dog and scooped him up in his arms. Bobby cried in pain and licked Patrick's face at the same time.

"Bobbo, what are you doing here? Are you all better? You poor guy. I missed you, too!"

Rosie realized with a stab that Patrick was crying, too. With every fiber, Rosie wanted to run to them and throw her arms around her dog and the man she loved. But she didn't because she remembered why Patrick was here.

Instead, she stood and re-crossed her arms. "Please be careful with my dog," she managed to say. "He's still got broken ribs."

"I know," Patrick said. "He told me."

Rosie felt like slapping him for being so insolent, but she tried to glare at him, instead.

"How'd your dog get hurt?" Al asked. He leaned on the hood of his car, folded paper in his hand. She assumed it was the warrant. She stared at it, but tried to convince herself that she didn't care.

"It was the sprite," Patrick said. "Bobby was defending Rosie and her dad. He got too close."

Al just nodded and watched as Patrick carried Bobby back to the wagon next to Rosie. He set the dog back into his nest and tucked the horse blanket around him.

"Now, you stay like a good boy, okay? We'll talk later."

Bobby thumped his tail happily and looked from Rosie to Patrick. Then he stopped wagging his tail and looked at the both of them again. He whined.

"Later," Patrick said, looking at Rosie.

Her mouth suddenly when dry when their eyes met.

After a long moment, Al said, "Ma'am?"

Rosie tore her eyes from Patrick and blinked at Al. She shooed him off with a wave of her hand. "Go ahead, Al. Sorry for the trouble before."

He tipped his hat at her. "Patrick? Want to show me where this stuff is?"

Rosie looked up at Patrick, but he had already turned to follow Al. She watched him walk away and then knelt on the ground next to Bobby and buried her face in his fur. The joy of the spring sunshine was gone, and she felt like a brittle, empty husk. She felt like nothing was in her control anymore. Kua Fe was going to be punished for doing the very thing he was designed to do, and Rosie couldn't protect him. Alix couldn't protect him. And without Patrick's help, she couldn't even attempt to explain to the sprite that he was in danger.

"I've failed him," she said to Bobby's fur. "I can't save him, and I've lost Patrick because of it."

Bobby whined sympathetically and licked her ear. Then Rosie felt him stiffen. The low growl rumbled against her forehead, and Rosie froze.

"Is it the sprite?" she whispered. "He's come to get Patrick and Al, hasn't he?"

Bobby growled again, louder, and stood up. Rosie sat up and looked in the direction of the barn where Al and Patrick were rummaging around the evidence from under the tarp. They were fine.

Bobby barked once. Rosie saw he was looking the other way, toward the horses. She followed his gaze and saw Sunny next to the fence in the far end of the light-filled pasture near a spreading big leaf maple tree.

Bobby barked again, and Rosie saw something move in the branches of the tree. Then it leaped over the fence and onto Sunny. The horse began shrieking.

"Patrick!" Rosie shouted. "Cougar!"

She took off running without looking back, Bobby shooting in front of her as if he weren't hurt at all. Sunny was flinging herself around the pen, trying to shake the cougar from her shoulders, while the cat hung on with its claws and tried to get a kill bite on the back of her neck. Rosie heard Patrick's anguished cries as he ran after them.

"It's too far," Rosie thought as she climbed over one fence. "She'll be dead before I can get there."

Bobby was halfway there, barking, but he was slowing down as his own pain became too much for him. Sunny's golden sides were streaked with blood from the cat's claws and she screamed like a terrified woman. The cat finally got a chance to bite, and Rosie stopped running and breathing.

Then the air around the far end of the pasture went black as if night had fallen on that one spot only. There was a crackle and Bobby slid to a stop. A moment later, Patrick and Al were at Rosie's side, but they stopped, too.

At the end of the pasture, Kua Fe stood next to the horse and the cougar, bristling. Sunny stood frozen in place, but the cougar yowled at the sprite. It let go of Sunny's neck and swiped at the sprite with its claws. Kua Fe snorted, pawed the ground once, and then hooked the cat with one of his horns. Kua Fe flung the cat over his shoulders and onto the ground. Then he spun with supernatural speed and dispatched the cat with a swift kick and stomp. The cat lay still and dead in the darkness.

Satisfied, Kua Fe turned to Sunny, who stood stiff with pain and fear. The sprite snuffled the horse, smelling her thoroughly, as he had the bunny, and then began licking her wounds. When he was done with one side, he moved to the other, licking as a cow would her calf with his great black tongue until all the blood was gone, and Sunny stood relaxed and head-down, almost dozing.

With that done, Rosie and Patrick and Al watched as Kua Fe sniffed the dead cat once more and then disappeared, taking the darkness with him.

Sunny shook her undamaged coat and walked down to a grassy area far away from the tree and began grazing again.

After a moment, Al said, "You two saw that, too, right?"

That was when Patrick pulled her into a tight hug. She felt the zings in her body and clung to him tighter.

Rosie poured coffee for everyone and set the bottle of whiskey on the counter. "I think I need an Irish coffee," she said. "How about you two?"

Patrick smiled, and Al shrugged from the dining room table.

"I don't care if I'm on duty or not," he said. "It's been ... it's been a day."

She mixed some sugar and liquor into the mugs and floated a little cream on top. They clinked mugs and sipped. Rosie wrapped her cold fingers around the mug. She really hadn't processed what she'd seen. After the shock, as soon as they could move again, Rosie ran to Bobby and carried him back to the wagon. Patrick caught Sunny, who gleamed in the sunshine like she'd been brushed for hours. They all marveled at Sunny's scar-less hide. She'd never looked healthier, actually. Then they brought the horses back inside. Al took some pictures of the cougar carcass, and then with some silent agreement, they all went into Rosie's place.

Bobby sat with his chin on Rosie's thigh, and she rubbed his ears, thinking how good it felt to have her brave dog back home. She looked across the table at Patrick and thought how good it was to have Patrick back, too.

"So, um," Al began. He set his mug onto the table and fiddled with the handle, not looking up. "You all did see what I saw, right?"

"We didn't say so outside?" Patrick said.

"Not out loud."

"I know what I saw," Rosie said. She watched Patrick. "What did you see?"

Patrick held her gaze a moment, then turned to Al. "I saw a wild cat attack my horse. I saw the cow sprite defend her, the horse, and kill the cat." He swallowed.

"I saw that, too," Rosie said. "I'm sure that's the cat that's been taking my neighbor's calves this spring," she said.

Al nodded slowly. "So, a cat that attacks a large animal like a horse in broad daylight in sight of people, that's a problematic cat." He looked at them carefully. "That's a cat that is a danger to people, too." He looked first Patrick, then Rosie as he said this.

Rosie nodded, getting it. "That cat might have hurt someone," she said.

"That cat might have already hurt someone," Al said.

They both looked at Patrick. Bobby moved under the table, and Rosie saw his head poke up under Patrick's elbow. Patrick rubbed the dog's head and took a long drink.

Al turned to Rosie. "I also saw the sprite dispatch the cougar, exactly the way sprites are supposed to," he said. "I did a little reading last night. I didn't think I'd get to apply that learning so quickly..."

"So, Kua Fe was just doing his job?" Rosie said.

"He did it very well," Al said. "It would be a shame to ... hinder the cow sprite."

Patrick put his head in his hands. "What do you want me to say?" he said. "It killed Nan."

Al put his hand on Patrick's shoulder. "Yes, and from what you told me, your aunt was practicing a black art she wasn't even licensed for. She was intentionally enhancing a supernatural being, and it defended itself and those in its charge. Right? Isn't that what you told me?"

Patrick looked up at Rosie, his eyes bright.

"Kua Fe saved Sunny," she whispered. "If he hadn't been here, we'd have a dead horse, or at best, a badly injured horse. He's helping us. Even when Nan ... he was helping us."

"But, the one in Iraq. It just stood there!" he said, teeth clenched. "After the horses died, it just stood there!"

Rosie said. "I still think it was grieving."

Al nodded. "I read that sometimes sprites do that."

Patrick shook his head. "How can something that vicious have emotions?"

"Dude." Al put his arm across Patrick's back. "I saw action, too, remember? I saw casualties, innocent and not-so innocent. I've been vicious when it was my job to be. We have emotions."

"We're human. Not demons."

"Where does it say that the supernatural don't have emotions? People say dogs don't have emotions. You know for a fact that isn't true."

Patrick rubbed Bobby's head, and the dog thumped his tail.

"Listen," Al said. "If Nan had bothered a baby bear and the mama bear killed her, we'd have to move the bear, but we wouldn't blame the beast, would we? She was doing what she was supposed to: protecting."

"We can't move Kua Fe," Rosie said. "But we can forgive him and let him do his job."

Patrick swallowed. "I won't trade my aunt for my horse."

"No one is asking you to," Al said. "She did something very … ill-advised … and got herself killed, Patrick. Listen: this is a force of nature that is not good or evil, it's just fulfilling its purpose. It hasn't even gone rogue as far as I can tell. It was inert until you two tried to remove its home, right?"

"Right," Patrick said slowly. His face didn't change.

Rosie thought a moment. "You know when the stallion threw Ben? When I found him in the ditch, I was so devastated, I considered … I thought about shooting the horse."

"What?"

"Oh, it was only for a moment. It wasn't the horse's fault. I knew that. But even if it had been, it wouldn't have been a just punishment. It was Ben's fault for being overconfident. He knew it was dangerous to take the green broke stallion out on the trail by himself. But you couldn't talk sense to that man."

Patrick wiped his eyes and looked at her. "It wasn't the horse's fault."

"It wasn't the horse's fault," she repeated.

He stood and looked out the window at the shed.

"The rogue mountain lion must have killed Nan," he said. "Kua Fe has killed the lion. I guess, I guess…"

"That's that," Al said. He stood and so did Rosie. "I'll go write up my report, leave you two to, well, I'll be in touch." With that, he picked up his hat and let himself out.

Rosie and Patrick stood awkwardly for a moment.

"I don't know what to say." She picked up her mug and set it down again.

"Me neither. I'm going to need some time to … I need to think about all this."

"I know." She hugged herself. "Take all the time you need."

He looked at her askance. "Are you dismissing me? Do I need to go?"

"Oh, no. Please don't go," she said. "I just assumed ... you said you needed time."

"No, not about you. I need time to wrap my head around Kua Fe. Not you."

Patrick stepped around the table and took her hand in his. She watched as he ran his thumb across her knuckles.

"I'm sorry," she said.

"What are you sorry for?" Patrick said. "You never once did anything wrong."

"Heh. You've met me, right? I'm the stubborn one who won't listen to reason or believe things that are right in front of her."

"Yeah? Well, I'm the one who is so stuck in the past that I can't tell that the present is different."

"No, that was me," Rosie said.

He smiled and tucked imaginary hair behind her ear. "We can both own that one, I guess."

She kissed him and held him in her arms until Bobby couldn't stand it any longer and joyfully wedged himself into their hug.

October

Rosie twitched her calf and the stallion beneath her flicked his ear. She did it again and the animal thought for a moment. Then he stepped deftly to one side, crossing his striped forelegs as he moved diagonally across the indoor arena.

His name was Ruger, and he was the surprise of the herd. Of the five mustangs that arrived on her ranch after all the drama with Kua Fe, Ruger was the one that Rosie expected to be the most difficult. She based this judgement on how much of a pain in the ass he was on the trailer. He nearly kicked the door out before they had a chance to open it into the outdoor paddock.

"Crap," she said to Patrick. "I was hoping that they'd all be reasonable creatures."

"Who says he isn't?" Patrick had said. "Give them a while to settle down, and I'll go talk to him."

Of course, Ruger had just been acting as a protector for his mares in the only way he knew how, as Patrick eventually explained. Patrick had to chase the herd around the little paddock behind the indoor arena until they slowed enough to listen to him. Wild horses have no idea some people could talk to them.

Ruger had an innate talent for dressage. That sport requires the horse to perform maneuvers in such a way that the cues from his rider are nearly invisible. Rosie realized early on that someone who could talk to his mount and ask for the moves without moving at all would have an advantage in competitions, but Patrick insisted that he had no interest. He also said it might be unethical for him to compete with that advantage. Rosie had to agree.

However, it didn't bother either of their consciences to coach Ruger using Patrick. Ruger was intelligent, athletic, and enjoyed the challenge of dressage. Patrick explained the move, and helped Ruger understand what was wanted as Rosie gave the correct cues. It was a genius combination.

Rosie leaned over and clapped Ruger on the neck. "Good boy!" she cried, scrubbing his mane in just the right spot. The horse licked his lips in pleasure.

"I think we'll be ready for his first competition next week!" she called to Patrick who was leaning against Sunny's shoulder, feeding her carrot sticks. He tossed one to Bobby who swallowed it after one crunch.

"You two will be great!" he said. "Brains and Beauty!"

She laughed and didn't bother to ask which one she was. Rosie dismounted, snagged some carrots from Patrick, and led the horse to the cross ties. She fed him carrots and unsaddled him, chatting the whole time about how proud she was of his progress. Ruger rumbled and held his head a little higher. Like some people, Ruger liked to have his ego stroked.

After she put the young stallion away, Rosie stepped into Caesar's stall. "Ready for the trail ride, old man?"

The horse swished his red tail at her, making her laugh. "Oh, all right. I won't call you that anymore." Then she sidled up to her friend and slipped him a handful of carrots. "You know no one could ever replace you, right?"

Caesar snorted but took the carrots from her and followed her out to the cross-ties.

Rosie carefully groomed her friend because she knew it felt good, and because she was proud of him. He had taken to his role of trail ride leader with gusto and liked leading the herd around their property. Caesar had helped pick the trail horses Rosie and Patrick had brought to the ranch to carry the magical tourists, so everyone got along and enjoyed their work. At least, that's what they all told Patrick, and he still insisted that animals never lie.

"How many riders do we have today?" Rosie asked Patrick when he and Sunny appeared in the doorway.

"Ten including our friends. I'll ask who wants to get out on the trail today." He whistled and horse heads appeared over every stall half-door, ears at attention. Then a few horses turned back.

"Daisy and Custer say they are tired, and Monty has a headache," Patrick said. "Everyone else is game."

"Great. Let's get them saddled. And remind me to give Monty a little something for his head."

An hour later, a dozen horses including Sunny and Caesar stood dozing in the morning sunshine, awaiting their riders who stood munching on cinnamon rolls and coffee conjured up by Cooky. Her resume had claimed she was "a magician in the kitchen." Rosie now knew this was not hyperbole. Buster hopped under the table, munching up dropped bits of roll.

Richard, the contractor who fixed her torn-up house, made the steel-clad bunkhouse. He also put steel siding on Rosie's house practically for free as a consolation present for the loss of Auntie Nan, whom he had a thing for once. Neither Patrick nor Rosie had felt the need to inform him or anyone else of their theory that Nan had intended to take over Rosie's ranch. Thanks to Al, even the police investigation had ruled her death an accident. Besides, Rosie now suspected there were very real reasons one wasn't supposed to speak ill of the dead.

"Is everybody ready to ride?" Rosie called out, clipboard in hand. A general cheer answered her, so she began calling out names from the clipboard and assigning people horses. "Amy is eleven? Princess will be happy to carry you, sweetie. She likes to be scratched between the ears, so be sure to do that before you get on. Oscar, my, you really are a giant, aren't you? You'll have Rocky. When he grunts as you get on, don't take it personally. He's just messing with you.

"Meg, you're on your own horse, right? He's still a little stiff on his right side, but he said he wanted to go today."

"Okay, Rosie," Meg said as she swung her leg over Talent and scratched his neck on the left side so he bent his head around to her. "That'll help you stretch, big guy."

"Molly? Dad? You guys can ride Beezus and Ramona over there. Don't let them eat too much grass, though."

Rosie smiled as her dad and his wife pulled themselves onto the backs of the mustangs. The horses were, in fact, sisters, and they bickered sometimes. Hence, their names.

"You could have called them 'Kate' and 'Bianca,' after *Taming of the Shrew*," Lew said.

Rosie just rolled her eyes.

"You sure you don't want to ride, Ed?" she asked. She smiled at her neighbor and his wife who were still sitting at the picnic bench, finishing cinnamon rolls.

"No, thanks, Rosie," said Ed. "I gave that up years ago."

"I've got the equivalent of a Cadillac for you to ride."

"Nah," he said. "Between Mabel's hip and my back, we're one fall from the hospital. You go have fun. We'll sit here and help Cooky clean up." Ed and his wife both helped themselves to another roll each.

"Suit yourselves," Rosie said, smiling.

When all the people were mounted, Rosie and Patrick swung up into their saddles and led the group into the cherry orchard. Rosie took the lead with Bobby at Caesar's heels, and Patrick brought up the rear. Sometimes he'd trot up and down the line of horses, chatting with people, pointing out landmarks and spirit sinks they might have missed, and answering questions. He stopped to say hi to Rosie's friends.

"How's Talent feel, Meg?"

"He feels good. What's he say?"

"Just happy to be here."

"Patrick, is the pond spirit around today?" Lew asked.

"Don't know. She's probably around because the ducks are migrating, and they say she likes to visit with them."

Several feet behind the last horse in the line, the wind played in the trees, and a soft snuffling could be heard. The grass parted gently and swished back into place, and huge hoof prints weighed the grass down, only to let it spring back undented. Bobby kept his eye on the Kua Fe and was never close to him, but they tolerated each other as necessary.

What Auntie Nan had said was very true. For a reason no one had been able to figure out yet, Rosie's property and much of the cherry orchard and Ed's place were saturated in spirits. Aside from Kua Fe, who was a recent arrival, and the oak and spring spirits, there were more tree, water and earth sprites in their little hollow than anywhere else in the state. In the hills, there was even an air spirit who rested in a cool little bubble over a waterfall. She was the highlight of the ride.

Once, Rosie sought out a Native American elder and asked her about the spirits at her ranch. The elder stood at the foot of the old oak tree and scowled at the cowshed and shook her head. "That's a very old place," the elder said and pointed up into the hills. "Great-great grandmother's parents used to visit once a year and leave berries at the waterfall."

"Why?"

The old woman shrugged at Rosie. "Who can tell? Great-grandma used to make up all sorts of shit. She lost her mind when I was little."

Still, Rosie had a basket of fat blackberries in her saddlebag. She tossed one to Bobby who caught it mid-air and smiled a dog-smile in thanks.

When they arrived at the pond, Rosie and Patrick paused the group to do a tack check on everyone. Oscar, the giant seated on Rocky, stopped Patrick. "I was wondering," he said. "I mean, not to be too personal, but that little Rosie, what's her talent?"

Patrick tightened Rocky's girth and the huge paint horse grunted. Patrick patted him and then smiled (way) up at the rider.

"You mean magical talent? She will tell you she doesn't have one." He glanced at Rosie over his shoulder. She was adjusting a stirrup and laughing with little Amy whose wings you could just make out if you squinted right.

"So, I'm confused, then," Oscar said. "Why does she own a magic dude ranch?"

"That's a really long story," Patrick said.

"Well, how did she come to know about magic?"

"Same long story." Patrick leaned against the horse. "The short version is in the brochure, but the shortest version is that she met me, and there was a spark."

Oscar grinned. "Oh, I see. So, because of the spark, you assume she's not entirely without magic?"

"Oh, she's magic, all right," Patrick said. "Even if there hadn't been a spark, that woman is magic. She does every little thing on her own terms, and somehow makes it all work. Plus," he said. "Have you seen her ride a horse? Magic!"

The pond was covered in ducks and geese on their migration south, so the pond spirit was ecstatically bubbling around the visitors' paddling feet. He had even worked up a froth at the shore. Bobby helpfully barked at the birds from the shore.

"He's too busy with the ducks today to say hello," Rosie explained to the riders. "We'll pass on the way back. Maybe he'll be less distracted then."

The group made its way up the mountain side toward the air spirit. The horses climbed the hills, grass swishing out of their way and earth rising to meet their feet. In a shady copse that was still shady with colorful leaves, deer appeared on the trail to the delight of the riders. The people were perfectly aware that Patrick had called the deer and promised them apple slices, but the graceful creatures were still a treat for the city folk to see. The group stopped and fed the deer the apples from Patrick's saddle bag.

Then they entered the forest at the base of the largest hill and wound their way up toward the top. The trail was steep, but the footing was good this time of year. Aside from a few "low bridge" branches hanging across the trail (chest-level for the giant), the ride was merely steep through the thick woods. The underbrush was turning the distinctive red-of-fall color.

"There's some poison oak!" she called over her shoulder. "I have plenty packaged for sale at the ranch, so you don't need to dismount here."

"Oh, I'll want some of that for sure," said a pretty young woman three horses back. "I'm making evil repellent sachets for Christmas presents."

Rosie nodded. She wasn't used to magic folk or the weird things they did yet, but she was happy to cater to them. They were no more or less weird than "regular" people. And if they wanted to pay her for poison oak, all the better.

As they rounded the next bend, Caesar chuffed at her. Rosie looked up and threw an arm up in the air to stop the line of horses behind her.

"Look!"

Rosie pointed over Caesar's head to an impossibly white unicorn standing in the middle of the trail munching on fallen acorns. She didn't have to turn around to know the rustling and clicking behind her was the sound of camera phones taking pictures of the rare creature.

She smiled to herself. The unicorn was named Jacqueline, and she was neither wild nor native to Rosie's forest. As far as Rosie knew, the closest thing to a unicorn in the Northwest was a herd of white deer that lived on the coast. However, through a series of Patrick's connections, a unicorn who had immigrated to the New World contacted them, looking to relocate. She wanted to retire from show business.

Rosie was happy to have her. Jacqueline slept in the warm barn at night, ate hay with the horses, and then wandered happily in the woods until it was time for her "appearance" during the trail ride. She was good at not being seen, or at least making herself seem ordinary so everyone was surprised to see her. Rosie and Jacqueline were both delighted with the arrangement.

When Jacqueline moved on, off the trail, Rosie led the group on to the waterfall at the top of the hill. When they arrived, she noticed the water sprite was in a murky mood. She dismounted and examined the water carefully. Bobby stepped into the water, and Rosie shooed him out quickly.

"What's up, ma'am?" Patrick asked stopping by Rosie's side. He slid his fingers down her spine and she smiled at the tingle.

"I think a herd of deer walked through the pond," Rosie said. "The water sprite is still grumpy."

Patrick nodded. "And where is Airy?"

Rosie looked around. She didn't feel the breeze today. She frowned. The spirits were free to come and go as they pleased, but she didn't like disappointing her customers. Out of the corner of her eye, she saw the glimmer, the wave in the air that marked Kua Fe settling in to wait for them by the rope where the horses would be tethered. Now that she knew he came on every ride, she had begun to look for him each time. She had to admit that she felt safer when she knew the sprite was there with them. That admission had taken far less effort than she expected.

"It looks like the air sprite is on an adventure today," she called to the group. "Go ahead and dismount. We'll take a break here, have a snack, and maybe Airy will come back. One thing," she added. "Don't go in the water or let the horses step off the shore. The water sprite is trying to clear his stream, and we don't want to make more work for him."

Rosie took the basket of berries from her saddlebag and placed them in a heap at the edge of the water. She saw Molly and her dad watching her, so she shrugged. "Why not?"

Lew laughed. "So, no hope I can have some of those with my granola?" Molly said.

"Ew. They're on the ground." Rosie laughed with them and pulled carrots for Caesar and a fairy bar for herself. She tossed Bobby a bite. She didn't know what the fairies put in the bars, but they were tasty and filling and Rosie had learned not to ask questions she didn't want the answers to.

Twenty minutes later, Airy hadn't returned, so Rosie helped everyone back into their saddles and prepared to take the downhill trail home. As she swung her leg over Caesar's back, he pricked his ears and said "Look!" in a way she understood.

Hovering high above the pool near the waterfall, a shimmer rippled in the air. Something sparkled, and Rosie smiled.

"There's Airy!" she said quietly to Patrick. "Pass it on."

Soon, all of them were looking up at the sky, watching the sparkle drift down gently until it hovered just above the spray of the waterfall. Something like a whisper hovered there, too. Finally, Airy touched the water, sending a ripple over the surface. The mud in the water fled to the shore in front of the ripple, leaving clear water behind. The ripple lapped up the berries at the edge of the pool until they were all floating in the water.

The group of people cheered, and a cool, happy breeze tickled the horses' manes and tails.

Rosie smiled at Patrick. She might now live in a magic world still largely alien to her, but at least her corner of it contained this kind of magic, and Patrick.

THE END

About the Author

Maren Bradley Anderson is a writer, teacher, and alpaca rancher in Oregon. She is the Editor in Chief of *The Timberline Review* and has written plays for the Apple Box Children's Theater. Her writing has appeared in *The Christian Science Monitor, Alpacas Magazine,* and *The Timberline Review.* Her new novel *Sparks* (July 2019) and alpaca ranch romance *Fuzzy Logic* are available online and through your local bookstore.

Connect with her on Facebook:
https://www.facebook.com/MarenBradleyAnderson
Twitter: @marenster
or her website: http://www.marens.com

Special Thanks

Thanks to the team at Not a Pipe for loving *Sparks* as much as I do. Thanks to Therese Oneill for telling me that Rosie and Patrick needed their own book. Thanks to Gigi Little for the fantabulous cover. Thanks to Rick's Café in Monmouth, Oregon, for keeping me and the local Liars' Club well-caffeinated. And thanks to the old farmer who first told me that it was bad luck to tear down a barn, but never explained why.